J. H. Fletcher is the author of several best selling novels as well as being a successful scriptwriter of plays for radio and television, which have been produced by the BBC and the South African Broadcasting Corporation. The author also writes regularly for the *Singapore Straits Times*.

J. H. Fletcher was educated in the UK and travelled and worked in France, Asia and Africa before emigrating to Australia in 1991. Home is now a house within sound of the sea in a small town on the South Australian coast.

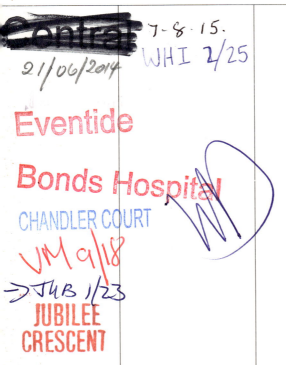

WINGS OF THE STORM

Cal Jessop returns to his home on the South Australian coast, still blaming himself for what happened one fateful evening in Paris. Once he was regarded as one of Australia's most promising young artists. Now, the future is bleak; his work, like his life, devastated by guilt . . . Kathryn Fanning's future seems secure. Everyone, Kathryn included, expects her to marry Charles Chivers, the local doctor. Unexpectedly, Wagner intervenes. When Cal and Kathryn meet at a performance of *RHEINGOLD*, their futures are changed irrevocably . . .

J. H. FLETCHER

WINGS OF THE STORM

Complete and Unabridged

ULVERSCROFT
Leicester

First published in Australia in 2001 by
HarperCollins Publishers
Sydney
Australia

First Large Print Edition
published 2003
by arrangement with
HarperCollins Publishers Pty Limited
Australia

British Library CIP Data

Fletcher, J. H.
  Wings of the storm.—Large print ed.—
  Ulverscroft large print series: general fiction
  1. Large type books
  I. Title
  823.9'14 [F]

  ISBN 0–7089–4786–7

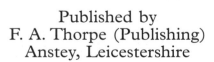

Published by
F. A. Thorpe (Publishing)
Anstey, Leicestershire

Set by Words & Graphics Ltd.
Anstey, Leicestershire
Printed and bound in Great Britain by
T. J. International Ltd., Padstow, Cornwall

This book is printed on acid-free paper

To Brad, who took me there in my mind,
and to Jennie and Scott.
And to David, who also helped.

Art provides the wings that enable us to
ride out the storms of human experience.
— Marie Desmoulins (*Sun in Splendour*)

Love . . . sustains the artist.
— Henry Matisse

Amenhotep, protector of artists,
guard me now.
— Ancient Egyptian invocation

1

The day was dying as Cal Jessop fought *Jester* northwards through rising seas towards the coast that had to be lying just over the horizon.

The sloop, main and genoa well-reefed, climbed the lurching waves and crashed in a welter of spray into the troughs beyond.

Two kilometres to the east, a dense bank of cloud pointed towards the invisible land. Cal kept his eye on it; when the storm came it would be from that direction and the broken waters ahead were strewn with rocks. With night falling the sensible course would have been to put about and head back out to sea, but his hands on the wheel did not falter.

Let the gods decide, he thought.

Three days earlier, the pressures of existence once again beyond bearing, he had sailed out into the Southern Ocean. So often had he done it in the past, seeking the terminal storm to exorcise the demons that, twelve months after Gianetta's death, still plagued him. Always he had been unsuccessful; always, after two or three or four days, he had abandoned the search and turned northwards once more.

Now, sunset buried in cloud, wind increasing with every minute, it looked as though he might have found his terminal storm at last.

The irony was that this time things were different. The storm he had been seeking had not been in a gale, but in the arms of the woman he had brought with him. Stella — waist-long black hair, lean and ardent body — was thirty-two, three years older than Cal and, for the past six months, his frenzied, soul-starred lover. She was married to Hennie Loots, a chopper pilot who worked the Outback, a trusting man who would have called Cal his friend. But Hennie hardly ever came home and Stella, a sprite of the sea with no interest in the Outback, had moved on long ago.

As though his thoughts had conjured her, there was movement below. Stella, storm anorak drawn close, stuck her nose out into the wind.

'Where are we?'

'Somewhere south of Bushranger.'

Bushranger Head lay to the east of Kidman's Inlet, the tiny coastal settlement, one hundred kilometres south of Adelaide, where Cal and Stella lived — Hennie, too, when he was home. The rock-strewn harbour was no place to enter in foul weather, yet that was what they would have to do if the storm arrived before they did.

'Somewhere?' Stella echoed. 'Where?'

'We'll be seeing it directly,' he hoped.

Perhaps they would, if his dead reckoning was right, if the rapidly-falling darkness did not beat them to it.

Stella came and sat beside him in the spray-soaked cockpit. 'Can't see a thing,' she said.

Which made two of them. There was a beacon on Bushranger. It should have been visible by now but was not, which meant that in truth Cal had no idea where they were. Once again he felt the sickening lust for death that had plagued him for so long.

Perhaps this time, he thought.

He knew he could not permit it. Stella, lover or not, had nothing to do with any of this. The Bushranger was there or it wasn't; the coastline was there or it wasn't. Within the next hour or two, they would certainly raise them both.

Jester lurched and shook, her wooden hull complaining at the hammer blows of the sea, but still her bowsprit rose streaming from the troughs as over and over again she climbed the dizzy slopes of the waves.

Stella drew herself tighter into her anorak and shivered.

'Why don't you go back below?'

Cal had to shout for her to hear him above the exultant scream of the wind. She turned to stare at him; in the dying light the spray seemed to spill the blue of her eyes across the stark whiteness of her face but he saw that she was laughing, exultant.

'And miss this? Not in a million years!'

It made sense to stay on deck, in case they capsized, but to enjoy it . . . It took all sorts.

A blink of light appeared through the spray. It was high up, well above the masthead.

'There she is!'

A damn sight too close, too. Even as he spoke, the headland loomed out of the darkness. It was half a mile ahead, no more, and closing fast. Swiftly Cal spun the wheel and *Jester* changed course to windward.

'Now what?' Stella asked.

'We're going in.'

'Is it safe?'

He grinned at her, a ragged grimace through salt lips. When the wind backed to the east, as eventually it must, it would be very far from safe.

'We'll have to wait and see, won't we?'

There were underwater rocks just off the headland but there was nothing he could do about them. Deliberately, he put them from his mind. Wheel hard over, only yards to spare, *Jester* rounded the corner and ran for home.

Three miles to safe harbour; they had covered less than half when the storm struck like a flail out of the south-east, putting the yacht almost flat in the water and shrouding the coast in driving spray.

Cal brought *Jester* up into the wind.

'Take the wheel!'

She was an old boat with no automatic furling. He ran forward to ease the halyards and get the remaining sail off her.

The brutal thrust of the gale tore at him. He wrapped an arm around the mast, the hull rearing and bucking beneath his feet. He eased the halyard, stiff with salt; the sail thundered like cannon as it came down. He grabbed it and lashed it roughly to the boom.

The main secure, he went forward to deal with the genoa. In the bow the movement of the hull was horrendous, climbing skywards only to come crashing down again. Each time it hit the water it rattled the teeth in his head.

He was clipped to the boat by his safety harness, or the sea would have swept him away. All the same, it was not the safest of tasks, wrestling the foresail down while the gale tried to prise it from his hands and the tack's heavy shackle flailed like an armoured fist. A blow from that, in this wind, could break bones.

The bucking sail subdued at last, Cal broke out the storm jib, clipped on halyard and sheets, hauled away. Even that was too much sail, but they had to have something to steer by or they would never get in.

Assuming the sea would permit them, in any case.

The wind tone had risen to a manic scream that battered the ears. No longer was it a force of nature but a vindictive, intensely personal attack upon their sanity and their lives.

That was what you wanted, wasn't it?

Yes, but alone. It had never been the plan to take anyone else with him. Furiously he clenched his fist, yelling his challenge at the gale.

'I'm taking this yacht in!'

Stella was watching him from the cockpit. She would be alarmed; she had been born inland but the sea ran in her blood. Superstition decreed that you never challenged the sea, particularly in the midst of a storm, but Cal cared nothing for that. Superstition implied faith, and faith had gone out of the window when his life had collapsed twelve months before. Not faith alone;

humility, too, had been a victim, replaced by arrogance, and love by bitterness and anger.

At least be thankful for the anger, he thought. That's what you'll need to get you in now: anger, guts, skill. And luck. Lots and lots of luck. Let's go for it, then. Let's make our luck.

He crawled back to the cockpit, took the wheel and spun it to bring the yacht back on course.

Stella slipped the jib sheet over the winch and cranked it home. The tiny sail filled with a crack (*Don't let her blow out!*) and held. The yacht heeled until the rail was buried in the water and began to surge through the waves.

In this weather the mouth of the inlet would be a wall of broken surf, turbulent and deadly. No yacht could hope to survive it, but they had no choice. Pinned between the Bushranger and the land, they had to get into Kidman or perish.

For a moment he took his eyes from the seas to glance at Stella's face. 'You okay?'

'I'm fine.'

I'm fine. If the yacht broached, they would sink. If they were driven on the rocks at the harbour mouth, they would sink. If that happened, their only hope — a damn slim one — would be to be swept clear of the wreck and through the entrance into the harbour. And Stella said she was fine.

Again Cal flung his challenge at the gale. 'I'm taking this yacht in!'

Blasphemy. Hubris. Challenging the gods of sea and wind. No other seaman he knew would dare.

But I will dare. I will challenge anything in heaven or hell. I will win, gods or no gods.

He clung to the wheel, holding the kick of the rudder against the sea's violence, angling the yacht towards the gaping mouth of the harbour. Now he could see the white bar of surf closing the entrance, its voice audible even above the wind.

We are coming, he told the white tumult, jaws clenched so tightly that the muscles in his cheeks ached. *We are coming.*

Slowly, the entrance drew nearer. The gale screamed. If the storm jib blew out, they were dead. If the rudder gave beneath the assault of the sea, they were dead. If they picked up a cross wave in the entrance, if he was out by even a fraction in his course between the rock-strewn headlands, they were dead.

Cal risked a glance at the woman crouching beside him. Water cascaded off her, but she did not move, seemingly mesmerised by the wilderness of broken water in their path.

What could live in those waters?

We can. We will.

All the same . . . 'Fetch us a couple of life jackets.' Cal bawled the words in her ear.

Stella turned to stare at him.

'If I get it wrong and she goes over, we'll have a chance with life jackets. We won't manage with one of these.' He flicked the safety harness securing him to the yacht.

Stella nodded, wrestled the hatch open and disappeared below. Almost at once she was back with the jackets.

'Put one on.'

Stella struggled into the jacket, secured it. Silently, she proffered the other to Cal.

Cal shook his head, hands busy with the wheel, eyes on the storm jib taut as a drawn bow, on the thundering avalanche of waves.

'No time.'

He would just have to get it right, that was all.

The entrance loomed. To starboard, Wally's Reef was invisible beneath the surging water. Between the narrow headlands, the waves swooped, reared and broke in a froth of foam.

We're here. By guts. By skill. As I said. Now it's time for the luck.

'Come on,' he screamed at the water. 'One big surfing wave!'

He looked over his shoulder. A huge mass

of grey water, slashed with white, reared behind them. Wally's Reef was abeam. The tumult of the breaking seas was all around them. Waves crashed and roared along the deck. Cal set his feet, grasping the wheel with all his strength, shoulders tense, and felt the stern lift to the onrushing sea.

The surfing wave. As ordered.

It picked them up like a toy, the yacht tracking true between the headlands, and flung them like a cork into the waters of the harbour beyond.

A cathedral hush descended. The wind still blew, the waters of the harbour were alive with the chop of waves but, after all they'd been through, it was as though they were awash with silence. It was dark now, but Cal knew his way blindfolded and eased *Jester* between the handful of moored fishing boats, his father's among them, until Stella could go forward with the boathook and pick up the buoy. The soft pad of her bare feet upon the deck seemed loud in the stillness.

After all the frenzy, an intense weariness had descended upon them both. Below decks was a mess. Water had come in when Stella opened the hatch and now slopped half an inch deep above the cabin sole. The contents of the cabin had been flung about by the violent movement of the yacht: clothes, cushions, sleeping bags, a saucepan — fortunately empty — all hurled together in a heap.

They pumped ship, wrung out the soaking clothes as well as they could, re-stowed the mainsail neatly along the boom. After the wind's roar, the silence of the harbour bellowed.

'Want anything to eat?'

She shook her head.

'Let's get ashore, then.'

Only after they had reached the jetty did they look at each other, sharing not simply the recent tumult but everything that had gone before, limbs entwined in what passed for love under the yellow eye of the cabin lantern. They could share the past; for the moment, the future was something that neither of them wanted to think about.

'Well . . . '

She smiled — just. 'Yes.'

He leant forward to kiss her. At the last moment she turned her mouth away. His lips grazed her cheek.

Cal was having none of that. Deliberately, possessively, his hand squeezed her breast. Then he stood back and watched as Stella picked her way up the path that led over the cliff to her house by the sea.

Her husband was supposed to be his friend. No doubt he should feel guilty, but did not. Friendship, like so many other things, meant nothing. And Stella had been at least as willing as himself. She was traumatised now but not for long. She would be back.

Up to Hennie to keep his own house in order.

Cal stood motionless, a dark-haired man clothed in dark thoughts, until Stella's outline cut the sky at the top of the cliff. She disappeared and he turned away, walking to the car that he kept in a ramshackle lean-to near the jetty.

He climbed in, turned the key in the ignition and drove home.

The cottage stood in a hollow of the cliffs, three kilometres along the coast road from the harbour. At night, from the summit of the hill behind the house, he could see the lights of the town spilling in a blaze of diamond points around the bay; in daylight the ocean was a sunburst of azure light. That was the first thing the critics had noted about his paintings when he had begun to get a name for himself: the trademark sheen that cloaked his work in its shimmering blue mist.

Cal had bought the property with the proceeds of his first one-man show in Sydney, which had been a huge success. He had been as dazzled by it as by the all-pervasive azure

12

light; it had opened the door to prospects that previously he had not dared imagine.

Dexter Holt had made it a success. Dexter — Dave to his friends — was world-famous, the most respected art critic in Australia. He had been behind Cal from the first, thought of him as his protege. What he had written about Cal's work had set the international art world on fire.

The only real artist to come out of Australia within the last twenty-five years.

So he had written, with the enthusiasm that characterised everything he did, and the gurus of the visual arts had taken note. Within days Angela Scales, Cal's agent, was getting enquiries from Paris, Tokyo, New York; Cal had sat back to watch with bemused eyes as the price of his work went into orbit.

The cottage had stone walls and a sturdy roof to withstand the winter storms that left salt encrusted over the windows in a rime of sparkling light. There was an old barn at the back that he had converted to a studio. He had bought a more reliable car. He had bought *Jester*.

He had won awards at Royal Melbourne, at Oyster Bay, at Mornington. Paintings were bought by galleries in Adelaide, Perth, Singapore.

With the money he had bought an air ticket, gone to Paris to study engraving. Originally he had planned on six months; in the end had stayed far longer, until catastrophe had swept him away.

Cal stopped at the gate to grab the post out of the box, then drove on to the house. In the room he used as an office, he sat at the battered desk and flipped quickly through the mail.

'Damn . . . '

All the stamps were local; the letter he had been awaiting so impatiently was not there.

He grabbed the phone, dialled the number that he had known by heart for three years now, but Angela Scales was not in. He left a message on her answering machine.

'That letter from New York still hasn't arrived. What's going on?'

He banged the receiver down, angry as he so often was these days and seeing no reason to hide it.

He was hungry; he went into the kitchen and opened a couple of tins, heated the contents in the microwave. He ate standing up, spooning the stuff in without registering what he was eating, then went out of the house again and over to the studio.

He switched on the lights. He had spent weeks experimenting, trying to ensure that

14

they were all in the right place; now the interior of the studio was as brilliantly lit at night as it was during the day. The reek of oil paint assailed him; at one time he had worked mainly with ripolin on masonite, but recently had gone back to canvas and oils, trying to find a new method to derive meaning from a world where all meaning had been lost.

He studied the unfinished painting on the easel. Returning to his work had once been like coming home, renewing acquaintance with an aspect of himself that was discoverable only through the medium of his work, familiar yet always new. Always the critics had commented on the personal nature of his paintings, the way his personality came through. In those days it had been an advantage, but those days were gone.

He studied the painting closely, shifting it this way and that. No use; it was like meeting a stranger. There was nothing with which he could identify; nothing, it seemed to him, of value.

Anger, stark and brutal, blazed from the canvas.

He studied the work with the dispassionate eye of the artist. It had strength, certainly; the colours were powerful, the explosive energy manifest in the silent room. Yet they were the strength and power and energy of a madman, a barely-controlled passion that said more clearly than words, *I hate you.* Even worse: *I despise you.*

He detested what it revealed of the man he had become.

He hesitated, fingers itching for the brush, but the painting was like an unwelcome stranger whose acquaintance he had no wish to renew.

Perhaps he would feel better in the morning.

He switched off the lights and went back to the house. Overhead a scattering of stars blinked through the wild hair of the wind-blown clouds. Against the tender night, his memory of the painting's angry pigments blazed like a furious and unforgiving eye.

He went indoors, had a shower, went to bed.

Images.

Jester, climbing the mountainous seas, the darkness filled by the storm's frenzy, the cold green waves laying their hands upon the yacht. The gold of lamplight, limbs pearl-coloured, the warmth and texture of love. Stella's ecstatic features, her limbs sinuous beneath his own. A glitter of stars above a white-flecked sea that stretched for thousands of miles to the realm of ice. The screech of tyres. The echoing thud of destruction.

Eventually he slept.

He woke to the sound of the phone. Grabbing the receiver, he squinted in the sunlight spilling into the room.

'Hullo?'

'Angela.'

'New York. You told me the Stuyvesant would be writing to me about next year's show. It's November already and I haven't heard a word. What's going on?'

'Nothing's going on. I spoke to the Stuyvesant last week. They said they'd come back to me, but so far they haven't.'

Cal had no interest in excuses. 'What are you planning to do about it?'

'I suppose I could contact them again.' But did not sound very enthusiastic about it.

'You'd better do it, then, hadn't you?' God knew she got paid enough to afford a phone call.

'I'm not sure it would be wise to pressure them too much — '

'If you don't push them, they'll leave everything to the last minute and then, all of a sudden, they'll be yelling for action. Just call them, okay?'

And slammed down the phone.

The conversation had unsettled him; it took so little to fire him up these days. Even the trip on *Jester* hadn't helped. Blame Stella, he thought. I should never have taken her with me. That sort of trip, I need to go alone. Next time I'll remember.

He knew it would be no use trying to work until his head was right. Instead he walked along the road until he came to the cliff path and followed it to the end. There was a way down to the shore from this point. Hardly anyone knew it was there. It was a bit of a scramble but safe enough if you knew what you were doing, and Cal had been using it since he was a kid.

At the bottom a patch of white sand was ribbed with rocks the colour of dark sapphire; he came here often when he wanted to be alone. This time, to his disgust, someone had beaten him to it. Two boys, both about ten years old, were crouching side by side at the edge of a large pool. Mantis-like, forearms lifted, they were poised motionless, as though frozen by the sunlight into statues of the most delicate bronze. Their eyes were fixed on something in the water, and they did not hear him approach.

He recognised neither of them; guessed they must be from the holiday park on the far side of the headland. He was hopping mad to see them there; all the same, at once he started assessing the angle of the light on their bodies; the pose of the heads; the tension that held them both, with the pool and rocks, in a single dynamic whole. He knew there was the making of a picture here and his mind was busy with possibilities: the boys' heads superimposed against a background of burning buildings, the shattered span of Sydney Harbour Bridge, the soaring, soot-stained tower of a vast crematorium. Past and future, he thought. Life.

The idea improved his mood, if only momentarily.

'What are you looking at?' he asked.

The nearer of the two boys glanced up at him and then quickly back, eyes tethered to whatever it was they were watching. Neither spoke.

Cal came a little nearer, peering over their shoulders into the weed-fronded pool. Momentarily the light on the water dazzled him, then his eyes adjusted and he saw below the surface the pale shadow draped over the dark rocks.

'An octopus,' he said.

'Devil fish.' So said, importantly, the bigger of the boys.

His companion nodded eagerly, wanting to please, to belong. 'Devil fish,' he echoed.

'It won't harm you.'

But this was not gothic enough for the children.

19

'My dad says they get their arms round your foot, they'll pull you under and drown you.'

'It's not big enough for that.'

But saw they wanted to believe the worst, to polish their justification for killing the creature whose alien characteristics threatened so powerfully.

'What are you going to do with it?'

But knew, without the boys telling him. Again the smaller of the two shot him a sly smile, offering complicity. Cal understood that by inflicting death, they would become whole, if only for a moment, and again saw their rapt faces against a background of destruction: the looming chimneys, the stark and dangerous watchtowers garlanded by wire.

Suddenly he was sick of it, sick of everything and everyone. He turned and walked across the glaring white sand that crunched like sugar beneath his feet. Let them get on with it, then. Kill or not, as they chose.

Thus Pilate, he thought, washing his hands.

At least Pilate had cared enough to try, if only briefly, to save a Jewish troublemaker. Cal cared nothing: neither for the boys, shouting now in shrill excitement, splashing ferociously through the weedy water on their mission of destruction; nor for the fish; for nothing and no-one upon the face of the earth.

Kill it and be done, he thought. Maybe then I'll get some peace.

He stripped off his shirt and lay on his back upon the harsh sand, feeling the sun bite into his chest. His eyes were closed against the hot glare but, through the blood-flushed darkness, he continued to see a moving kaleidoscope of images: the children's faces, the healing and destructive energy of the sea, a narrow flight of stairs fleeing downwards into the consuming night.

He heard the triumphant cacophony of the boys' voices and opened his eyes to see them running pell-mell across the beach, the broken octopus trailing tentacles of flesh and slime across the yielding and indifferent sand. The sapphire rocks quaked beneath the booming assault of the sea.

The two figures clambered between boulders towards the open and more popular beach half a kilometre away where, no doubt, their parents lounged beside the lazy waves, unknowingly destined to become recipients of the trophy wrested from the sea.

The ceramic fragility of their laughter faded. Silence seeped soothingly into the space where the boys had been.

Cal lay, prisoner of sun and sea-surge, of the images that for twelve months had never left his mind, that leaked on to canvas and masonite only to renew themselves endlessly.

★　★　★

In Paris, texture and depth became Cal's universe. For a month he stayed in digs; after that managed to get hold of a one-room flat above a grocer's shop in the Rue de la Huchette. For three months he lived there alone; afterwards shared it with Gianetta Frachesi, a sculpture student from Milan with whom he was in love.

Every time he opened a book it was her face he saw upon the page. Every minute was enlivened by his awareness of her existence, the certainty of his feelings and the knowledge that they were shared. Even the veins that carried his blood were aware of it.

With his tutor he studied the work of Dürer, of Goya and Picasso and Cezanne. He visited the Louvre and spent hours observing the simple profundity of Honore Daumier, and a dozen others. When he was not working, Cal read the poems of the French romantics, telling himself the French had great reputations as lovers. He spent hours battling with the works of Baudelaire, that great artist with his doomed love and Creole mistress riddled with syphilis. The English poets had also managed to capture the emotion and pin it miraculously to the page, so that its beauty and truth and life survived even that capture. Theirs was a great art and somehow, in pigment and stone and ink, he knew he must attempt to achieve something of the same.

Simplicity revealing truth. The sculpted shapes of Gauguin, the taste for the barbaric, the massed colours, raw and vibrant. The Elizabethan dramatists or the King James's version of the Psalms. *Then was our mouth filled with laughter and our tongue with singing.* It was a sentence capturing all there was to be said of glorification and praise. It was what Cal felt, it *was* the emotion, incarnate on the page.

In the place of words, he would have to find the line, the texture, the spaces between the lines, to express what he wanted to say.

Why were the simplest things the most profound?

Contrast, contradiction, conflict.

Yet he felt no conflict with Gianetta, nothing but certainty and peace. There were no shadows.

He told himself he should write to his parents; he wanted to, he wanted to tell the whole world about her, shout it into the sky, but could not bring himself to do so. He had read that the Malays were afraid to speak the tiger's name, for fear of summoning him. He felt something of the same: speak too loudly of what was precious and the gods of destruction and of envy would arise.

Cal lay in the room, listening to her breathing, his eyes open to the almost imperceptible beginnings of the dawn.

This was the best time. Sleeping, in quietness together, she was his. Making love, they belonged, not to each other, but to the passion that consumed them both. This was the best time.

Yet it was precisely for that reason, because it was best, that he could not remain still. He had to express it, to share the moment. So his hand moved on her, his palm caressed her skin until she woke and turned to him.

Drowning, the moment passed.

To Cal she was everything beautiful: long-legged, slender-boned, startlingly blonde for an Italian. Regardless of colouring, the temperament was unmistakable. There were moments of rage, violence. She knew how to raise her voice at him; knew how to throw plates, too, although not often and fortunately ill-aimed. Her temper was part of the whole; he accepted it in that context.

One evening he was late. He had stayed hours in a cafe with two friends, discussing politics, art, women. The Tour de France was on; they watched it on television. When the broadcast was over they talked some more. More politics, more art, more women.

He felt in a benign mood as he strolled home through streets crowded with traffic. It was a fine summer evening, the air full of the smell of warm dust and leaves, grazed by falling pollen. Only as he climbed the single flight of stairs that led directly from the street to the room did he remember that today was the anniversary of their first meeting, that he had promised Gianetta he would be home early for their own private celebration.

She had prepared a special meal; now it was ruined. Cal was full of apologies but she smelt alcohol on his breath and erupted into screaming rage, hurling abuse at him until he, too, lost his temper and started yelling back. She snatched up a plate and hurled it; it crashed to pieces on the wall behind him.

'For God's sake, stop acting like a child!'

He grabbed her wrists; she ducked her head swiftly and bit his hand.

'Christ!'

Furious at the sudden pain, he let her go. At once she slipped away around the table.

His raging eyes abused her. 'You stupid

bitch! Why don't you shove off and leave me in peace?'

'You think I want to stay with you, you drunken animal?'

Which he was far from being. The awareness of injustice stoked his fury.

Tears of rage ran down her face. She whirled and disappeared down the stairs. He chased her to the top of them. She was halfway to the open door leading directly to the street. He followed her, bawling:

'And don't bloody well come back!'

He never knew if she heard him or not. She ran blindly on and through the door. Following at her heels, he was in time to see her run straight out into the roadway and under the wheels of the fast-moving lorry.

Dear God. Dear God.

★ ★ ★

There is a patch on the wall by the bed. They say I stood there, striking the wall with my fist, hard, harder, harder, until they took me away. It should have been my head; I should have killed myself, but could not. I cannot. I have murdered once. I cannot do it again, and I have no friend to do it for me.

I have no friend.

'You've nothing to reproach yourself with. Nothing.'

'An accident. Shocking, of course. But an accident.'

'She always was a temperamental girl. Always. To fly into a rage like that — '

'You've nothing to blame yourself for.'

'She can't have looked at the traffic at all. And in that busy street — '

'You've nothing to blame yourself for.'

'It must have been instantaneous, that's one thing. She can't have known a thing.'

'You've nothing to blame — '

A scream, rising in the head.

Dear God. Dear God.

2

When Cal got back to the house, Dave Holt was sitting on the grass outside the studio. Cal's heart sank. He owed Dave lots, but this business of rocking up uninvited had always exasperated him. Today, in particular, he could have done without it. It was bad enough having his own doubts about the way his life was going without someone else getting in on the act. Which, he knew only too well, was why Dave was here. Again.

Cal had discovered that the world was divided into those who believed in him and those who did not. After 'Coastal Sequence', the series of paintings that had established his reputation, the believers had far outnumbered the rest. No longer; over the last twelve months, the new harshness in his palette had scared people off. Nowadays, Cal thought that Dave was the only one who still had faith. Sometimes even he seemed to be wavering.

Cal told himself he didn't care, that no artist could afford to be influenced by what others thought. The creativity was still there; it was only a matter of time before people came to understand and accept his new style.

He wasn't sure he believed that himself, which didn't help. Was pretty sure that Dave didn't, either.

Dave Holt had backed Cal from the first. He had done more than anyone to push him forward, but recently had been warning him that influential people in the art world were beginning to lose faith.

'Never imagine you're bullet-proof,' he had said, wagging his finger. 'Even your show at the Stuyvesant could be at risk.'

If Dave were right, that could be serious; the show was supposed to announce Cal's arrival as a major player upon the field of international art.

Scornfully, Cal had refused to accept the warning. 'They'd be turning their backs on reality. Chocolate-box vision . . . '

Yet in his heart, had known that it was he who had turned his back, that with Gianetta's death, he had lost his vision or any belief in the future.

All, all gone into the dark.

Which did not mean he wanted another lecture now.

'Come to give me a hard time?'

'Of course.' Grinning, refusing to acknowledge the bleakness in Cal's tone. 'Why not?'

Unique among critics, Dave was a jolly

man, but Cal had learned to tolerate even that. It even served a purpose; his laugh, effervescent as bubbles, provided such a contrast to Cal's anger and despair that it gave them added weight.

'I've been watching two boys on the beach,' Cal said. 'They were smashing up an octopus. I destroy, therefore I am. The SS would have been proud.'

He shoved past the critic and into the studio, thought of slamming the door behind him but did not, insufficiently interested to bother.

Stella, he thought, that's who I need now. Yesterday he would have said he'd seen enough of her to last for months, that indulging self-hatred in the texture of her most intimate flesh had lost its appeal. Now he knew better. Turning your back on destruction only prolonged the agony.

Dave Holt and Stella Loots, he thought. The light and the dark. Of which, always, I shall embrace the dark.

Cal knew by the changed texture of the light that Dave had come into the studio behind him. Without turning, he said savagely, 'You want to look, that's fine. But don't go telling me how lousy they are. You reckon you can do better, buy a canvas and do it yourself.'

For all the notice Dave took, Cal might not have opened his mouth. He wandered around the studio, inspecting each painting in turn, until that, too, made Cal wild.

'Well?'

As though it mattered what the critic, what anyone, thought.

'They're strong. They're harsh. The technical use of — '

'You don't like them.' Flat, like an accusation.

'No one could like them.'

'The symbols of a sick society?' Cal jeered. 'Isn't that the politically correct thing to say?'

'They're nothing to do with society,' Dave said. 'They're about you. Your heart upon the canvas. It's always been your greatest strength. And weakness.'

Cal told himself he welcomed Dave's rejection, that it made him strong. Yet, in his heart, did not believe that.

Now Dave was studying the incomplete painting on the easel, the slashes of black and red like a symphony of death and blood. Almost casually, he discarded it.

'New York won't touch them with a ten-foot pole,' he said.

'I haven't sent them to New York.'

'It's the same. Since you came back from Paris — '

'I've been painting my heart,' Cal said savagely. 'As you keep telling me. Nothing has changed.'

'Everything has changed.'

Cal would give no ground. 'Are you saying there's no room for hatred in art? What about Goya? George Grosz?'

'They hated what they were portraying. Cruelty. Selfishness. Bigotry. The firing parties. The porcine officials. 'There,' they were saying, '*there* is your enemy.' But the artists themselves . . . Always, *always*, they were on the side of truth. Of goodness. Of what humanity can become.'

'Wagner? The anti-semite?'

Deliberately Cal brought in the composer's name, knowing how Dave shared his admiration for Wagner's music.

'But the message was sublime. What you're doing is glorifying the hatred itself. The darkness.'

Especially to himself, Cal would not acknowledge that Dave might be right.

'I paint the truth.'

'No.'

'As I see it.'

'Not even that. That is in your earlier work.'

'Chocolate box,' Cal repeated.

Dave turned away, stared through the open

doorway. 'That rumour I warned you about
. . . I hear the Stuyvesant's definitely having
second thoughts about your show.'

'They can't. We've got a contract.'

'With an escape clause. There's always one
of those.'

'I've heard nothing from Angela.'

'I've a nasty feeling you will.'

It would certainly be a blow. Cal told
himself that artistic integrity was what
mattered. But without a market . . .

He had the need to savage himself through
the medium of someone else. Dave made a
convenient target.

'Why don't you keep your beak out of my
affairs?'

'Because I feel responsible.'

Which was a bit bloody cool.

'To me?'

'To art. I've always believed you have the
potential to be one of the great artists of the
twenty-first century.'

'Freudian slip,' Cal said unpleasantly. ' 'I've
always believed . . . ' You saying you don't,
any more?'

'I think you're off target. What happened in
Paris — '

Fury clenched its fists. 'Leave Paris out of
it, okay?'

'The talent is still there. But you're going

in the wrong direction.'

Cal's voice was jagged, with blades. 'And naturally you plan to re-direct me?'

'It's not for me to do anything. You know the truth as well as I do. It's up to you what you do about it. But the way you're headed at the moment is wrong. Wrong for you, wrong for your art.'

Rage like a coal, burning. 'Thank you so much for telling me. And if I say you don't have a clue what you're talking about?'

Would have said more, gathering the words like spittle around his tongue, but Dave beat him to it.

'I'll do a deal with you.'

'Deal? What are you talking about?'

'You mentioned Wagner . . . '

'What about him?'

'I've got a spare ticket for *Rheingold*. I thought you might like to have it.'

The Ring Cycle was being performed in Adelaide for the first time. Cal had thought to go, but hadn't got around to booking. It was a generous offer; the tickets cost a packet.

Cal was suspicious. 'Why? What's the idea?'

'Just to come with me to the opera. Nothing else. Maybe it'll do you good to immerse yourself in the work of another great artist.'

'In opera?'

'Emotion.' The word fierce, a votive offering to a god of great yet unknowable power. 'Bathe yourself in it. Surrender yourself to it. Who knows? It might help get you back on track.'

'And if I agree?'

Dave laughed. 'I won't badger you any more.'

A good deal, indeed. Too good; Cal remained suspicious. Yet the idea of immersing himself in another man's artistic experience had an odd appeal.

What the hell, he thought. What harm can it do?

'Good on you, Siegfried,' he said. 'Just don't try marrying me off to any Brunnhildes, that's all.'

Dave was rounded, soft, with an apologetic moustache, a rotund joviality that he sprayed like spit. Anyone less like Siegfried would have been impossible to imagine, yet heroic elements remained. As now, come to beard Cal in his den.

Cal turned suddenly and caught the critic watching him with an expression at once concerned and apprehensive, as though Cal had been wired to explode at any moment.

'Don't worry,' he said. 'I'll come.'

★ ★ ★

The Arts Centre beside the Torrens River was spilling with people. Some had come to see, many to be seen; there might even, thought Cal sourly, be one or two who had come for the music.

Beyond the refreshment tents, starched-looking and brilliant against the emerald lawns, the river reflected the imploring branches of trees. The evening sunlight gilded the bandstand on its little mound, two racing skiffs slid downstream and, beyond the cricket oval already announcing the dates of a forthcoming test match against England, the twin spires of the cathedral pointed the road to heaven.

Cal walked with Dave Holt at his side, a glass of free champagne in his hand and the music of *Rheingold*'s first act thundering in his head. Soon the bells would summon, they would return to the twilight world of myth and truth, heroes and frailty, an emotional intensity that stripped the skin from his susceptibilities, bringing them raw and bleeding into the light.

It was too much. Cal had a sudden longing to be away from here, to be alone in a canyon walled with stone and silence, the rocks as red as heat and pulsing in the light. From nowhere, standing beside the cool river, the gritty fire of the Red Centre summoned him.

He thought, Perhaps *there* I can regain my peace. More important still, my sense of mission.

Sidney Nolan had done it. In his own way, so had Russell Drysdale. Aboriginal artists without number had produced paintings that reflected their personal vision. Cal felt the urgent need to follow them, to seek contact with the spirit of the land in the same way that Wagner had created from legend a universe of mystery and myth. It was no more than a fleeting glimpse, a glint upon the rock to hint at what might lie beneath, but he turned restlessly, staring down at the tranquil river.

Now the sun had set. The city's buildings shone golden in the dying light. It was still hot; along the river the trees looked cool and inviting. Cal stood amid a clattering chatter of people as a flight of ducks planed in from nowhere to land upon the water in a gash of foam. Again Cal wished he could be away from the city loud with voices and traffic, to escape the pressures that had squeezed all hope and creativity from his spirit. The Centre's red heart flared between the willow trees, along the olive coolness of the water. The darkening sky shone with the first blink of stars yet, above the theatre's yellow lights, it was still blue, pulsing with heat and ardour,

a sense of awakening purpose. He felt the lust
and hope of renewal.

Dave cried, 'I don't believe it!'

And stood staring, hand clapped theatrically to his head, his other arm outstretched
to embrace the figure of a young woman who
had paused in front of them. She was wearing
a white dress that reflected the last of the
light; her suntanned face laughed beneath a
cap of dark, short, gleaming hair.

'Where have you sprung from?' Dave
asked. He turned to Cal. 'My niece. Kathryn
Fanning. I've mentioned her to you often.'

Cal knew that Dave had never mentioned
her at all, but smiled anyway.

'The truth,' Dave said. 'Your name is ever
on my lips.'

Kathryn smiled, tolerant of her uncle's
ways.

'Enjoying it?' she asked Cal.

'Very much.'

'I wouldn't have missed it,' she said. She
turned back to Dave. 'I was keeping a lookout
for you. I thought you might be here.'

'And now you've found us.' Dave spoke as
though it were the most astonishing thing.
Again he slapped his forehead. 'My dears,
please excuse my manners . . . Kathryn, this
is my dear friend, Cal Jessop.' He defined him
further, speaking in capital letters. 'Cal

Jessop. The Artist.'

As though Kathryn would have the slightest idea who that was.

Astonishingly, she did. ' 'Coastal Sequence',' she said.

It was the one thing everyone remembered, the series of paintings that had brought him to the attention of the art world, first here, then overseas. What had started as a series of coastal studies had developed to embrace the spirit of the land. Those who had come first and their successors; the coastline at first denying and separating, then uniting, casting a noose about the land and all it contained; the people one amid a flight of X-ray birds and fishes, enfolded by the encompassing sea. As Nolan had sought to define the country through his paintings of Ned Kelly and Bracefell the Convict, so Cal had sought a unifying definition of the land, comprehensive and entire, by painting the coast.

The 'Sequence' had brought him his agent, friendship with Dave Holt — even, it now seemed, a name beyond the world of art. The next step had to be a new and still more profound expression of identity for which, since Gianetta's death, he had been searching without avail.

' 'Coastal Sequence' was five years ago,' he

said shortly. It irritated him that no-one ever seemed to think beyond the past. 'I've moved on since then, let's hope.'

Although doubted whether he had. A doubt that it seemed was shared by others, in particular by the Stuyvesant Gallery in New York.

'Cal is a great artist,' Dave said. 'At least, in the making.'

Cal smiled, razor-edged. 'Your uncle's great at giving compliments and a slap in the face at the same time.'

He did not want to talk about it to this stranger. He studied her with his artist's eye. Grave, attentive face, slender arms darkened by sunlight, the combination of warm skin and cool dress seeming to encompass both aspects of the dying day: the sunlight and the shadows flowing like the river itself between the motionless trees.

She said, 'I'm sorry.'

For her to apologise for his rudeness was too much.

'For what? I'm the one should be sorry.' He heard the sharpness in his voice and forced a smile. 'Please . . . Let's start again. Tell me how you're enjoying the opera.'

And was relieved to see her smile.

'At the beginning I wasn't sure,' she said, 'but once I got over the bare stage and modern dress, I thought it went very well.'

The warning bell began to ring inside the building.

'Heading for the last round-up,' Cal said. He found that he did not want to lose contact so quickly with this woman. 'You rushing away afterwards?'

Her dark eyes regarded him gravely. The crowd began to flow in a chattering tide towards the entrances. The febrile noise made their own silence all the more intense, and he found himself wanting very much to see her again.

'We could have a coffee,' he offered.

Again the silence hung between them, while in the background was the maddening, insistent clamour of the bell.

'That would be nice,' she said.

He was delighted, unreasonably so, as his earlier irritation had been unreasonable.

'I'll meet you by the bandstand,' he suggested. 'We'll be out of the mob there.'

She smiled, touched his hand with a butterfly brush of her fingers, then turned and walked away through the press of people. He watched her go, the slender back and long, coltish legs, the gleaming cap of dark hair, and was very glad that he had asked to see her again and that she had agreed.

'We'd better get in if we don't want to miss

the rest of it.' There was what sounded suspiciously like a laugh in Dave's voice.

Cal grinned at him. 'I'd forgotten all about you.'

'So I saw.'

Cal laughed outright. They walked back into the theatre, the music kindled its incandescent images and, all the time, behind Cal's eyes, the vision of the Outback pulsed, raw and vital and compelling, the means of restoring vision and spirit to his work.

The final curtain. The applause. Euphoria soaring in the auditorium's enclosed spaces, the air grey with the exhalations of the audience yet alive and crackling with the fulfilment of the music. Cal tried to see Kathryn in the crush but could not.

Outside, the cool night lay like dew. He turned to Dave.

'I've got to thank you — '

'Thank me in your work. You have a date. Enjoy it.'

Cal ran down the steps and across the grassy slope to the birdcage framework of the bandstand. The music pulsed and roared within him, a lingering surge of energy and emotion arching triumphantly between himself and the glittering compassion of the stars.

There was no-one by the bandstand. He watched while the river slid silently. One or two people passed, some coming from the opera, their voices loud with the echoes of Wagner. The sound dwindled. Harsh-breathed, a jogger pounded along the footpath. A distant drifting of figures.

She has changed her mind.

Cal paced a few steps, restlessly; came back again.

The grassy expanse was still empty. He waited.

A figure emerged from the shadows beside the opera house. He watched. Pale dress. High, coltish stride. As it approached, he saw the dark hair shining in the darkness.

Kathryn came close. A gleam of teeth as she smiled.

'I met someone I knew. Couldn't get rid of them.'

'It doesn't matter.'

Nor did it. Even to himself, Cal would not acknowledge how certain he had been she would not come, the happiness he now felt at being proved wrong.

'Do you mind if we skip coffee?' she asked. 'It's a lovely night. I'd sooner walk.'

So they did, making their way slowly along the path beside the river, past banks of reeds where waterbirds stirred with liquid plash and stammer of wings. He felt her presence, the slender, sun-brown arms, the column of her neck, the glint of light in her eyes, felt . . .

He did not know what he felt. Only that, in the communion of silence, there was a warmth and fulfilment he had thought gone forever. He wanted her to speak yet was glad she did not, silence more eloquent than speech.

Until at length, where the river narrowed, they stopped as though by unspoken agreement and looked at the water, the light running in veins of silver upon its dark surface. He felt her presence beside him, the warmth of her arm and body, yet did not move, aware how their senses were touching although their skins were not. It was a good feeling; a sense of gratitude that, after the strident day, the enriching music, the soft, slow flooding of the stream, he had emerged from turmoil into an unexpected place of rest.

She smiled at him and, again, he saw the gleam of light upon her teeth and eyes.

'Peace after storm,' she said.

For a moment the words, so much in keeping with his thoughts, startled him; then he understood she had been talking about the music.

'Right . . . ' Peace after storm, indeed.

They paced slowly back the way they had come, while the river flowed silently beside them, barely visible between its banks of reeds.

Now, as though her words had unlocked the silence, they talked. Of the music and the evening's performance, of nothing and everything. Cal and the girl whom he did not know, yet to whom he spoke as though to an old friend. In no time they were back at the opera house, shuttered now against the night, and he found himself regretting very much that the evening was coming to an end.

'Where are you parked?'

Now that they had reached the point of parting Cal, who had never been short of words with a woman in his life, found he had nothing to say. By her car they turned to face each other. With something close to desperation, he said, 'It's been nice . . . '

The words died weakly in the silence.

'There's an exhibition,' she said. 'Ancient instruments. I thought, if you were interested — '

'When?'

'Tomorrow. Eleven o'clock.'

She told him where the exhibition, in which he had absolutely no interest, was being held. He recognised neither the street nor the building, but would find them. Nothing was more certain than that.

He had not planned on staying in town and

had nothing with him. Now, after midnight, it was too late to do anything about it, so he drove back to the coast as though he had never met Kathryn at all. It didn't matter. The night was cool, the air like silk; he drove with the windows down, the rush of air lifting the hair from his forehead. It was over an hour's drive and, in the morning, he would have to come all the way back again, a journey that in daylight would be clogged with traffic. And it did not matter at all.

Beyond the city the countryside was dark yet in his mind Cal could see the tranquil paddocks stretching away, the undulating contours of the distant hills, the sea at journey's end burnished beneath a sickle moon. Apart from the rush of wind, the engine hum, it was quiet. There was no other traffic at all and, for the first time since Paris, a sense of peace began to heal the jagged edges of his mind, soothing away the hatred and loss. The moon rose over the distant ranges and shone upon the sleeping land and, in his head, was the reverberating wash of the sea and the girl's slender body, watching.

★　★　★

As she drove away, Kathryn watched Cal in her driving mirror until she turned the corner of the ramp and he was gone.

Yet was not. The night was peopled with images. The ecstatic thunder of the music. That, above all things; yet through it, like diamond points of light, gleamed other memories: the man, tall, long-armed; his strong mouth and sun-dark skin. The sun had always drawn Kathryn, despite, or perhaps because of, its dangers. Hair that was almost black. Emerald-green eyes that in certain lights would glitter like ice or burn, like the sun. They drew her, despite, or perhaps because of, their dangers.

An intolerant man, she thought, impatient when she mentioned 'Coastal Sequence'. Impatient of her? Or of the paintings? From which he claimed to have moved on? Arrogant, too, then.

Oh dear.

Her uncle had called Cal a great artist in the making, and in matters of art Dave knew what he was talking about. She had heard other things, too: a litter of broken affairs that the media had reported gleefully; a punch-up outside a pub that might have ended in jail. Yet his impact remained. He was air blowing where until now her life had held no air.

She drove up the hill past the cathedral, the Children's Hospital.

Most people would have envied her. She

had a secure, comfortable life. If she chose, she could look forward to a future neatly wrapped, with little chance of unpleasant surprises; a future, moreover, where she knew she would be adored, if only in moderation. Charles Chivers was not a man for excess, especially in emotion, but, to compensate for what might otherwise have been disappointment, Kathryn knew she could handle him. Had been handling him, in fact, since he had first dated her three years before, when she had been nineteen and he twenty-six.

Then, and since, she had permitted him to touch what she knew she could have forbidden him, had she chosen. It had meant so little to her, yet was the way things seemed to work. Her friends said it was how to catch a man without being caught oneself — although a lot of them seemed to end up caught, all the same. Kathryn had not, nor intended to be, and knew how to say no when necessary. Mostly Charles had gone along, although he had rebelled a little, from time to time, most recently over the Wagner.

The mid-north was no place for the unconventional, and Charles had wondered audibly about the wisdom of spending so vast a sum on going to an opera. In which none of their friends was in the least interested. Charles liked Kathryn to stand out from the other eligible females of his parents' acquaintance, yet there was a line beyond which individuality became suspect.

Kathryn had told him, defiantly, that she was going anyway.

He had conceded that it made sense, once you'd bought the ticket, not to waste it, but expected that on another occasion she would know better.

It was absurd to talk of being hemmed in when the countryside was so vast, when rains fell and crops grew on schedule.

The man she had met tonight had no place in any of this, yet when he had asked her to meet him after the opera, she had not hesitated — at least not at the time. Leaving the theatre, having had the opportunity to contemplate the dangers, she certainly had hesitated. Cal Jessop was dangerous, every instinct told her so. The fact that he was so attractive only made things worse.

So she had walked for a time alone, testing the darkness with her doubts. In the end, it was the offering of air that had decided her, the opportunity to breathe.

She had walked to the bandstand, had found him there, as promised. That had been her last chance: that he might have grown tired of waiting and pushed off. But she had seen him and known, with trepidation and delight, that she was glad he had not.

They had walked beside the silent river and said little, and in the silence had said a great deal.

Peace after storm, she had told him, knowing that he might think she was speaking only of the music. Which could have been a catalyst, she supposed.

After their walk, not wanting the evening to end, she had grabbed at the one thing she could think of, had suggested paying a visit to the exhibition of antique instruments. She had not cared whether he might be interested or not, but after he had said yes, had hoped he was not interested at all, because that would mean . . .

She would not permit herself to consider what that might mean.

It was all too soon, she told herself as she turned into the side road that led to her friend's place. Too soon for the turmoil of ifs and buts and maybes, for imagining things when there was nothing between them but incompatibility.

There was certainly that. Herself and an artist, even a good one . . . What could they possibly have in common? It would be an experience, certainly, something different, but daring to be different was a danger to a future where being different had no place.

She had seen two of his paintings. One of the 'Coastal Sequence' was in the Adelaide Art Gallery; the other, the portrait of an unnamed woman, she had seen in an exhibition in Melbourne.

This was the one she remembered now. It had been a chromatic painting, planes and exclamation points of colour everywhere, yet somehow had combined breath-taking sensuality with an emotion that had seemed close to adoration. What she remembered in particular was how the integrity of the subject had been in no way subordinated to the feelings of the viewer, so that all three — emotion, observer, subject — had existed in their own right, a celebration of the potential and fulfilment of human love. She had turned away from it, startled to find tears on her face.

This was the man with whom she had walked beside the river, whom she would be seeing in the morning.

She parked in the street outside the unit.

To say nothing of all the other things she'd read. Womaniser, fighter, drunk — she certainly knew how to pick them.

She went indoors, closing the door softly so as not to disturb her friend, who would have needed no disturbing had she had any idea of the confusion warring inside Kathryn's head.

51

Because the fighter was also the painter of the portrait. That frightened her. The painting depicted an intensity of emotion beyond anything she had known, a mingling of spiritual and physical that had left her breathless. What could she offer a man who was capable of producing such a thing, a man who had — how clearly each brush stroke proclaimed it! — endured and gloried in the fire?

Who was the woman? she wondered as she got ready for bed. Where is she now?

To which questions neither the darkness of the room, nor the steady beating of her heart, gave reply.

★   ★   ★

Next morning, very early, Cal went into his studio. He looked at the unfinished painting on the easel and saw all sorts of things wrong with it that he had not seen before, saw that it was, in fact, beyond redemption. As he had believed himself beyond redemption. As, indeed, he might still be although, for the first time since Gianetta died, he was less sure of that or anything. For so long he had wanted death, yet now saw that to die would prevent him from producing the body of worthwhile work that was the only reason, he believed, for his ever having lived.

He took the painting and stood it on the floor with its face to the wall. He replaced it with a piece of board and pinned a sheet of drawing paper to it. With quick slashes of a sepia crayon he drew a sketch of Kathryn Fanning as he remembered her from the previous evening: the slender, sun-bronzed arms emerging from the summery dress, the graceful column of her neck, the dark eyes watching him from the tanned face. She came to life; he felt the tremor of her breath on his hand as he sketched, the liquid glint of light upon her eyes. Behind her the river flowed in tranquillity and, all around, the peaceful night held its breath.

He stood back, studying it dispassionately as he studied all his work, then did another drawing, confident strokes creating out of air and memory the likeness of the girl. A profile, this time: the angle of nose and cheekbone, the close-fitting cap of dark hair poised above the graceful neck.

Again he studied the drawings, recognising the quality of both, then went out of the studio and climbed the path to the cliff. There was a wind blowing and bright sunlight: a starched, clean day. He looked down at the breakers bursting in spouts of spray against the boulders far beneath. The wind flattened his shirt against his chest. The sky was a brilliant blue, the air crackled with salt and over everything — sea, sky, cliff — lay the golden blessing of the sun.

He turned, went back down the track to the house. He took a shower, pulled on clean clothes. He rolled up the two sketches he had made of Kathryn, went out to the car and drove back to town.

3

The guide was trilling in an appropriately flute-like voice about the characteristics and merits of serpent and sackbut, of lute and claviharp and dulcimer.

Cal and Kathryn watched, sort of, and listened, perhaps, as he wafted them, and others, through the shuttered silences of the exhibition. All the time Cal was conscious, not of the instruments they had supposedly come to see, but of Kathryn beside him. She was very small, the top of her head reaching barely to his shoulder. Very upright, too, yet she walked with liquid ease, limbs flowing as effortlessly as the river beside which they had strolled the previous evening. She was wearing a shift of oatmeal-coloured linen. It hung straight, barely disturbed by the contours of her body. The effect was one of sensuality and grace and Cal felt an attraction that was both sexual and devoid of sex, a mingling of purity and desire that he had known only once before in his life.

'The playing of these instruments,' the guide told them, 'required a discipline entirely alien to the times in which the musicians lived. A combination of military precision and feminine grace,' he proclaimed, melodious as any sackbut.

Kathryn risked a sideways glance at Cal's face. His expression was impassive yet, in its stillness, offered the hint of a sardonic smile.

The guide pirouetted, beaming at the half-dozen sheep he had succeeded in mustering into the dusty paddocks of the exhibition hall. 'Now upstairs we have — '

Cal caught Kathryn's eye. 'Let's get out of here.'

Laughing in the street amid the hustle and shove of shoppers, the belch of traffic, Kathryn stared at him accusingly.

'You weren't interested in the exhibition at all.'

'Not at all,' he agreed.

He grinned; she grinned; again they were laughing, joyously, without reason.

Only yesterday he would have been defensive, alert to what might have been criticism. He would have scythed her down and lost her. Now he was filled with the lightness of knowing that she had not been getting at him at all; on the contrary, she had been sharing with him her laughter at the pompous little man with his pompous little phrases. The sense of lightness became one with the magic of the previous evening. Cal felt inexpressibly happy, kindly disposed even towards the flute-voiced guide, and laughed again. He wanted to seize Kathryn's hand, to run and run. Instead they crossed the road, most decorously, and walked until they came once again to the Arts Centre. They crossed the grass to the river bank. The water flowed, lovers walked with interlocking hips, joggers ran lightly, or doggedly, leaving upon the air an imprint of sweat and clutching breath.

There was a restaurant by the bridge. Cal had eaten nothing all day and was hungry.

'Fancy some lunch?'

They sat at a table by the window. They barely spoke, but watched the river and, occasionally, each other: skipping glances, while tentative smiles touched the corners of their eyes. Which remained cautious, nonetheless.

The silence flowed like the river, separating and uniting them. Kathryn knew that she could drown so easily in its depths. She commanded herself to consider all the things that made up her life: the friends, the man who would marry her, if permitted, the expectation of an ordered and fulfilling life. They were eminently desirable and as nothing.

I am helpless, she thought, and did not care.

The food came. Now they talked, their tongues of trivia, their eyes of what mattered. Even now there were long minutes when they said nothing at all but sat, and looked, and experienced the moment.

Over coffee Kathryn said, 'My uncle phoned this morning.'

'Dave? What did he want? Checking up to see I haven't kidnapped you?'

'He said you might be having a one-man show in New York.'

'He could just as easily have said might not.'

'Why should he say that?'

'He warned me. The gallery over there doesn't like the stuff we sent them. Nobody does.' He toyed with his spoon. 'I don't like it myself.'

There was a sense of shock in saying it, in acknowledging that all this time he had been wrong and the others right. Relief, too, that by admitting it he had created the opportunity to sort things out at last.

'About bloody time,' he said.

'What is?'

He did not answer, sat staring at the shadowed water, the boats, the people walking. Now it begins, he thought. Then corrected himself. Not now; early this morning, when I did the sketches.

He wished he had them with him. He wanted to touch them, to trace with his eyes the movement of crayon on paper, to re-live the emotion that had guided his hand when he drew them: the moment, he recognised now, of re-awakening. He had always hoarded his work, but now wanted to show them to Kathryn, to let them speak for him in the silence that had once more come down between them.

Which, later, they did.

They stood beside his car in the parking garage. He handed her the sketches. She unrolled them, looked at them silently.

Now he was embarrassed by what he had done. His mind seized words that would be frivolous enough to dilute the awkwardness but, at the last, watching the dark head lowered over the sketches, he said nothing.

She looked up at him. A slight frown puckered her forehead, and he saw she was trying to guess his motives in offering her the drawings.

'I did them this morning before I left. I'd been painting something else, but decided it was no good. So I did these instead.'

'They're lovely,' she wondered.

'Ten minutes work,' he said. 'No big deal.'

It was important she should understand that the sketches really were a gift, that accepting them would commit her to nothing that she did not wish for herself.

'You could stick them on a wall somewhere.'

Or in a drawer. Or even in the fire. Because it was the offering and acceptance that mattered, not the drawings themselves. This he did not say; yet something in his tone must have resolved her doubts. Her face cleared.

'Thank you very much. They really are beautiful.'

And looked at them more happily.

He did not want her to go, but knew she must. She had told him she lived a hundred kilometres north of the City, whereas he was the same distance to the south. He wanted to see her again very soon and hoped she might feel the same, but the patterns of their lives made it difficult. The thought troubled him. Their two meetings would come to nothing unless they did something about things straightaway.

He knew nothing about her life or commitments. Last night and again today these things had not mattered, but now that they were going to be apart, they would matter very much.

He was determined to stop things fizzling out.

'You could give them to a friend,' he said, watching her.

She rolled them up, her slim hands clasping them to her. She smiled at him. 'I shall keep them for myself.'

He walked with her to her car on a different level of the same garage.

'Here we go again.'

She looked the question.

'Yesterday and now today. Watching you drive off.'

'I can't very well sit here forever.'

He looked at the concrete ramp, the rows of other cars. 'Not much of a view,' he agreed. 'Not like the river.'

'Thank you for the lunch.'

'I've no idea what I ate,' he confessed.

She burst out laughing. 'Neither have I.' And was again sober.

'The exhibition,' he said. 'I remember that, all right.'

'Military precision and feminine grace,' she said. 'He was pretty graceful himself.'

'Not to say feminine.'

Shared laughter warmed them.

He said, 'I would like to see you again. If that's possible.'

Now was the chance for her to say, No, I'm sorry, I don't think that would be a good idea.

'Fanning,' she told him. 'You can always phone me. We're in the book.'

A handful of words, yet filled with light and hope. And, yes, joy.

'I shall.' He took her hand in his, feeling the slender fingers smooth and cool against his own. 'Thank you again. It's been wonderful.'

'And you will phone?'

'I shall.'

Once again he watched as she drove away. Except that this time, as she went down the ramp, her arm waved at him through the open window. He raised his own hand, then she was gone. The dying hum of the engine, the squeak of tyres; silence.

Certainly I shall phone, he thought. Yes, indeed.

He drove home for the second time in successive days, seeing in daylight the hills that had been invisible the previous night, seeing superimposed upon them once again the dark-haired, smiling features of the girl.

Cal had been home an hour when Angela Scales arrived.

He heard the crunch of tyres on the gravel and went out to see her hauling her flab out of the little sports car that seemed too small for one of her heroic proportions.

One look at her expression, concerned and

apprehensive, and he knew why she had come. Anger and resentment returned in full measure, like a sickness. He stared at her silently, with no intention of making things easier for her.

She gave him a bilious smile, nerves showing. 'How you going?'

He waited.

'I was passing. Thought I'd drop in and surprise you.'

Sure.

He twisted on his heel, turning big shoulders on Angela's crap, and went back into the studio. Along the walls the stacked paintings flourished their sombre fire. A momentary loss of light as Angela came in behind him. Cal did not turn but stood with his back to her, waiting.

Like Dave before her, she wandered up and down, glancing at a painting here, touching another there. The light pulsed with their anger; hatred struck like a blow. And, far worse than hatred, self-pity.

Cal parked his backside on a stool and watched her — and them — silently. Thought, no wonder nobody likes them. If someone else had painted them I wouldn't buy one. I wouldn't have them as a gift.

Now, looking at them as Angela waddled to and fro, it seemed to him that they had indeed been painted by someone else, that he had neither patience nor connection with them or the man who had painted them. With the realisation came the awareness that he was sick of playing games, that he wanted this whole wretched business behind him, so that he could get on with his life and his art all over again.

He said, 'New York.'

And watched her shoulders slump.

'They don't want them,' she told the stacked paintings. Then she turned to face him, chin defiant. 'They say the paintings we sent them aren't up to the standard of your earlier work. They say they doubt there's a market for it. At this precise moment in time.' She mimicked an American accent, shrugging helplessly. 'You know how they talk.'

So.

David Holt had warned him. He had even had the chance to wonder how he'd feel, being turned down by the Stuyvesant after all the hype, the excitement.

Now he knew. He didn't give a damn. Rejection gave him the chance to put away all that had happened during the past year. His feelings for Gianetta would remain always, a glory of light and fulfilment in his life, but the manner of her death, the corrosive hatred that had destroyed both himself and everything it touched, was gone.

Yet now he found the habit of anger more enduring than anger itself.

'We have a contract. In case you've forgotten. Or,' he amended, 'you told me we had.'

He saw her eyes harden at his tone.

'You know we have. You've got a copy.'

'So enforce it.'

Her expression said, Don't be a fool.

'We could,' she agreed. 'At the moment all they're saying is try again, send us something new, we think you're on the wrong track here. They're embarrassed by it. I had Ira Roth himself on the phone. He wanted to take them but said he couldn't, it wouldn't be in our interests or theirs. They understand what happened, what you've been through. They have every sympathy — '

'Short of honouring the agreement.'

'At the moment, the door's still open. Hold them to the contract and we've lost them for good.'

'So what use is the contract? Or you, either, come to that?'

Angela was sick of him and his mindless petulance. 'The art world is full of spoiled brats. The way you've been since you got back from Europe I'm beginning to think you're one of them.' She stalked him across the studio and he saw how angry she was. 'I've made allowances. We all have. We know how bad it's been for you. But we've had enough. You've got to move on, Cal. You must.'

'Let the dead bury their dead?' A viper smile. 'And what happens if it's not so easy to do that?'

'Then you're finished. Because what you're doing now is wrong — wrong for you, wrong for the market. And if you're not willing to take my word for it, then you're right, I'm no use to you, either.'

She was blazing; he nodded at her, unsmiling. 'And that's telling me.'

'You'd sooner I lied to you about it?'

No, he would not sooner she lied, knew that she was telling him only what he'd been telling himself for the last two days. Yet to acknowledge it remained hard. In a perverted way, it seemed like a betrayal of Gianetta. Whom he had killed.

Perhaps he could meet her halfway. He gave her a crooked smile. 'Want a drink?'

It wasn't much, but enough.

'Just what I need.'

What they both needed.

Whisky, quickly replenished, unlocked his tongue.

'I've been thinking of taking a trip into the Outback. Do some paintings of the desert.

The Flinders Ranges, maybe.'

At once she was interested. 'Like Sid Nolan?'

'No.' He smiled, feeling the creative juices stirring, exultantly. 'Like Cal Jessop.'

'Tell me about it.'

He hadn't thought it through, was not sure he was ready to talk about anything, but had brought the subject up, after all. He had a go, hesitantly.

'I thought it might make a series to complement 'Coastal Sequence'. Sea and Outback. The circle, encompassing, and what it contains.' So he fumbled, images and ideas as elusive as mist. 'The other aspect of the continent?' he hoped.

'Technically you've come a long way since 'Coastal Sequence'.'

She was right. But . . . 'I don't see that as a problem. I haven't thought about it properly. Just a few ideas. Floating.' He smiled apologetically. 'Gone off half-cocked. Sorry.'

'Don't be. I'm glad to hear about it.'

At last. She did not say it, but he heard it clearly. She would be glad of anything that might bring him out of the cul-de-sac in which he had trapped himself. Two days ago the implied criticism would have angered him but now he felt only relief that he might indeed be coming out of the shadows at last.

★ ★ ★

The next day he phoned Stella.

'Heard from Hennie?'

Her laugh mocked his question. 'Still up at Moomba, I'd say. If you really want to know.'

It was true that he was usually more interested in knowing the coast was clear than anything else. But this time he'd rung for a different reason.

'I need to get hold of him. I'm thinking of taking a trip into the Outback. I thought, if he's got any leave coming, he might be interested in ferrying me around.'

'You saying that really is the only reason you rang? To find out about Hennie?'

Bloody hell.

'Of course not. But I have to get hold of him, right?'

'Phone him at the plant. If he's not there, you can leave a message. He might ring you back. I wouldn't know; I haven't tried recently.'

'Thanks.'

'It is all you wanted,' she accused.

Now he was tumbling over his feet, tongue busy with denials. 'You know very well it's not.'

Lies and shut eyes, he thought. Knew that the only way to avoid a row was to go along.

The last time, he told himself severely. The very last.

For the first time in a year, he had seen what might be light. In the new series of paintings, the company of the girl. He'd better be right; the Venusberg had released Tannhäuser once, would never have done it a second time had he gone back. Cal had only one chance of salvation and Stella, he knew, would never be any part of that.

Yet he went anyway and afterwards . . .

'What's wrong?'

Panting, sweat streaming, he stared down at her, at the body beautiful as damnation.

'Wrong?'

She laughed, long nails set in his flesh. 'Come on, lover. Lie to anyone else, but not to me, not now.'

He set his teeth, his mind, his heart. 'I don't know what you're on about.'

And rode her down the dark path.

Afterwards, they lay side by side, not touching. They were separated by less than an inch, by the infinite distance of their unrelated lives. Beyond the closed curtains, the sea broke in smoking pillars upon the quaking land. Here, from the still corners of the room, Cal was watched by eyes that he would not acknowledge, a river flowing under green and peaceful trees.

'Something's happened to you.'

Stella's fingers traced paths along his thigh. 'Nothing's happened.'

'Don't try and fool me!' Anger sharpened her voice, her fingernails dug deep. 'When we went south in that boat of yours, you were violent, like a maniac. Mad at yourself; at me, too, maybe. Not that I cared. You were like the storm, sweeping us both away. Now . . .'

The talons worked their path. Deeper, harder, as he had earlier savaged her flesh, seeking what could not be found. It was unbearable.

'I'm sorry I wasn't up to expectations.'

Knowing that was not it.

Now the gouging fingers were still. For a minute they lay inert, then withdrew as Stella herself withdrew. He felt her leave him. He should have been relieved; instead, felt only desolation.

He turned, desperately, seeking consolation. For himself; for her too, perhaps. He placed his hand on her breast, he kneaded the sullen flesh. Would have ripped it in his efforts to obliterate the memory of all they had shared through the dark months. Convulsively, she shoved him away.

'Stop it!'

Now it was his hand that lay still, acknowledging helplessness, but Stella was less ready to forgive.

'You think you can use me, even in that?'

She had helped him through the darkness. For her own purposes, no doubt, had turned her back on a husband who loved only flight, who should never have married, least of all a sprite of surf and storm. In his absence, she had turned to Cal. In need himself, he had come to her; now — in spirit if not yet in body — was gone again.

He thought he had given nothing in return for what she had given him.

Had used her, indeed.

It was impossible to stay, yet there was guilt even in doing what was right. As always, the woman found the way.

'I think we've come to the end of something . . . '

'No . . . ' But with no force in the denial.

'I'm not just a quick screw. I thought you knew that.'

'Of course I know it.' The words died like dust; protestations of innocence had no place. 'Shall I see you again?'

'Sort yourself out. Then we'll see.'

Cal crossed to the mainland over the bridge that spanned the smoking surf. From the far side he looked back. Stella was standing upon the furthest pinnacle of rock, garlanded by the spray that flashed its rainbow brilliance in the sunlight. Her spread arms embraced the sea that tumbled its massive rollers at her feet. Her back was to Cal, to the land, and the spray burst about her. She had returned to her true love.

His feet groping between slippery rocks, Cal walked away until sea, island, woman, were lost to sight.

Back at the studio he sat on the floor, feeling his paintings, past and future, pulse in the air about him. A sea sprite, spray-drenched, held her arms aloft. Against the green silence of a river, eyes watched beneath a close-fitting cap of dark hair.

Tomorrow, he thought. In the morning I'll make a start. I shall work, I shall find myself again. I shall be whole.

Until Paris he had trained himself to a ritual of work, iron-hard and resolute. This, too, had gone. He had drifted, his life unboxed, spilling its contents aimlessly. Now he would change that.

Tomorrow, he thought. Tomorrow the world begins.

★　★　★

In the pale flush of dawn Cal went out of the house. On the cliff top was a granite slab, another at its back, that he called his chair.

He sat and stared out at the vast expanse of sea and sky. This I am, he thought, but knew there was more. Visions filled him; red and umber sand, stone polished by the wind, screaming in an oven heat, an emptiness peopled by time. The land itself, eternity at its back, in its face. Beneath the ancient sea it had remained while the mountains were ground into shallow stumps by the aeons' weight.

We, black and white, are nothing, he thought. Eternity exists in the spaces, the rocks, the boiling wind. It needs nothing more. It needs nothing at all. It is.

This he would paint. He would capture the wind and space, the heat. Eternity. He knew how great a task it was, would accept it not vaingloriously but in humility and fear. This is how the old priests must have felt, he thought, the worshippers of the infinite. No longer; religion is like everything else, tidied into boxes. It has lost touch with the universal, which is true eternity.

I shall try, he thought. More than that is impossible.

One thing more he knew. He could not do it alone.

When he got back to the house, the phone was ringing.

'Angela.' The fat voice breathed in his ear.

'I'm having a little dinner party next Thursday. I wondered if you'd be free?'

So she also believes in my new vision, he thought. Angela's parties were famous in the art world. It was the first time she had invited him to one for almost a year, since shortly after his return from Paris. Then everything had been as fragile as porcelain. Words and glances had tiptoed around him with dreadful tact, but the invitation, once she had seen the new work emerging from the abyss, had not been repeated. In the way of business, Angela would pay homage to the dead, but once only. The living had a prior claim.

The fact that she had invited him now was a signal. Three days ago, he would have rejected it. Now he did not hesitate.

'What time?'

★　★　★

An elegant unit, seven floors up, staring at the Gulf — which, in the quality and cost of its embellishments, it attempted to outshine. Most of the guests were equally valuable, at least in their own estimation. Cal as much at home as a limpet on a silk shawl.

He didn't care. He knew the type of hangers-on that Angela gathered about her. He had nothing in common with them but they were harmless, for the most part, the bray and twitter that passed for conversation no more than a mild irritant. All the same, he was glad Dave Holt was here, or Dexter Holt, as he was known in this company. Dave greeted him with a knowing smile that at first Cal misunderstood.

'I've been hearing things . . . '

'Right?' Thinking, *Kathryn.*

Wrong.

'Angela says she hasn't seen you so enthusiastic about a project for a long time.'

'All I said was I might go poking around the Outback . . . '

But he *was* enthusiastic and did not mind in the least that it showed.

'Looks as though *Rheingold* may have helped, eh?'

'Something like that.'

Certainly the music might have set the mood.

'When are you going?'

'Soon.'

'How are you going to arrange it?'

'I've got a mate. A pilot. He ferries supplies for the Moomba gas plant. He's been working the Outback for years. Knows every nook and cranny. He's probably got some leave coming; if he has, I'm hoping he'll agree to ferry me around.'

Talking about it, Cal found that he was eager to get his eyes and hands around the new project.

'I also hear you made a hit with my niece.'

Cal brushed it away. 'We talked. We went for a stroll. That was all.'

Was warm in the knowledge that it had not in the least been all.

Dave laughed, high-pitched. 'My dear, did I say anything? Do what you like with her, far as I'm concerned. It's a free world, or so they're always telling us.'

'She's gone back now.'

Dave shrugged. 'It's her home. Can't imagine how she tolerates it, but there you are. Besides, she has a boy there.'

An instant's absolute silence, freezing the air. Somehow he said, 'That right?'

The shrill background voices echoed remorselessly.

'Local doctor. Seems harmless enough. They have an understanding, I hear.'

Angela was calling them to the dinner table but, for a moment, Cal did not move. Far out in the darkness, the lights of a vessel moved steadily across the Gulf while overhead the stars held their breath.

They have an understanding . . .

'Tell me about him.'

'Nothing to tell. I haven't met him. My

sister says he's a nice boy. Steady. A doctor, as I said. With prospects.'

'Come *along*,' Angela said behind them, 'or everything will be cold.'

The dining table was long, of glass and brass. Around which we have all set our arse, thought Cal savagely. He looked around at the other diners. Feeding. He could have tipped over the table and everyone around it.

They have an understanding.

There was no reason why Kathryn should have told him; none. Yet in his heart felt betrayed by her silence.

A nice boy. Steady. With prospects.

Any mother's dream son-in-law. Suddenly it seemed outrageous that he did not even know what this nice boy was called. Dave was seated at the far end of the table. Tough.

'What's his name?'

Cal's raised voice cut the decorous gabble about this and that, about me and me and me. A shocked silence. Everyone present would have acknowledged the theory that true creativity has its own rules but, in practice, things were different. In the silence eyes gathered indignation around them, like a cloak. Which Cal disregarded.

'Dave, what's his name?'

'What's whose name?' The blank look of one who truly did not understand. Then his face cleared. 'I believe . . . Charles Chivers. Why?'

'Just curious.'

But knew it was more than that. Charles Chivers. The nice boy. With prospects. Learning his name gave strength.

They have an understanding.

We shall see about that.

Conversation was beginning to patch the silence. The extraordinary interlude, so tasteless, was over.

After dinner Angela sought him out.

'When are you going into the Outback?'

'Couple of weeks. Give or take.'

'Then I probably shan't see you before I go.'

He did not understand. 'Go where?'

'My dear . . . ' Angela laughed. 'That's what this bash is all about. Didn't I tell you? I'm going away. Three months touring Asia.'

'What on earth for?'

'Looking for treasure. Asian art's flavour of the month. The Americans are in there already. I'm going to see what I can dredge up before it's too late.'

Suddenly, unreasonably, Cal was angry. 'For three months? Just when I'm starting a new project?'

Tantrums were wasted on Angela. Her expression did not change.

'You're not the only pebble on the beach, dear. Just as well. Way things have been the last twelve months, I'd have starved.'

Deliberately Cal turned his head, surveying the wreckage of the meal, the plates, the puddled glasses.

'Thank God there seems no danger of that.'

'Small thanks to you.'

And moved on, leaving Cal to his futile anger.

Betrayed twice in one evening . . .

It was a child's reaction, egotistical and unreasoning; he despised himself for it but it remained, for all that. Made him, if anything, angrier than ever, his re-awakened confidence still too fragile for such shocks.

He found Dave. Whom he was quite willing to blame, though for what would have been hard put to say.

'I'm out of here.'

Angela overheard. 'I wanted to introduce — '

'Skip it. I'm not in the mood.'

The spoilt brat stalked down the corridor, a plush hush like a millionaire's casket, and hammered the button to bring the lift. Already, too late, he was having second thoughts. It was the sort of conduct he despised in others, the hooligans who insult in order to demonstrate to themselves their own importance. In which no one else believes. It would serve me right if Angela dumped me, he thought.

'I shall ring her,' he told the silent lift as it whisked him to the ground. 'Make things right.'

As for Doctor Charles Chivers . . .

Have to sort him out.

It had been raining. He headed south on slick roadways, gunning the motor despite his good intentions. On South Road, just past Flagstaff Hill, picked up a stream of slowly-inching traffic. After five minutes he passed the flashing blue lights crowded around a wrecked car that had left the road and overturned. The CFS was working, had already hosed down the highway where fuel, it seemed, had been spilt.

Cal glanced briefly as he edged past. It looked bad, the remains of the car a crumpled ruin. There was an ambulance, but no activity, the car's occupants presumably still trapped inside the wreck.

He drove home. He parked the car and walked up the path and stood on the cliff edge, letting the wind blow away the residue of the evening's anger. It had diminished him, not in the eyes of the other guests, who did not matter, but in his own. Self-perception had become important, linking what he was to what he must become if he were to carry out the work that once again had become important to him.

'I really will ring her,' he told the night, and this time meant it.

Half an hour later, back in the house with his feet up, the phone rang.

'Hullo?'

'Thank God! Thank God!'

Dave's voice, strangled by alarm even as he laughed.

'What's the problem?'

'You, man! You! I thought it was you!'

Heaven preserve us, thought Cal. 'Thought what was me?'

'There was an accident on South Road.'

'I know. I saw it.'

'It was on the late news. A man, they said, driving alone. Driving like a maniac, by the sound of it. Lost control on a bend. Stone dead. They haven't identified him yet.'

'Why did you think it was me?'

'The car. A red Commodore, like the one you drive. And the way you left the party — '

Cal felt a cold finger touch him. Dave was right. He remembered the car upside-down beside the traffic-choked road, saw again the revolving blue lights, the CFS crew working, and knew how easily, in his mood and those conditions, it might indeed have been him.

Walking with Kathryn beside the green-shadowed river, he had discovered for the first time in a year that he no longer wanted to die. Now, holding the phone, he knew that things had gone much further than that. Now, most ardently, he wanted to live.

That brought an awareness of danger. When he had sailed south in search of his ultimate storm, danger had not existed. Now things were different. Shortly he would be flying with Hennie Loots around the Outback. There was danger in that, the potential for disaster. How ironic it would be if, having searched so long for death, he should find it now, when he wanted so much to live!

'Hullo? Hullo?' Dave's voice squawking in his ear.

'I'm here.'

'I was so shaken when I saw it. I rang the newsroom but they said they didn't know who he was.'

Cal was smiling: at Dave's relieved agitation, at the darkness beyond the window, at the blood coursing richly through his veins.

'You know what Mark Twain said. When a newspaper reported he'd died?'

Cut off in full flood, Dave floundered. 'What? No.'

'Reports of my death are grossly exaggerated.'

He was close to laughter, not that a stranger was dead but that he, gloriously, was alive. Nothing will take that away, he thought. I shall not permit it.

Now Dave was laughing, too. 'I'm glad. There's another party you might like to go to, if you can face it after tonight. Next weekend at my place.'

'Don't say you're rushing off as well?'

'Just a quiet evening with friends. My niece will be there.'

★ ★ ★

Not only Kathryn; Margaret Videon was there, too. Cat's eyes and spiteful smile, legs that went on forever. Seeing her brought back memories which she was quick to proclaim, hinting, nudging, laughing in the high yip-yip that, now he had been reminded, he recalled with much distaste. To hear her talk, they might have been the best of friends, as — hard to believe — they had indeed been once.

'Sydney,' Margaret told the room. 'My God, darlings, shall I ever forget it? Cal had just started in those days. Even then I could see how different he was from the rest.'

And smiled, publicly sharing a past. They had been together for only a few months. The relationship had little to do with art, a great deal to do with chemistry. Twelve months after they broke up Cal had started to make a name and for this Margaret would never forgive him.

'Sex and creativity,' Margaret said. 'They say they go together, don't they? I'll tell you, darlings, Cal has always been very creative.'

And laughed, drawing the room into a joke with nails in its paws. Perhaps imagined that Cal, with Kathryn beside him, would be a soft target. But that was something he had never been.

'One thing about Margaret,' he said, sharing the laugh, 'she may not be creative, but she's always been one for sex. Ask anyone.'

Which shut her up, and the laughter.

After dinner, as soon as there was a moment, Cal and Kathryn slipped away. They stood outside the door in the cool darkness. Down the drive moonlight shone on the surface of the parked cars and, at the bottom of the hill, the bay was a blaze of fairy fire.

'I'm sorry about that.'

'She was jealous. It's not important.'

Looking at her, Cal believed her, that for her the ugly exchange across the dinner table had not been important at all.

They walked silently along the track, past the occasional wind-beaten tree supplicating the stars. There was a stone wall with a gate in it. They passed through the gate and came out on the cliff.

He put his hand on her arm. 'Listen . . . '

In the darkness the breakers gnawed.

'We are very high here,' Cal said.

He took her hand and walked forward until they were on the very edge. Beneath them was nothing but crumbling stone and air. The cannonade of the breaking seas echoed dizzily. He felt her tension.

'I grew up here. I know what I'm doing.'

And felt her relax as she surrendered herself into his care.

For a few moments only; soon they turned and walked back down the path to Dave's house. Both knew that the moment of trust had done something to seal their feelings, had brought them beyond acquaintance into something a good deal more important.

At the door he paused, hand once again on her arm.

'Where are you staying?'

'Here. With my uncle.'

'I'll come and see you in the morning. If I may.'

The gleam of moonlight on her teeth as she

smiled. 'Will you? Truly?'

'Will seven be too early for you?'

If it was, she gave no sign. 'I'll be ready.'

Before he knew he was going to do it, he put his arms around her. It was the first time he had touched her so intimately and, for an instant, he felt her stiffen. Then, as on the edge of the cliff, she relaxed and came closer into his arms.

Cal was filled with a fearful, tremulous joy. He drew her close, feeling her body pliant and amenable against his, the ardent length of thigh and belly and breast. There was an essence there, something free and unattainable. It was the core of her being, could be captured or even touched by no-one, yet the need to do so was great. He yearned for her, and for it, as some men yearn for the remotest realms of space; forever there, forever dear, forever unattainable.

He kissed her hair and released her, the fragrance of the kiss in his mouth.

'Coming in?'

The idea of plunging back into the spiteful pool of Dave's party, of being indoors at all, appalled him. What he needed now was freedom. Freedom to walk, to breathe, to be.

'Say sorry for me.'

He touched her cheek gently with the back of his fingers, saw the warmth kindle in her

86

eyes. He turned and walked away up the path. Somewhere behind him the door closed. He was alone — to run, to shout, to brandish arms and spirit at the moon.

He returned to the place on the cliff top where they had stood minutes earlier. Beyond was a ledge, no more than a few centimetres wide, angling steeply down the vertical face of the cliff until it levelled out twenty feet below. No handholds, no bush or tree to grab in case of a slip. Below lay nothing but a swoon of air, a lonely crying of gulls, the resonance of the distant surf. He had edged along it in daylight, had sensed stones along the path edge falling like crumbs into space. It had been dangerous, then; at night it was madness. Which was the point. Life welled within him, needing the exultation of danger.

He walked purposefully forward, set his feet on the steeply-angled path, inched downwards into the plunging dark.

In the darkness, memory.

While he had been studying in Paris, he and Gianetta had taken time in their one Christmas together to go to England. In London they had visited the galleries, had explored with their eyes and ardent breath the masses of Moore, ponderous yet light as air, the pre-cubist explorations of Cezanne.

They had gone west, to Exmoor. Had stayed in a farmhouse far from roads and people.

★ ★ ★

A track sketched in mud probed the moor's dark roots. One night, after a day of rain, they went out at dusk and followed the track until they reached an amphitheatre between great rocks.

Alone, Cal clambered to the highest point, stood with his face to the icy wind. The temperature was plummeting, the clouds promised snow. He knelt to be one with the structure of the mud, touched where the imprint of a hoof revealed a horse's passing. In the compression of the mud sensed the animal's heat. He smeared the mud on hands and face, trying to discover its essence as, earlier, he had tried to discover the essence of the girl. Again he failed.

Ceremoniously he stripped, white skin shrinking in the ice-edged wind, while from the track below Gianetta screamed of danger, folly. Which was the point, the ultimate sharing with oblivion.

★ ★ ★

On the ledge he paused, the cliff's vertical face propelling him outwards, while a cascade of loose stones fell silently. Gravity sucked. One more step. Another. He reached the end. Heart and brain sang, on fire with life. Terror was one of many flames.

A gull's wing brushed the darkness. Cal inched around until he faced the sea, space. He stood straight-backed, not permitting himself to touch the cliff behind him. He took a deep breath and raised his arms, like a diver. Stood motionless, free, upon the ultimate brink of oblivion. Again his mind went back to the ecstatic moment, naked upon the frozen moor.

★　★　★

A movement. In the ardent wind, a fox, loping. It reminded him of a tale told him by a writer he had known back in Oz. Half-drunk at a party, the man had talked of a fox he had seen crossing a paddock near his home, how the sighting had triggered a series of images that he planned to incorporate in a novel. Now Cal watched the silhouette of the animal as soundlessly it crossed the path. A momentary glimpse, so close, then it was gone, leaving upon the darkness its rank stench, the texture and memory of movement like an owl's cry painted upon a frosty canvas.

Ceremoniously he lay down, spread-eagled upon the turf, feeling the awe and oneness of creation, its ardent singularity.

With desperate speed he dragged on his clothes. Hauling Gianetta protesting behind him, returned to their room in the isolated farmhouse, at once began work on the painting that critics later hailed as a new departure, a giant step forward from the 'Coastal Sequence' that had made his name.

Fox By Moonlight.

A tree, the slash and zag of moonlight through naked branches, a bleak and snow-bleached hill rising into a black sky. The mask of a fox, superimposed. In the tree, the bundled shape of a koala. Upon the glare of the hill's white breast a nude study, in the blue of moonlight and spangled with frost, of Gianetta.

Making love to her with the brush as, earlier, he had made love to her with the flesh.

Three days later they went back to Paris. Where, in the following summer, she died.

The world, the glitter of ice, the promise of moonlight upon his ardent flesh, were dead. All, all, all dead.

★   ★   ★

Now, on the cliff, daring the edges of oblivion below the turning of the stars, Cal heard the night surge of the sea's slow offering and knew that life had returned once more.

Enough.

He had made his sacrifice of nerve and danger. Now the instinct to survive was strong again. He lowered his arms and edged back along the ledge. To what he willed would be safety.

4

The next morning, seven o'clock as promised, Cal went to call on Kathryn Fanning.

For no reason he laughed into her smiling face, his spirits on tiptoe this bright morning, and knew that in this, too, life was returning.

'Why are you laughing?' Laughing herself as she said it.

'Because I'm happy.'

Hand in hand, they went out into the day's promise.

'I want to show you everything . . . '

He did the best he could.

They went first to the summit of The Bushranger. They sat on the edge of the drop, feet dangling in a vertiginous swoon of air. All around them the sea was sparkling, brilliant.

'Had a bit of a scare off here, not so long ago.' He told her about the storm, the nail-biting return to harbour through the violent wall of surf, but nothing of his motive in going out, nothing of his companion. He pointed. 'That's the harbour where I keep my boat.'

'What's her name?'

'*Jester*. I'll take you out some time, if you like.'

Below them a sea eagle swooped with eloquent tilt of wings amid a screeching cloudburst of gulls. Far beneath, a sea lion glided along a line of buoys, sleek body gleaming, upturned flipper imploring the air.

Further along the coast, two islands sailed into the brisk wind. In the distance, anchored to the mainland by a causeway barely visible in the early morning light, was the island where at night the fairy penguins roosted. Much closer, the second island was little more than a pile of rocks. At which Cal would not look, nor at the roof of Stella's house, gleaming amid the boulders.

'Come on . . . '

They spent the rest of the morning exploring the coastline. He talked to her, awkwardly, about his work, how he tried to find the hidden significance in physical things.

'A tree standing alone in a paddock is more than a tree. It is loneliness, or at least solitude.'

'And a woman on a rock?' Kathryn pirouetted against a backdrop of restless sea, white-flecked. 'What is she?'

'Who can ever hope to understand a woman?'

Laughing as he teased her, joyously.

Suddenly serious, she turned to watch the waves. 'Sometimes I am afraid . . . '

He did not ask of what. Had no need to; happiness had its own terrors.

'We are all afraid,' he told her. 'That is why people worship. Some in churches, some in the bodies of others — '

'Some in paint.'

'Worship, yes. But not fear. Only that the work might be inadequate to convey — '

And paused, searching. *All there is to convey.* But could not find the words and gestured, helplessly.

A single breath consumed the rest of the morning. It was early; they were happy; the next thing it was lunchtime.

'Where's the morning gone?'

They grabbed a roll from a cafe in town, walked to a beach Cal knew, a kilometre away. To get there they had to use the path that skirted the cliff edge, dipping periodically almost to the rocks, crossing the beds of dried-up watercourses before climbing again. Below them the sea stretched like a piece of crumpled silk to an horizon blurred by haze. It was the path that ran past the island where Stella lived.

Kathryn paused. 'What a wonderful place to have a house!'

Cal did not look. 'Gets a bit wild in winter, I reckon.'

'Who lives there?'

'Bloke I know. Pilot. He's away most of the time, working in the Outback.'

'Why does he keep the house, then?'

Cal did not slacken his stride and Kathryn went with him, turning at the corner of the path to stare back with envious eyes at the little bridge connecting the island with the mainland, the house perched amid the rocks.

Cal watched her impatiently. 'Thinking of making him an offer?'

'I wish. It would be wonderful to have a place like that. So free . . . '

'Dare say Stella agrees with you.'

'Stella?'

'The wife. She lives there all the time.'

The path followed a bend in the cliff. The island, the house set amid the rocks, were gone.

'It could be lonely, I suppose,' Kathryn said. 'But if she's got the sea for company . . . '

'She makes out all right,' Cal said.

They came to a headland; beyond it, the path ran down to the beach, tawny, tide-rippled, deserted.

'You need to be careful here.'

They found their way down a slope where

wild flowers painted the cliff in patterns of red and chrome. They ran the last few yards, feet slipping in soft sand, and came out on the beach.

'It's a lot bigger than it looks from the top.'

It was big, two hundred metres wide and a kilometre long. The retreating waves had left a sheen of water, slick as oil, on the shelving sand, in which the reflections of clouds shone like the uncertain images of half-remembered dreams. The sand ended in a jumble of dark rocks against which the sea dashed in a welter of foam, even on a day as calm as this.

'You don't want to go in the water here,' Cal said. 'There's a tide rip just off the beach. Every summer people get drowned.'

'Despite the signs?'

There they were, all along the beach, warning people not to swim.

'They take no notice.'

They found a place among the rocks, stripped off shirts and shorts, lay on the sand in the sun. It was hot.

'Make sure you use plenty of sunscreen,' Cal said.

Kathryn lay on her back, eyes closed, skin shiny with cream.

'Bliss . . .'

He lay beside her, listening to the sounds of the sea, conscious of her at his side, the pleasant weight of the sun's rays on his body.

Suddenly, without knowing it, he fell deeply and completely asleep. It seemed only for a matter of seconds; the first thing he heard when he came to was the sound of the surf, exactly as it had been before. He opened his eyes. Kathryn was watching him. He reached out and took her hand.

'I've been sleeping.'

'You certainly have.'

'A minute. Two.'

'Try half an hour.'

'Never!'

'You were snoring.'

He was confused by the idea that he might have slept so long. Would not have credited it, but looked at the sun and saw that it had indeed moved, was now appreciably lower than when they had first arrived on the beach.

'I can't believe it.'

She laughed at his crestfallen expression. 'You must have needed it.'

It was true. For months he had felt close to exhaustion, yet now was alive, full of renewed energy, as though he had never known the meaning of fatigue.

'Come on!'

They walked side by side along the water's edge. The waves reached towards them, licking their bare feet with cool white tongues. Once a bigger wave came charging, soaking them almost to the waist. Kathryn shrieked at the sudden impact of the cold water. Like a ten-year-old, she kicked up her heels and ran, her laughter cast upon the air like a skein of bubbles. For a minute he let her go, watching the supple brown body, the long legs wet with spray, and felt the ache of desire deep in his belly. He set out across the sand after her, caught her easily, seizing her hand. She stopped, laughter ebbing like the surf, and turned to him. He kissed her and her arms went around his neck. He ran his hand down the long, silky flow of her back, feeling the structure of muscle and bone beneath the tender flesh, and turned slightly, cupping her breast, slipping his hand under the flimsy triangle of cloth that covered it. Her nipple was hard against his palm. She freed her mouth from his.

'Someone will see us.'

'There's no-one.'

'Yes, there is.'

He turned and saw a group of people coming down the dunes towards the beach. Four adults, two children swirling across the sand like blown leaves; the same boys he had seen tormenting the octopus.

'Damn.'

And stood back from her.

She smiled brilliantly up at him. 'Lousy timing.'

'You could say that.'

Hand in hand, they walked back to the rocks. Once again they stretched out on the sand. Kathryn turned on her front, face pillowed in her arms.

'Please put some cream on my back.'

Her skin was warm, dusted lightly with sand. He rubbed the sand away with his shirt, undid the cord of her top and worked the cream gently into the smooth skin. He was careful to touch neither the side of her breasts nor the taut buttocks but in his mind he touched them, hoping that the pressure of his fingers would convey his feelings to her. He continued to work the cream into her skin until she sighed and turned to face him. They lay with noses almost touching, looking into each other.

'You'll be all sandy again.'

'I don't care.'

And kissed him again, lingeringly.

Her top had slipped as she turned and now hung loose. He touched her breasts, very gently, then bent and kissed them. Her hands cupped the back of his head and pressed him against her.

He felt himself respond, grow enormous

beneath his bathers.

He smiled at her. 'I won't be able to stand up.'

She felt. 'Oh dear.' Felt some more. 'What do you do about it?'

'Nothing I can do. Not here.'

'It might be a bit public.'

He sensed laughter beneath her solicitousness, said crossly, 'All very well for you . . .'

'You think I don't feel the same?'

'At least you don't show.'

The screeching children were very close, now. He kissed her again, briefly; she re-fastened her top. He turned on his back and soon things were back to normal.

He raised himself on one elbow, smiling ruefully. 'Bloody hell . . .'

She had no sympathy with him at all. 'Maybe it's just as well.'

'How do you work that out?' And reached for her once more.

'Do that,' she warned, 'you'll just get in a state again.'

There was another scream from behind the screen of rocks. It took a minute before he realised that this time the sound differed from what they had been hearing before.

He stood, abruptly.

The holidaymakers were clustered in a knot at the edge of the surf, halfway along the beach. In the water, twenty yards out, a head. One arm raised.

Cal was running. Kathryn was somewhere behind him, but he had no time to think of her. As he ran he counted. Four adults, three up to their knees in the surf, one woman a little further out. One child, silent now, hanging behind what was probably his mother. The woman in the sea was screeching, thigh deep. Her outstretched hands implored the waves. Cal arrived as she took another step, tentatively, and almost lost her footing. The water swirled, clutching at her.

Another yard and we'll be having to drag her out, too.

'Stay where you are!' Cal bawled.

He dashed into the water. The boy was further out now, arm no longer raised, but head still clear of the waves. Yet even as Cal watched, a breaker reared and buried him.

He made a running dive through the surf. At once the current wrapped its python length about him. He knew at once there was no chance of reaching the boy, who was already much further out, beyond the cavalry charge of the waves. The problem was going to be how to save himself, never mind the child. Even close inshore the current was terribly strong. There was no way he could fight it. His one chance was to surrender himself to it, let it carry him where it would and pray there was no undertow. Any undertow and he was finished.

A toppling wave fell upon him, and he went under for the first time.

The world became nightmare: terror and darkness and bubbles, the bitter tang of salt. He was blindingly angry. All these months looking for death and now, when his life had regained its purpose, it had come for him and for the wretched boy who meant nothing to him, who had got into difficulties because of stupidity. Now he would die, as would Cal, who wanted so much to live.

The wave passed. Sunshine and light came back. Opening his eyes, Cal saw that the beach, with its imploring, frantic knot of people, was further away than ever.

The water dragged at him, another wave buried him. It passed in its turn and, when he returned to the light, he heard the sound of spluttering, gasping breath and knew that it was himself, that already, beneath the sun's bright eye, a sky full of light and life and promise, he had begun to drown.

Something bumped against his leg. He thought *Shark* and, for the first time since entering the water, knew panic. He convulsed, trying to thrash away from this new threat. An arm struck him limply across the face and he realised that it was not a shark but the boy, that somehow the waves had brought them together, after all.

The child's body was inert. Cal wrapped his arms around him, knowing there was little he could do to save either of them. Neither sun nor light would make any difference now. Kathryn, the anguish of the boy's parents, life itself, had no bearing on whether they survived or not. The sea would kill them or release them. Nothing else was relevant.

With his acceptance of that reality came stillness. Now he could hear neither the roar of the surf nor the screams of the boy's mother. He had entered a realm of utter silence. He sensed the waves, the froth of bubbles exploding over and around him, but heard nothing. Peace, like the water, enfolded him. Mind and body grew still and he felt himself go under for the third time.

When he returned to the surface, Cal was aware of a change. For a moment, dazed and half-drowned, he could not work out what it was. The waves still rose and fell, the fiery salt still burned eyes and throat, the golden beach was no nearer. Then he realised that the current had relaxed its grip, that he was free to regain the land. If he could.

Now the beach seemed a million miles

away. The figures were still clustered at the edge of the surf, but far away, indescribably remote, and he knew he would never be able to make it back on his own.

He thought, Can't they see it's safe to come in and get us?

The figures did not move, but it didn't matter. Nothing mattered. He gave a few feeble kicks with no discernible result. That, too, did not matter. Realisation brought lightness, like laughter. You were, or you were not. Either way was the same.

A wave surged past. Another. In his arms, the boy's body was absolutely still. He could not tell if he were alive, but that, too, no longer mattered. He, too, was or was not.

It was a moment of total surrender. To the sea, to life, to death, to everything and everyone that ever was or would be — all focused in the single, burning instant of acceptance and unity and peace. It had been what he had been trying to achieve in all his work, the place that was and would be forever.

Another wave.

His eyes were closed. He surged with the water, with the golden reality that had come to him. He no longer knew or cared if he were alive or dead. It was the same.

Something bumped gently beneath him.

Again. The water ran bubbling on either side of his body. The sunlight was brighter, hotter. Sound returned: the faint, distant screaming of gulls, of people. A rush of feet, thudding on sand. Voices laughing, crying.

Somehow, out of eternity's golden peace, the silence of the universal, the sea had returned him effortlessly to land.

With the return came brilliance — of light, heat, sound — amid confusion. Arms dragged him up the beach, the sand abrasive beneath his body. He was afraid that somehow, in those last moments before coming ashore, he had lost the boy. The idea that all the effort and danger might have been for nothing was unbearable. He tried to sit up, but could not.

Kathryn was looking down at him. Her skin burnished by the sun, she was warm, alive, was life itself. He wanted her with an intensity beyond anything he could have believed possible. Every sense was sharpened to a point of exquisite pain. His body was a furnace of salt, blazing beneath the sun.

Through the pain, a weariness that was like death, he said, 'The boy . . . ?'

'He'll be right.'

Nausea shook him. Just in time he turned his head. A scalding spasm spewed seawater. His eyes, throat, mind were ripped raw by the sea. He wanted to drag himself away to a quiet place, far from noise and people, to lie with Kathryn's arms warm about him, her body warm to cover him. He wanted her and life, the awareness and texture and glory of life. He wanted sex and fulfilment, the heat and blaze of being.

'Lie there,' she said. 'You'll be better in a minute.'

Eventually strength returned. He was able to move. The corrosion of salt remained, but the peace and golden glory of eternity were gone. He crawled up the beach, a yard, maybe two, collapsed again, head down in the sand. Arms turned him, he felt the roughness of a towel on chest and legs. There was life in that, too.

A harridan voice assailed him. 'It ain't right. They oughta fence the bloody place off . . .'

The boy's mother. Her hot eyes accused him.

He tried to say something in the teeth of her rage, but could not. He lay beached upon the sand. He could hear Kathryn's voice, as angry as the woman's, telling her to shove off. Kathryn: nothing else mattered.

★   ★   ★

Somehow she must have got him off the beach and into the car. Somehow she had got him home and to bed. Memory was fragmentary, a haze that afterwards seemed more like a dream. He knew and did not know. Only that he woke in the morning, mauled and aching, but alive — gloriously, exultantly alive. He turned his head painfully to look about the room but she was not there. He had no idea where she was.

He got out of bed, so stiff he could hardly move. He was naked. She must have taken care of that as well. No surprises left, he thought. And grinned. My God, I must be feeling better.

He staggered to the bathroom, found a towel, wrapped it around his waist. Looked in the mirror. Shadowed eyes the colour of strawberries looked back at him out of a white face.

My God, he thought again.

He went through the house, seeking her. Nothing. Perhaps she'd dumped him here and taken off. Spent the night at her uncle's place. For all the use he would have been to anyone, she might as well have done that, yet he found himself hoping she had not.

There was only one other place she could be. He went out into the cutlass blow of daylight and opened the door of the studio.

Surrounded by the glow and clamour of colour, the piled racks of paintings, wrapped in a blanket, Kathryn slept.

As he watched her, he felt his head running over with tenderness. This woman who had come into his life . . . This healing miracle . . .

He could think now of Gianetta and what had happened; with pain, yes, but without the hideous self-hatred that had weighed upon him for so long. Always he would regret her, but now it was a clean sorrow without any of the bitterness he had felt before. This was indeed a miracle, and Kathryn had brought it about. He thought that he would never be able to repay her for what she had done.

There was a pad of drawing paper and some crayons in a drawer. Moving quietly so as not to disturb her, he got them out, sat there in the stillness sketching her asleep. When he had finished he propped the drawing beside her and added a note:

Out on the cliffs.

He went outside with the pad and crayons and walked up the path. He found his granite chair among the rocks. He sat and watched the sea waving its blue flag far beneath, heard its voice — muted, now, deceptively gentle — and thought how yesterday it had nearly taken him, as over the years it had taken so many others. Countless thousands. Millions, maybe. Of their bones are corals made. But not mine, he told himself, not yet. I still have a lot of living to do.

He thought of Kathryn asleep in the studio, of everything he had done and still hoped to do; all the work, the concerts to hear and places to visit, the mountains and deserts and oceans, the heat and cold, rain and snow. With her beside him, all things would be possible, a celebration of life. Now that he had come so close to losing it, he had learnt to value it all over again.

He thought of what had happened yesterday, what had so nearly happened. Like revisiting a dream, he remembered through mist the sense of serenity and acceptance that had come upon him, the idea that death and life were the same and that nothing that could happen mattered.

Life was a dream within a dream; he had read that somewhere. Yesterday, on the brink of death, he had understood what it meant. Now, thinking of Kathryn and all the things he wanted to do in his life, he understood no longer.

Life, he thought. Ultimately, that is all that matters. Let me celebrate living.

And began to work, trying to capture on paper the thoughts and feelings that had come to him in the water and since.

What he was trying to do was so hard. He had one go; dissatisfied, put it aside; tried again, put it aside; was deeply engrossed in the third effort when he became aware, returning from a great distance, that he was no longer alone.

He looked up. Kathryn was sitting on a rock a few yards away from him, staring at the sea.

She sensed his movement and looked up, smiling at him, this man who had come from nowhere into her life, had so nearly left it. A man whose vitality burned like a dark and dangerous flame. Before sleeping she had examined the paintings stacked about the studio, felt the anguish and anger and self-hatred. She could understand why the New York gallery had turned them down. All the same, she thought they were wrong. These paintings plumbed the depths from which Cal, God willing, had now emerged. The intensity of the emotion was a measure of the man. The idea that yesterday the sea had so nearly swallowed him was unbearable.

Two weeks ago I had never met him. Now he has become my life.

Five years earlier she had paid a visit to the snows, had gloried in the white peaks blazing against a cerulean sky. Closer to the mountains, she had seen the roughness of the scree that made up the lower slopes, the huge boulders, many times the size of a man, over which it would be necessary to find a way before coming out on the flank of the mountain, far above, where the snow began. How she had longed to do that, to force her way up to that purity, to the electric glare of the ice, the deathly cold of the wind that could invigorate and kill.

I have always wanted it, she thought. To live life to the limit, dangerously. The valleys can be beautiful, they are certainly a great deal safer, but always it has been the peaks that beckoned. I had forgotten that feeling. The mid-north has no mountains, but now I know that nothing less will satisfy me. If I lost my legs and could no longer walk among the mountains, I would still wish to sit with my face turned to those realms of ice and glory.

Cal said, 'I didn't hear you arrive. Have you been there long?'

'A few minutes. I didn't want to disturb you.'

'You do. All the time.'

'I'm glad.' Smiling.

It was all there: in the looks, the words, the tone of voice. Below them the seas ran smoking up the beach, the cliffs were gold and brown and green between the contrasting blues of sky and sea. Seabirds like scraps of torn paper flew white and brilliant in the sunshine.

All this, she thought. All this we have this fine morning when we came so close to having nothing at all. The glory was precarious, so all the more precious.

Her heart filled her breast, her knees felt uncertain; she stood and walked across to him.

'Thank you for coming back to me.'

His smile filled his eyes. 'Any time.'

His arms pressed her close. He felt her breasts against him; she felt the strong, slow beating of his heart; they were so close; now only one step remained. They looked at each other. She felt him pressing hard against her. So much she wanted him, the man.

She shook her head. 'No.'

His hands cupped her breasts, exquisitely. 'Why not?'

Her body was trembling. She was moist and open to him. There was no reason. Yet still she would not.

'Go into the Outback,' she told him. 'Do what you have to do. Then come back to me.'

'And then?'

She concealed doubt with laughter, thankful that he had not been offended, as she had feared he might.

'Then we'll see.'

Later, she could not understand herself. Knew only that she had not been ready, was committed yet not committed, was waiting still. For what, she could not have said.

She came back to the realisation that Cal was speaking to her.

'Margaret Videon . . . '

It was a shock, after all that had passed. She didn't like being so little trusted that explanation was needed.

She turned away, but Cal ignored the signal.

'Please, I want to tell you — '

'What about her?' Ice.

'You heard what she said. I wouldn't want you to think — '

It was amazing how much his doubts hurt.

'Why should I care?' Hating herself, even as she said it. Stop it, she thought. All this means nothing. *Stop it*!

'No reason at all.'

Humility was an unexpected stranger in his voice; this, too, she hated.

'That's all right, then, isn't it?' Then could bear it no longer, came and put her arms about him. 'Oh God, I'm sorry . . . '

'It's all right. All right.'

'I can't bear it when you don't trust me. To trust you, I mean. I don't care about her. Or anyone. It's you I care about. You and me.'

And everything was right between them again. Again he touched her, touched her, yet she, nearly swooning, still said no.

I must be out of my mind.

Only knew that, for the moment, it was the right thing.

Later that morning they parted. Kathryn drove north; yet again Cal watched her go, then went back into his studio.

Why should I care?

Why, indeed.

She had still not mentioned Charles Chivers, the nice boy. With prospects. Let us never forget his prospects, he thought savagely. Which are so important. He looked around at the studio, the sunlight spilling through the open doorway. The boy's presence was everywhere, overwhelming the bright and sparkling day. Something had to be done; he had told himself so already, any number of times. But what? When she had never even mentioned him? What could he do?

The idea of being helpless annoyed him. You should have it out with her, he told himself. Ask the question, find out what's going on. Yet he knew he would not. To ask would be to leave himself vulnerable, and he was not ready to risk that. No, he thought, rather let things ride for a while, and see what happens.

5

Two weeks after getting home from Adelaide, Kathryn went out onto the verandah of her parents' old farmhouse. The paddocks were a blaze of sunlight. In one corner of the garden, beyond the tree-shaded tennis court that with summer was already grey and threadbare, a clump of shaggy-headed lavender drew a bumble-buzz of bees.

Until her trip to the opera, her life had been mapped out clearly. Conventional, certainly, but with security, which she had been taught was the highest reward that life could afford. You had only to look at those who lacked it: improvident families, single-parent families, husbands with a weakness for booze and fists, the bodies of other women.

In the mid-north, the conventions were iron-hard.

Deviate, even by an inch, and look what happens to you.

Cal the possessor of fists and, rumour said, of many women. She had mentioned it, most casually, to Dave Holt, pretending both to him and to herself that Cal and his behaviour were utterly unimportant to her, but asking the question, nonetheless. Dave had told her that all that was history, but everyone knew that history had a habit of repeating itself. She did not want to be the latest in a queue. No danger of that with Charles Chivers, decent son of decent parents. With status, too: everyone respected a doctor. A husband, if that was what he was to become, on whom she would be able to rely, always. A sensible future.

Why should I be thinking about Cal at all? she wondered. Seeing I have not heard.

She wandered restlessly the length of the verandah, eyes averted from the paddocks' brassy glare. She could hear in the distance the treble wailing of lambs, the deep-voiced responses of the ewes. This was her life, laid out before she was born, before her parents were born. It was easy to believe in predestination in a landscape where nothing ever changed.

Charles Chivers. Her father would have preferred a farmer, but Mrs Fanning was a great believer in grabbing what you could get. Kathryn's view: Charles was as good as any, better than most. No basis for romance, of course, but the mid-north was suspicious of romance. Without it some might have conceded there wasn't much of a basis for marriage, but for life . . . That, surely, was what mattered.

Everyone agreed; Kathryn, of all people, would be lucky to land a fish better than Charles Chivers. Because the mid-north did not look kindly on eccentricity and Kathryn knew she was regarded as odd. Not barking mad, nothing like that, but different. This enthusiasm for music, for a kick off . . . And something more alarming still. As a kid, before she had learned to keep things to herself, she had laid claims to having what could only be called second sight. At first people had thought she was showing off, but one or two things had happened to make them wonder. Announcing the arrival of a friend before anyone could have known she was coming: things like that. Everyone had known that such things happened, of course, but having them on the doorstep, so to speak, had made them uncomfortable. For years, now, she had taken care to say nothing about it — although it still happened, from time to time — but she knew people hadn't forgotten. No, there were plenty who'd say she would be lucky to end up with anyone half as worthy as Charles Chivers.

She rested her hands on the verandah rail and stared out across the valley. Worthy was the word for him, and the problem. There was an echo in the name, tedious, repetitive, just as Charles himself, at twenty-nine, could be tedious and repetitive. Formal, too; thus Charles, never Charlie. She could imagine him wearing a collar and tie in bed. Could imagine that more easily than his doing anything else in bed, perhaps. A man whose stability could not be denied. A reliable man.

It was foolish to undervalue the importance of that.

★　★　★

Across the valley a shadow sped like a dark wind. From the gum trees beside the house came a raucous explosion of galahs, but the wedgetail eagle was not interested in galahs, whose shrieking would have availed nothing had it stooped.

From the bread-smelling kitchen, Marge Fanning watched, seeing more than her daughter suspected. She approved of Charles, did not intend to let him escape.

Charles was not rich but would always be comfortable, which was to be preferred. His fingers were white, pinkish about the knuckles beneath a dusting of gingery hair. Pinkish, too, along the jawline where no stubble, gingery or otherwise, would be permitted. She had seen a photograph of the artist in the paper. Cal Jessop's dark jowl threatened a virile aggression, undeniably sexual in nature, although Marge would acknowledge no such considerations.

She sighed as she dished up tea. She was burdened by her knowledge of what was right. Her face was withered by it; body, too, perhaps, although none could have suspected her of owning anything as coarse as a body.

It was not that she wanted much, only what was best for her daughter. Which, most certainly, included no artists.

She blamed that teacher, years ago, for stirring up ideas. Music. Opera. If it hadn't been for him, Kathryn would never have gone to this shindig in Adelaide, would never have laid eyes on Cal Jessop. As for her brother, who had introduced the pair of them, deliberately . . . Shooting was too good.

Now look at her. Mooning. Marge could read the signs, while denying her own memories of that age. Memories had no place. This was serious.

She would see what she could do to push Charles. A definite offer might work wonders. She could hear Claude washing up in the lavvy. He was Kathryn's father, after all. She'd have a word with him, later.

'Tea, Kathryn!' She added her own screech to the galah chorus. 'Tea!'

119

★   ★   ★

Cal's reputation was enough to give anyone second thoughts.

Kathryn had denied caring what Margaret Videon had said. A lie; of course she had cared, had wanted to deny the woman's existence, absolutely. Which was why she had been so sharp when Cal had tried to talk about her.

Margaret had been jealous; it did not mean that what she said was untrue. Men played games, everyone knew it. Especially men like Cal Jessop. Others, in the past, had believed in men, perhaps in Cal Jessop, and been proved wrong.

How could one be sure? Of anything?

Her mother was calling.

'Tea, Kathryn! Tea!'

'Coming . . . '

Uncle Dave had hinted at something in Cal's past that had changed him. It did not matter. What mattered was what he had become. And that was something that she still did not understand.

★   ★   ★

Cal had to shout into the receiver. 'That trip we talked about? Into the Outback?'

'What about it?' Hennie's voice was faint, burps and bleeps on the line mangling the words.

'You still game?'

'You're not thinking of going now?'

'Why not?'

'Hot as hades, this time of year. You can bet your life you'll get rain, too. Like standing under the Vic Falls. Hundred per cent humidity and ground like glue. Much better wait until autumn.'

Cal was not interested in waiting until autumn. The idea of the new sequence had bitten deep and he wanted to get on with it now, no mucking about.

'You saying you won't take me?'

'Don't talk crap. You want to go, my mate, I'm your man. Only don't say I didn't warn you.'

'When can you get away?'

'Gimme another week, sort out a few things. I'll fly down and meet you in Marree; save you driving all the way up here.'

★ ★ ★

Two days later; a Sunday, Kathryn and Charles together.

Charles was an honourable man, had explained his position to Kathryn on a number of occasions.

They would make a good team, he had told her, and was right. A doctor should have a wife; it reassured the lady patients, added weight to his image; was, undeniably, good for business.

Which was not to say he did not care for her. On the contrary, he cared greatly. He had told her this, too; a man who believed in putting his cards on the table.

Now he told her again.

Kathryn thought he was saying he would wait, but not forever. She didn't blame him. Plenty of girls would jump at the chance of being Mrs Charles Chivers.

She tried; it was over two weeks now and still she had heard nothing. As in the old days, she let Charles touch her. Those clean pink hands had touched many women in their time. In the way of business, no doubt, but still . . .

'Doesn't it excite you, sometimes, doing the things you have to do?'

Excitement was not high among Charles's priorities. Nevertheless he smiled, willing to humour her.

'Not at all.'

'Why not?'

'It's different.' And hoped that was the end of it.

'In what way?'

It seemed she could not let the subject alone. It was distasteful, but he endured, patiently.

'There's no feeling. It's simply flesh.'

He smiled bravely, but the questing fingers quested no longer and presently she refastened buttons, a little sadly.

Back home, Kathryn stripped naked, stared at her body's reflection in the mirror.

'And I? Aren't I flesh?'

So much she wanted to be flesh. To be loved, certainly, but also desired. I want to be bruised, she thought, to be worshipped in the temple of the flesh. There were so many things she wanted from a lover. Love, adoration, consideration, but other things, too. To participate in the violent sundering of the flesh . . . The idea excited, undeniably.

Admiration was important, too. So many doctors had forgotten they were in a service industry; they patronised their patients, seeming to believe that only inferiors became sick. Charles was not like that, was willing to visit, where necessary. Willing to serve. That was certainly most admirable.

He was also brave. The time of the bush fires . . .

Flames a hundred feet high. Heat to crinkle eyeballs in a day that had been over forty degrees when it started. A wall of fire with a north wind behind it, careering like a runaway herd. Four thousand sheep, two hundred kilometres of fencing, ostriches, emus, sheds and equipment. Four houses. Eight people. All destroyed.

There had been the injured, too, for whom something could be done. A CFS van had been caught by a wind change. Before it could get out, the flames had savaged. Two dead, three badly burned. Charles, somehow, had been there. Amid toppling, exploding gums, the howling terror of flame, he had carried on doggedly, giving aid, comfort.

There had been talk of a citation.

'What nonsense!' he had said.

'You deserve it,' Kathryn had told him.

Charles wouldn't have a bar of it. 'It's my job. I did it. Nothing remarkable in that, I hope.'

Charles had the deadly knack of making even the offering of his life mundane. Kathryn felt admiration and exasperation in equal measure. But admiration was not love and exasperation fuelled a sense of guilt, which was not love either. Charles was admirable, indeed, but lacked fire; and fire, she had come to realise, was as vital to her as breath.

There were alternatives, of course. Most

couples seemed to manage very well, the spiritual elements of fire uncommon in the mid-north. There was sport, line-dancing. For an elderly handful, the church still held a place. The seasons of wheat and canola, of peas and beans and barley, came and, ponderously, went. The footy club, of which Charles would one day be president, flourished. Fire there, certainly, for those who followed it. Kathryn would have wished to be one of them, but was not.

'Dunno where you get your highfalutin ideas from,' her father had told her once, hurtfully.

Claude Fanning hoarded his feelings like gold; from him such criticism had shown how perplexed and disappointed he was. With no son and a farm that had been in the family for a hundred years, even Charles was small consolation.

In place of footy, Kathryn had found delight in music, to which she had been introduced by a teacher who should have known better. For a time her mother had been supportive, no doubt permitting herself to dream of a career, of bouquets bestowed before an adoring audience, but Kathryn, who from birth had seemed determined to disappoint, had lacked the talent. Now she worked three days a week as assistant in the music department of an Adelaide University, helped her Dad, listened to her music. Wagner was her favourite.

When she heard that the Ring was coming to Adelaide, she would have liked to go to all four operas but, with the prices they were charging, that was out of the question. Instead she saved up, splurged on a single ticket, for *Rheingold*. Where she found Cal, and more than she had bargained for.

Marge Fanning, at her wits' end with such a daughter, had made only a token protest. Charles had no interest in music but would, she hoped, understand or at least accept. Then Kathryn had come home with talk of an artist, and that had been a different matter.

She had found out what she could, which was altogether too much. Booze and women and once, eight months before, an appearance in court after a punch-up outside a pub.

'You must speak to her,' she instructed her husband.

Who was chivvied, with great reluctance, into a gesture.

'Your mother's worried . . . '

'I need something. Fulfilment?' Laughing as she said it, to make the word seem less terrible.

'Fulfilment?' He groped dubiously, a man

126

walking on eggs. 'I'd stick to happiness, I was you.'

If pressed, he would have been at a loss to define the word. For her part, Kathryn knew that the conventional choices her parents would accept were like the rivers of Australia, all too often petering out in sand.

Claude reported back to his wife, confirming that he had spoken. But Marge, doubting not his word but his efficacy, decided to speak to Kathryn herself.

'We want what is best for you. We hope you realise that.'

'Yes, mother.'

'We'd like to see you settled. We're getting no younger, after all.'

'Yes, mother.'

'Your father's a worrier. As you know.'

'Yes, mother.'

'Charles is a fine man. Everyone looks up to him. A real pillar of the community.' Although the citation, much to her sorrow, had not materialised. For which she blamed Charles himself, whose attitude had been at fault.

'Yes, mother.'

Kathryn did not scream. Had learned, like a choirboy, to look alert during the sermon without hearing a word. In addition, she remained tolerant, or at least resigned; in her own way her mother did indeed want what she believed was best for a daughter who persisted in not recognising opportunities, even when they shoved themselves at her.

Of artists, or an artist, of the dangers and pitfalls of artists, Marge did not speak. While Kathryn guarded her thoughts and feelings and said nothing at all. But she remembered: the music; the thunder of the surf; Cal's hands, kindling fire.

★   ★   ★

Kathryn said sharply, 'Because I don't want to!'

Sparks flying in the mid-north. Charles, alerted to danger by what his mother had heard from Marge Fanning, was suggesting they should team up with a couple of mates, head across to the West Coast, spend a few days on the beach at Streaky Bay. Now. Tomorrow.

'Chuck a line in the water, see what we can catch . . . '

Of which fish, Kathryn knew, would matter least.

'It's too far . . . '

'Seven hours. No big deal.'

Distance was not the problem. Cal had promised he would phone; stubbornly, with

128

little faith, Kathryn was still waiting. Yet now it was nearly three weeks; she did not want to be left high and dry. She liked Charles, too, which made things difficult. She sought another avenue of escape.

'It'll be too hot over there.'

He seized the opening. 'We can go somewhere else, you'd rather. Darren and Lucy won't mind.'

Nor would they; the fishing they were planning had nothing to do with the sea.

Suddenly Kathryn was indignant with Cal, who might have been playing with her. She opened her mouth to say, Sure, why not, let's go. At the last moment, stuffed the words back into her mouth.

'Give me a couple of weeks, okay?'

Of course it wasn't okay. Charles's pained expression tried to come to terms with what she was not telling him.

While Kathryn was thinking, It'll be five weeks by then. If I haven't heard from him, I never will.

Charles remained dubious. 'I don't know what the others will say . . . '

'Do we need the others?'

Her bribe came from nowhere. If that was what it was. Certainly she understood the implications, her heart going pit-pat.

For Charles it was like a dam breaking.

Two weeks was suddenly acceptable; still too long, but for quite another reason. It seemed to him the moment to be serious.

'You know I care for you, Katie . . . '

Yes, she knew. It made things even harder.

'The practice is a good little earner. I thought maybe we could open more rooms in Clare. Place of the future, Clare.'

It was as close to a proposal as made no difference but, typically Charles, worded in such a way that he could pretend he had said nothing, if the need arose. All she had to do was show interest, and the question would follow.

Panic brought sweat. 'We'll talk about it later. Okay?'

And fled.

That'd be right, she thought, driving up the dirt road that led to the farm. Charles is so damn cautious I'll just about have to propose to him. Yet knew she was being unfair; any man who slung out an offer without checking the ground first would have to be a mug, and who needed that?

She felt suffocated, all the same. He has no life in him, she thought. No spark. The future everyone wanted for her would be like a box. Closed and dark, padlocked. She remembered a rock, slick with spray, herself posed theatrically upon it.

A woman on a rock? What is she?

The dark eyes, laughing back at her.

Rheingold's opening, the gathering momentum of the E flat major chord swelling from silence, spilling its message into the hushed auditorium. The darkness growing growing growing into brightness. The crash and thunder of fulfilment.

The concussion of the great waves, hurling spray.

A woman on a rock? What is she?

Two weeks, she thought. Could not determine whether it was prayer or threat.

6

Cal mooched, following the cliff path. Imagination burned, tantalised by half-formed images.

There was a stiff wind; the surf burst along the shore in salty pillars of foam, seemingly tumescent. Erections in the shape of water-spouts . . . His mind was busy with priapic visions. Form was everything; there had to be some psychic connection between objects that resembled each other so closely. Think of Marie Desmoulins, he told himself, the most famous of twentieth century Australian artists. When her friend Pete Marchant had killed himself over the woman Phyllis Gould, Marie had commemorated the event by a picture of his bier with, in the background, a funeral candle flame shaped like a brilliantly-lit vulva. In a single painting, she had mourned the dead man and celebrated the sexuality of the woman for whom the man had died. Jack Huggett, another of the group, had slept with Phyllis that same night. Putting his seal of approval on his friend's relationship? Or getting a slice of Phyllis Gould now that she was once again available?

Jack had been notoriously wild; from what Cal had heard, either motive would have been possible.

Images within images.

Kathryn poised upon the rocks, laughing. *A woman on a rock? What is she?*

A question above all questions that needed answering. The enigma of Charles Chivers tantalised. An old ballad unravelled its facile notes amid echoes of the pounding surf. Who is Sylvia, what is she?

What, indeed.

He scrambled down to a postage stamp of beach where no-one ever came. This, at least, he had inherited from his father, the kingdom of the sea. To it had added his own imagery, had sought to tether it within a noose of paint, capturing and revealing all.

Once this world had been enough. Then Gianetta, and the world had changed. Now it had changed again, the old visions tangled with other urgencies.

Cal had never been jealous in his life, but now was jealous of this unknown man whom Kathryn had never mentioned, the hidden life of which he knew nothing.

'There is no reason for her to have told me anything!'

So he accused the black and silent rocks. It was true; all the same, he resented it.

He stripped off, lay face down on the coarse and yielding sand.

I am a sponge.

That was how he had always thought of himself, a sponge soaking up the emotions and sensations of life. Now, feeling the sun's bite on his naked shoulders, hearing the rumble of surf beyond the rocks, he thought he was once again a sponge from which was draining all the fatigue and self-disgust that had choked him for so long. He dozed, dreamt of childhood, beginnings.

★　★　★

A brightness. He thought it was natural, that all boys saw the same vivid flare of colour that soaked him in ardour, recognised the significance of form that enchanted him. Soon he came to realise that it was not so, that others played footy with greater enthusiasm. He played himself; was no stranger to the surreptitious boot, the bright flag of blood amid the sweat of muddy battle, but even there constructed images in his mind, sought to render on paper the action, ferocity, exultation, pain.

Pain came from sources other than football.

His earliest memories were of his father.

The smell of brinestarched skin, tobacco, booze. Mick Jessop's face was like his fists, broken and scarred by violence, bearing also the purple-veined memories of booze-ups with mates. Mick had fished the coast, man and boy, and was not slow to say so, an iron man for the iron cliffs that tumbled in a welter of foam.

At sea he never drank; made up for it by never being sober on land, hitting the bottle and more than the bottle. Wife and son learned to lie low — not that it did much good. Cal carried his bruises to school, blaming doors, other kids. If the teachers doubted, they said nothing. They, too, had learned to lie low.

Cal picked up things from his ratbag Dad, all the same. How to endure, look out for himself. How to fish for snapper, whiting, cray; how to be one with the sea. Other knowledge came from nowhere: a sense of unity with everything about him. The need, and ability, to express it, and himself, in crayon and paint.

Mick, predictably, was disgusted.

'Painting? What the hell you want with that crap?'

Yet in truth was not much bothered, unable to take seriously anything so much at odds with his whole life's experience.

A schoolmaster encouraged Cal, introducing him to the fancy-pantsy garbage of poetry, music and — shit! — dance. A poor bloody bastard, that was for sure. Mick thought seriously about having a word but, in the end, let it go. The sea was Cal's blue destiny, as it had been his own and always would be until booze or storm carried him off. No poncy schoolteacher was going to alter that.

A day came for Cal, the first of days. Years later, it remained a haunted, haunting memory of what he still thought of as the Sea House.

A grey stone building, visible only from the sea, not far from Kidman's Inlet. Beneath a slate roof, its stern face weathered spray and gales, sturdily. In an adjoining paddock, sheep counselled the thin turf.

Mick had decided that this was the day he would bring his twelve-year-old son into the real world of work and fish and men.

Cal had been aboard his Dad's boat hundreds of times, had watched from the hatchway as the winches reeled in the nets with their cargoes of fish, but that had been different, make-believe. This time, and forevermore, he knew he would be expected to work, and Mick was not one to waste energy on instruction.

A clout round the head was the best teacher. He said it, and meant it.

Over the years Cal had learned to spot trouble coming; for the first time was reluctant to go aboard. Mick soon sorted that out, taking him by the scruff and hoisting him over the bulwark.

'Move your backside, lad! Let's go!'

Lesson One.

He was supposed to give Big Daley a hand. Big Daley the deckhand, his own hands as big as shovels, who nudged Cal, grinning, showing him what had to be done, while from the wheelhouse, Mick Jessop screamed a blue streak.

At last the nets were ready for shooting.

'Keep your feet out the way,' Big Daley warned, 'or you'll go with them.'

'I can swim.'

'Not with half a mile of net around you you can't.'

Cal straightened, looking towards the land, and saw the house. He stared at the solid building, the solid life, a place in the world for which he yearned, obscurely, not yet knowing what that might be.

★　★　★

After Gianetta's death, out of the valley of anguish and despair, Cal returned to that

137

moment. He remembered it, not as he had seen it as a twelve-year-old boy, but with the imagination and experience that sixteen more years of life had grafted onto his mind.

I dream of the house, of a sister, younger than myself, with whom I share a room, tenderly. The beds are neat, with white sheets. At night the moon throws patterns of white through the window. The sea is a distant beauty of dark and white, its voice a quietness filling the night.

I live inside the house, silently. I walk within the stone walls that separate the rooms, I slip between the crevices. On one side darkness and the growling sea, the other golden with light, or silver with the shadows of the moon. In the shadows she dances, the white girl my sister. Her robe is whiter than the moon, her skin is whiter still. A symphony of whiteness. The colour flows between my fingers, warmly.

★　★　★

Twelve-year-old Cal awoke from his daytime trance. The steel deck heaved. The sea roared in a cascade of frothing bubbles. From the wheelhouse, his father yelling.

'Move yer bloody arse!'

Secrecy guarded Cal's eyes. His heart lay

with the white girl. In the Sea House she knelt by the bed; white robe, white bed, white dreams in the white and sacred night.

One more thing: a magical event to end the day of magic. In the wide sea depths, something stirred. A form, lifting from the void. So close that it spilled its identity in front of him, becoming personal, at one with himself.

That night, the night of beginnings, Cal took a pencil, drew upon a piece of white card a picture of the house. He could not put words to the vision, did not understand it, yet somehow, within the drawing's lines, insinuated a hint of what he sensed but did not know.

★ ★ ★

Years later, Cal learned that the house was owned by a bachelor, a misanthropic farmer with bad teeth and breath, who never washed. Cal knew that if he had indeed been born in the magic house of dreams, he might never have become an artist, known the anguish and the glory. Always there was a story within the story, another destiny.

After the catastrophe of Paris, Cal looked back at an innocence long vanished, at his memories of that day. Evening, with the fishing boat approaching harbour, the grey and frowning house watching the sea. It had long become familiar to him, its magic gone, but that did not matter. In place of magic there had been another magic, newborn.

On that trip so long ago, close enough to see the barnacles on its flukes, he had seen a whale.

★ ★ ★

Mick had a squint at the drawing. Not bad, he supposed. As pictures go. But.

After Cal had gone to bed, he said to Cal's mother, 'Dunno what we do about him . . . '

Not that he was asking for advice. Mick used his wife as a sounding board, expecting his own opinions to come back to him.

Cal's mother was a case. Mixed-up Millie, not only in her husband's eyes. Her name, for starters. Known to everyone, herself included, as Em. Of whom she spoke as of a stranger:

'Em doesn't like the sound of that.'

'Em will walk out of here, one of these days.'

Although she never did. Had promised herself a hundred times she'd stick a knife in Mick's gizzard, but part of her believed a real man had to keep his woman in line. Was proud, masochistically, that the man cared enough to beat her.

She never let on, though. Screeching battles ricocheted off the walls of the small stone house. Made sure she dragged Cal into it, too.

'Look at him.' A voice to etch brass. 'Wanner grow up to be like your old man, eh?'

So that beery Mick, who had been intended to hear — who could not have failed to hear what would have drowned out a steam whistle — felt it his manly duty to leather them both.

Cal tried to teach himself to look into things. He studied a boat, a rock, a piece of wood, yet knew that until he could discover the essence of himself the essence of these objects would evade him. To do that he had to understand, and to understand he had to paint. Catch 22.

When he thought he was up to it, he had a go. He painted his old man at the nets, the steep, fish-slimed decks and donkey engine, stanchions corroded by rust, the ugly, lovely sea.

Mick scratched his head before a painting of machinery, of the man who looked more like an explosion of energy than anything you could call human. Did not recognise himself, but suspected, baffled.

'Never seen a bloke looked like that . . . '

As always, perplexity led to anger.

'Not a bloody poofter,' he threatened.

No son of Mick Jessop dared be that different.

Next bloody drama: Cal started listening to music. Not what everyone else listened to; what he called real music. Opera was his favourite. Wagner, for Christ's sake. Drove Mick bananas, hearing that racket thundering through the house, but at least it wasn't ballet. Would perhaps have sorted the kid out with his fists but Cal, eighteen now and strongly made, was beyond fists. As to being a poofter . . .

Cal knew the truth of that, as did several of the local girls.

'Fishing's a man's life, never mind this painting lark. Get you out there, we'll soon see if you're up to it. If you're a real man.'

So Mick challenged. Made sure that Cal, young from school, went to sea on the first tide.

'Get some fish scales on his hands,' he told the pub, 'he'll soon forget this other shit.'

Years later, Em reminded her son of the old days.

'Remember what I said, eh? About you growing up different from your Dad?'

He remembered, no errors. For better reasons than she knew.

As a small child, the ongoing drama between his parents had not worried him. Once he began to get a handle on what went on in the world, it was a different story.

Em, smiling at his father around a broken mouth.

Cal understood respect, or so he believed. A woman needed a man she could respect. But this new knowledge was greasy, disquieting. He saw that the concussion of fists and words was no more than a prelude. It kindled excitement in eyes that signalled hot messages to each other, led invariably to the concussion of loins that he had begun to visualise, the cries that in the small house he could not avoid. He learned to dread the squalls of fury, knowing where they would end.

He did not understand how one form of violence could lead to another, but promised himself that he, too, would punish his women when he was old enough. In time he did, although never with his fists.

A girl from the next town had hung around always, hoping he would notice her. In the end, he did. Screwed her on the cliff top, did a portrait of her that ripped holes in her psyche.

She studied it, turned to stare at him. She went out silently. He never saw her again.

'Doesn't pay to be that vulnerable,' he told the portrait. Felt bad, all the same; yet the painting itself had been true, and he did not destroy it.

There were others whom he had used. Margaret Videon, or so she would have claimed. Stella Loots.

★ ★ ★

'How you going, lover?'

'I'm good,' Cal said cautiously; after their last parting, he had not expected to hear from her so soon.

'Hennie says you really are going to fly with him.' The rich laugh he remembered, among other things. 'Ought to get your head read. Ever been up with him?'

'He's been flying for years. He's still alive.'

'God knows how. He's mad, you know that? His luck's bound to run out, one of these days. Just make sure you're not with him when it does, eh.'

'I'll try to remember.'

'When you going?'

'Next week.'

'Am I going to see you before you go?'

It would be madness; also, he had things to

do. On the other hand . . .

The laughter. The warm and ardent spirit, warm and ardent flesh. The mystic communion with the sea. All gone, or so he had supposed. Now was not so sure. Whatever else, she had been a part of his life.

As for Hennie . . . He liked him well enough, but there were limits, even to Cal's resurrection. Hennie wasn't his problem.

It would be madness. But.

The hot lick of lust caressed. He thought of Kathryn and Charles Chivers.

He said: 'When?'

★   ★   ★

The next morning, as usual, Cal got up early and went into his studio. He wandered to and fro, as Angela Scales had wandered two weeks before, studying a painting here, picking up a canvas there.

There was only one that he thought was any good; a minimalist canvas, a rectangle of black on a view of diminishing light, the darkness overwhelming the light. It seemed to him now that this stark painting represented everything he had felt in the first days after Gianetta's death, before sentiment and self-pity had poisoned his vision and his life.

As for the rest . . . The paintings were like a

collection of street beggars, pleading for sympathy.

He could not understand how he had not seen it before.

A year wasted.

He went out, watched the sun climb clear of the horizon. A new day, the first day of whatever time remained. The thought might have challenged but did not. The dead weight of despair was back. He feared that, by going to Stella last night, he had turned his back upon the new light that had come into his life.

Let me not slide back into the abyss.

He walked and walked, seeking to shake his mood. He crossed the causeway to the larger of the islands, followed the path to the seaward end, sat on a flat rock shaped like an altar amid other rocks, stared at the sea. For how long he did not know.

He heard the excited cries of children and turned to see a group of adults walking along the path, kids screeching in tangles beyond them. He relaxed; they would not see him here, he hoped.

He watched. The adults were stolid, heavy; he had no interest in them. But the petal children flowering among the grass . . . He felt the abyss that divided him from them and turned away once more to face the sea. How could he hope to paint when he was so cut off from life?

About him brooded a henge of monoliths, lichen-flecked. Beyond, the waves broke their heads against the rocks. They watched him and did not judge. Whereas he, sheltered from the wind upon the sacrificial stone, had sentenced himself long ago.

He had thought to drive directly to Marree, no stopping-off along the way. Now he changed his mind.

At least he could phone, he decided. It would be part of the renaissance, artistic and personal, that he would not allow to be destroyed by the backsliding of the previous night. He owed it to himself, the artist and the man.

Renaissance ... The first time around, there had been less at stake, things had been easier. A local art club exhibition had been what really got things going ...

★   ★   ★

Cal was not a member, but the notice said that outside submissions were welcome. He studied the members' work, the water colours and pastels of flowers and gum trees, of a sea lively as cardboard about Bushranger Head. Thought, bloody hell.

Still he hesitated about offering anything, not caring to display himself before the world. Then he told himself why not, sent in the one of his old man.

A twitter on the phone told him how excited the committee was.

'Do you have any more? Oils, perhaps?'

Neither Cal's budget nor technique ran to oils. Crayon, rather, on amber card. A harvest scene: the lorries standing, the field bins, the header belching dust. The sky was a weight of brilliant light, compressing the labouring men.

This, too, they accepted.

Cal told himself he wouldn't go, but in the end did so, apprehensively. Doubt wrinkled his neck. He saw his pictures, prominent amid the gum trees and the flowers. They looked like tigers in a mob of sheep. In the bottom right-hand corner of each, a tiny circle of red paper.

A lady, bones draped in a tasselled shawl, wafted.

'Can I help you?'

But clearly had little hope.

Cal pointed. 'What goes with the red sticker?'

She condescended to explain. 'It means the picture is sold.'

'Sold? How much?'

His tone said, Who'd be daft enough to buy them? At once she bridled. 'I'm afraid that's confidential. A local artist.'

'I drew the bloody things, after all.'

Which fluttered her grey-haired dovecots. Yet still she doubted. 'And you are . . . '

'Cal Jessop. Yeh.'

Smiles, then. The gushing twitter he had heard on the phone. 'So pleased . . . '

'How can you sell something isn't yours?'

'Mr Holt asked us to reserve them for him. Said he was anxious to talk to you. Most exhibitors are members of our little group,' she explained. 'When he discovered none of us knew who you were — '

'Who's Mr Holt?' wondered Cal.

Shock. 'Why, Dexter Holt. The art critic.'

Who was, it seemed, famous.

'Never heard of him.' Cal was suspicious of big names. 'He can phone me, if he wants. You got my number.'

Dave Holt rang that evening.

Cal, still inclined to be suspicious: 'Thought your name was Dexter?'

The critic laughed. 'That's for public consumption. Some people think Dave isn't smart enough for a critic.'

They agreed to meet. When he saw Dave Holt, sleek belly, silky moustache, Cal wondered what he was getting into. To his surprise, they got on.

Astounded, Cal listened as the critic described him as a major talent.

'A long way to go, you understand. But the talent's there, no doubt about it.'

'You're joking . . . '

'I'll show you how serious I am. How much d'you want for those two pictures of yours?'

Cal had no idea, had enough of the old man in him to be canny.

'Maybe you ought to tell me what you reckon they're worth.'

A sideways glance. 'I'll give you two hundred for the pair of them.'

A fortune. But . . .

'No.'

'No?'

'If I'm that good . . . Maybe I should get an agent.'

Not that he had any idea where to start.

'Agents aren't easy,' Dave Holt said. A speculative pause. 'I'll have a word with someone I know. If you agree to sell me those pictures.'

'Not for two hundred bucks.'

'How much, then?'

'That's why I want an agent. So he can tell me.'

Dave threw up his hands. 'I'll see what I can do.'

Except that the agent was a she, Angela Scales. Cal was sufficiently his father's son to be cautious of being told by a woman. In the event, Angela proved more assertive than most men, an anomaly that more than anything showed Cal this was a new world. Decided, for the time, to go along.

Angela wanted to see everything he'd done. Grabbed a study he'd made of the coast, studied it while Cal dithered, pretending unconcern.

'You've got the potential,' she said at last. Eyes skewered him. 'You willing to work?'

'I reckon.'

'Willing to be told?'

He gave her a look. 'Maybe.'

'You need to sharpen up your technique. The way you look at things.'

Cal was not so sure about that.

'If I'm going to act for you, you've got to trust me.'

In Cal's book, trust had to be earned. 'Maybe you'd better sell those two pictures, first.'

Which she did, to Dave Holt. He was, after all, a mate of hers.

'How much?'

'Five hundred each.'

He danced. 'You beauty!'

'They're worth more,' she said judiciously.

151

'Or will be, but for now it's a fair price. Much more important, he's going to write an article about you.'

'Dinkum?'

She smiled. 'I want him to think of you as his protege.'

7

When Kathryn got home, her mother was on watch. Gun-muzzle eyes questioned.

'Well?'

Kathryn parried. 'Well?'

'Did you see Charles?'

'Yes.'

Marge Fanning waited. Kathryn hummed a little tune, staring through the window at the sun-bright paddocks.

'Ann Chivers said something about a group of you going away for a few days.'

'I told Charles I didn't want to go.'

Marge managed to keep hold of her smile. 'You know it's your happiness we're thinking of . . . '

We. Claude Fanning's presence was often invoked when things were not going to plan.

Kathryn had heard enough from a mother who persisted in thinking her daughter was still in Year Ten. 'Sure you don't mean contentment?' Savagely.

Marge hated it when Kathryn got like this. But would resist. 'Contentment?' She assayed the word. 'Nothing wrong with that, surely?'

'Like a pudding.'

Now Marge was lost. 'Pudding?'

'A pudding would feel contented. If it could feel.'

Marge's eyes narrowed; she had always been a stern advocate of respect. 'We want what is best for you. Only that.'

Kathryn would have talked to her about the future's dark box, but knew it would be no use. Incomprehension was part of the darkness. Instead she made her offering. 'Charles and I may be going away in a week or two. Just the two of us.'

Was gone before her mother could question further.

That evening she went for a walk in the ranges behind the house. The ground was dust-dry; beyond the motionless gum leaves, the sky was an azure blaze that turned slowly to white as the sun sank. She stood amid the trees, feeling the silence gather about her.

I am wrong, she thought. This is my life. This country, this way of living. The dust and hanging leaves are as much a part of me as the blood in my veins. My friends, all my family, are here. Have been here, most of them, for generations.

It was enough. She would make it so. Would be content.

When she got back, the farmhouse windows golden in the darkness, her mother's tight mouth signalled a development.

'There has been a message. The number is on the pad.'

Kathryn did not ask who. She knew.

She went lightly to the phone.

★　★　★

'Kathryn?'

'Yes.'

'I'm going north. I wondered if I might stop off and see you.'

'Of course. When are you coming?'

'Thursday, I hope. If things go to plan. How do I find you?'

She gave him directions.

'I'll ring you later,' he said. 'Let you know for certain.'

'Will you stay over?' Hoping, but not willing to assume.

'If it's not too much trouble.'

Not to Kathryn. She returned to the lounge, where her mother waited.

'Staying here?' Marge's nostrils flared.

'Just overnight.'

'You might have asked, I suppose.'

'He can put up at the pub, if you'd sooner.'

If that was going to be her attitude, there was no more to be said. Besides, if they hid him up here, twenty kilometres out of town, it was possible that no-one would find out. Put him up in the pub, and there would be no hope.

'Consideration. That's all I ask.'

Kathryn went out into the darkness, stood looking at the lights of the other farmhouses scattered across the valley.

Cal is coming.

The soft tilt of the paddocks into the valley, the trees below the house, the line of distant hills — all were obscured by darkness, but Kathryn knew them too well not to see them now. All proclaimed it.

Cal is coming.

On Thursday. Another three days, he'll be here.

It was midday when Cal arrived. Mrs Fanning was not sure what to do with him, this dark-haired invader whose presence seemed to burst the seams of the room. He was courteous, she had to allow, but had no intention of permitting herself to like a man who threatened what was right.

Whatever attitude she chose to adopt, she was on her own. There would be no help from Kathryn; as for Kathryn's dad, he had scooted off, taking a mob of sheep to the block they leased five kilometres up the road.

They ate, Cal chatting, apparently at ease, Kathryn a-glow. There were times when

Marge Fanning could have hated her daughter. Afterwards, thank God, they went for a walk. Although there were dangers in that, too.

Cal and Kathryn walked through the scrub, surprised a couple of kangas that swung away, bounding fast between the trees. They came to the dam, the water reflecting light from its brown surface. Ducks rose and flew across the valley, necks outstretched.

They sat by the water. Beyond the dam the land fell in a long sweep until it climbed again to the distant hills. Across the valley, barely visible in the afternoon light, a header trundled in a cloud of amber dust but, on this side, the paddocks had already been reaped, the stubble pale tan under the sun's hot eye.

The heat hung motionless. As far as they could see, nothing but the header moved in an emptiness of earth and sky.

'The water looks cool,' Cal said.

'Why don't you go in? I've done it often.'

'Do it now,' he said.

'Nothing to wear.'

'So wear nothing.'

'A free show?'

'I wouldn't look.' But was grinning; a game.

'I would want you to look.'

Suddenly it was no longer a game.

'We could go in together,' Cal suggested.

'No.'

'I'll bet that dam's full of yabbies.'

'If the herons haven't pinched them.'

'Maybe we should check. I don't trust those herons.'

'It's not the herons worry me.' The teasing was making her itchy. 'You go. I'll sit and watch you.'

'No fun,' he mourned, but did so anyway.

Kathryn watched as Cal stripped to his underpants and jumped in, churning the brown water to foam.

He stood, wet skin gleaming, and called to her. 'Please come.'

She did not move. It was neither the herons nor Cal she distrusted, but herself, the urgent flutter of desire.

Eventually he gave up and came out. He lay beside her in a patch of sunlight. His eyes were closed against the brightness. She looked at him covertly; her body ached with longing, but she did not move, knowing how things would end if she did.

Cal's eyes were shut. In the hot sunlight the coolness of the water lingered like peace upon his skin. He could feel the pressure of Kathryn's eyes upon him. He wanted her intensely; was sure she wanted him, too. He thought he had only to open his eyes, to raise his arms to her. Yet did not move, content for the moment to wait.

After all the complications and self-hatreds of the previous twelve months, the future seemed clear to him at last. He would drive north, would fly with Hennie into the Outback. He would discover the essence of the country, would capture what he knew now he had been seeking all this time. He would come back to Kathryn, and everything would be very simple and very wonderful.

In a corner of his mind, a tiny voice warned of Charles Chivers. He disregarded it; no-one with a name like that was going to stand between him and his future.

Now Kathryn wished she had gone into the dam. Everything was hanging in precarious balance: her relationship with Cal, with Charles, with herself, her life — all suspended in an aching void of not knowing. She could bear it no longer. Either this man was her future, or he was not.

She watched the strong neck, the deep chest from which the water had now evaporated, the hard-muscled body. It was all she could do not to reach out a hand, to caress. She did not; what mattered was not the beauty, but the man.

I have to trust, she thought. To give myself in trust.

It was the only way. Yet this man, of whom she knew so little . . . She had expected him to make a pass at her; was unsure whether she was relieved or otherwise that he had not. Perhaps, after all, he did not care.

The thought should have made things easier but, emphatically, did not. I must know, she told herself, I shall have no peace until I do. But had no idea how to take things further without losing control of the situation, which she must not do.

Then she knew. For a moment rejected it as too radical. It would offend, drive him away from her forever. Desperation thrust caution aside. So be it, she thought.

Kathryn took her trust, her desire and unacknowledged hopes, and cast them upon the wind.

She said, 'My uncle told me something happened while you were in Paris. Something terrible. Do you want to tell me about it?'

A fist from nowhere, smashing.

The idea of talking about what had happened, the thought that people had been discussing him behind his back . . . It was intolerable, a knife sawing at the most secret part of himself. Brain and body went still; anger gathered its molten lava.

On the edge of outburst he paused, remembering. The stroll beside the river amid a dying splendour of music. Before that, the first meeting during the interval at the opera, the feeling as he looked at her that here was something new and filled with light, come unexpectedly into his life.

Shared laughter at the extravagances of the exhibition guide.

The day at the coast when he had shown her the places that delighted him, that would have revealed to her something of himself, had she the eyes to see.

He thought she had seen very well.

Now this.

It would be so hard to talk of it, yet perhaps she deserved to hear. Perhaps he deserved to speak of it at last.

He opened his eyes, saw her staring down at him. He recognised her anxiety, that she understood both the enormity of what she was asking and the risk she had taken in doing so. It was the final confirmation that he could and should trust himself to her, that there might be healing in telling her the story.

So he told her, simply, quietly, without rage even at himself. When he had done, there was a stillness.

She took his hand. 'Thank you.' Very softly.

His eyes had turned inwards to the anguish that had been Paris. Now he looked outwards and saw her face was grave, concerned not at what he had been but at what he was now, the man who had emerged from the fire.

He smiled painfully. 'It made me a bit antisocial for a while.'

He waited for her to utter all the platitudes. He was not to blame himself, it had not been his fault, he must put it all behind him and get on with his life — all the futile, agonising things that people say. Realised that in telling her he had been putting her to the test, as well as himself.

He held his breath, waiting.

She said none of these things, said nothing at all, but leant forward and kissed him tenderly, without passion, and ran her fingers gently down the side of his face. Then she sat back, her fingertips resting lightly on his chest. He watched her staring out at the dip and swell of the tan-coloured paddocks bathed in sunshine, the line of trees marking the creek that ran along the valley floor. This place had been her life, was still. Yet he knew, watching her, that everything about her was trembling upon the very edge of change, that even at this moment she might be bidding farewell to all that had existed in her life until now.

As I am, he thought. Because for him, too, everything was new. Even in Paris he had not known this overwhelming sense of tenderness, of desire as keen as a blade yet so much more than desire. It was an unfamiliar path down which he would walk in gladness, alone no longer.

He lay watching her until at last she sighed and turned and saw his eyes upon her. Her face coloured a little. She smiled, very close, and he lifted his arms. She came and lay with her head on his chest and, after a while, he rested his hand gently on her hair.

Later he got dressed. They walked silently back to the farmhouse. For the rest of the evening they barely spoke, letting their shared silence speak for them. Claude Fanning read the papers, growling throatily at the price of grain. Marge watched and watched and saw nothing.

8

Very early the next morning, Kathryn awoke and went out to the verandah, where she found Cal with a sketch block in his lap, watching the pellucid eastern sky. Night shadows still lay upon the valley, clustered about the silent conferences of trees, while along the horizon a rose flush turned steadily to apricot.

She stood at Cal's side and rested her fingers lightly on his shoulder. Presently he lifted his own hand and laid it on hers.

They waited, as the land waited, for the sun.

Colours deepened, emerging from stillness. Then, from behind the distant hills, came the first golden blink of light, needle sharp. A breathless instant before avenues of pure gold, pale and austere, opened across the paddocks, avenues into which the dusk drained. A pigeon fluted, a soothing, contemplative sound, and suddenly it was day.

The day in which Cal would be gone.

As though the same thought had occurred to him, he turned and drew down her head and kissed her. It was a kiss full of longing, at once gentle and on fire. She kissed him back, hard, while his hand shaped her breast and she felt her soul utter between her parted lips.

They strolled across the tennis court and into the patch of woodland.

Cal said, 'You remember the island I pointed out to you? The one where the penguins roost?'

'What about it?'

'At the seaward end there's a flat stone, like an altar. I was there the other day, trying to come to terms with things. There were children . . . ' For a minute he was silent. 'There seemed such a gulf between them and me. It was after that I made up my mind to go into the Outback. So I contacted you.'

'I'm glad you did.'

There was so much she did not understand. She was groping, groping, but to the darkness there seemed no end.

'The Outback,' she said. 'I understand you must go there. I don't understand why.'

'Because it's a rounding,' he told her. 'People think of the salt aridity of sea and desert.' His eyes shone at the vision of the silence that awaited him. 'They're not arid at all. They're the promise of hope. That's why I'm going. To get rid of all the trappings, to compress experience into ultimate simplicity.

Which is the most complex thing of all.'

She was trying to taste the meaning of his words, to share the vision. She was so close, yet the purity of the dream eluded her.

Cal tried again. 'I want to paint something so compressed that it is not there at all. Light and emptiness. Can you imagine it?'

Kathryn could, although more in the delineation of life's possibilities than in painting.

'And going into the Outback will bring you to that kind of light?'

'Or to ultimate darkness.'

He had lost her. She shook her head, helplessly.

'Ultimate darkness is where we escape completely from other people's vision. When we're alone, in new territory. Marie Desmoulins managed it, in the work she did in Kashmir. Matisse. Miró. Even Jim Nutt in Chicago. I want to see things in a new way, to have my fingertips touch what no-one has touched before.'

And thrust his outspread fingers so close to her that her spirit recoiled, although her flesh did not.

'To touch eternity,' he said.

I *will* trust, she promised herself. Then, perhaps, I shall understand. Yet the idea dissatisfied her. Trust implied surrender, and that had to be a two-way trip. She did not subscribe to the idea that a woman's place was to accept, mindlessly.

'And when you've been to this Outback of the spirit? What then?'

At last it had come. They looked at each other, eyes weighted by silence.

He said, 'I shall come back. If I may. If you are free.'

Light poured with a green purity through the trees, lay upon them silently.

'I shall be here.'

Four words, spoken lightly, yet with sober delight. Their weight was overwhelming. They bound her, absolutely and forever.

'You are so gentle,' he said in wonderment. 'I love the gentleness in you.'

She grinned back at him. 'Don't kid yourself. I know how to look after myself.'

And kissed him again, desire naked upon her tongue. She stood back from him.

'Go, now,' she said, and smiled at the unspoken question in his eyes. 'Sooner you go, sooner you'll be back.'

★ ★ ★

He was gone. Kathryn watched the plume of dust settling silently. When it, too, was gone, she went indoors. To be alone; to exult in the

167

joy and responsibility of knowing that never would she be alone again. Towards evening she went out again into the garden. She sat on the grass, looking across the valley to the line of hills.

She thought of the furnace into which Cal was heading, compared it with her life here, in the mid-north. It seemed to her that this expedition typified all the dangers that confronted them, the basic incompatibility of temperament and background. The differences would have frightened her, had she permitted.

Around her the garden was a pattern of roses and lavender, petunias and marigolds, whose gentle prettiness would be lost in the glare of the iron land. Everything neat and dear and familiar and stifling.

I shall have to fight, that is all. I shall have to overcome the differences.

Cal had told her that she was gentle, that he loved the gentleness he saw in her. It was what she would have wished for herself, above all things. Gentleness to please herself as well as him, but knew she would have to fight to acquire it.

I know how to look after myself.

Gentleness did not mean surrender. Her own life remained important, too, a life to be shared but not forsaken. I shall do what I must, she told herself. Whatever is necessary to achieve my life's desire.

★ ★ ★

Hours to the north, amid a wilderness of salt bush and silence, Cal stopped the car at the side of the road and got out. He stretched, making his spine creak, bent straight-legged to place his hands palm down in the dust.

He peed on an ant hole, watched them run.

He stared about him. He knew himself to be minute amid the vastness, yet at one with everything. The dusty earth, the tangle of wire-dry scrub, the dazzle of blue air. The scattered trees breathed stillness. Along the verges the plumed grasses grew silently amid a worship of sunlight.

The sun, low now, was still benign. Further north it would be a club to belabour the thirsty land. Few trees there, only scrub and patches of thin grass. Only the stones crying, and the heat.

The whole continent lay like an ambush, separate entirely from the irrelevant cities scattered along the coastal fringe. You had to come here to know the land's reality, to gain an awareness of perspective and scale.

Galahs flew screaming. Garlanded by the flock's raucous voice, Cal watched their wings, rose and grey, as they sped away.

I shall bring her here. She will see what I see, the wonder and the unity of life.

He drove until dark, slept by the road, continued in a rose-tinted dawn. Reached the Marree airstrip at nine. Hennie came charging to meet him, exuberant, back-slapping, voice to rival the galahs.

'How you going, my mate?'

9

Hennie slopped a beer, sighed and belched in satisfaction. 'Good to see you, my mate.' Winked. 'How's the old lady, heh?'

It was twenty years since Hennie had left South Africa, yet he still carried the accent, like a memorial to the Transvaal that he did not regret at all. He liked to play games, to pretend that Cal and Stella were having steamy sex behind his back. Had no idea of the facts. Cal went along, telling the truth while pretending to lie.

'Tires me out. Had to get away, or she'd have worn me to a frazzle. When you coming back to sort her out for me? Get her off my back?'

'Too much for you, heh? Not surprised. A real tiger, that one.'

Hennie was as proud of his wife's sexual appetites as though he believed what he was saying. Which, God and Cal knew, was true enough.

'Sure you won't join me?' Fiftyish, balding, shoving a beer belly, he scratched his gut and cracked another bottle.

Cal shook his head.

Hennie tipped his head back; the second beer followed the first. 'Gets blerry hot up here. Can't drink when you're flying, so in between times I likes to catch up.'

'So long as it's only in between.'

'No worries about that. I'm barmy, but not that barmy.'

Though he believed in pushing things to the limit, from what Cal had heard. When he had first suggested flying together, that had been part of the attraction, the death wish operating. Now things were different.

'Just get us back in one piece, I'll buy you all the beer you can drink.'

'Blerry rash offer. Don't worry, my mate, I won't hold you to it.'

But had a third beer, all the same. In a corner of the room, the packed fridge hummed boozily. Through the dusty window Cal could see a steel spider's web of pipes and valves and tanks, the high chimneys of the plant puncturing the sky. Beyond the perimeter fence, the parched and featureless land lay prostrate under the sun.

'Hot,' he said.

'I told you. Fifty degrees, last time I looked.'

'All the same, I might go for a stroll, bit later, see what's outside the wire.'

'Nothing you can't see from here. Might as

well be the blerry Free State.'

From a Transvaler, there could be no harsher condemnation.

'You through here?'

'Finished and *klaar*. Say the word, we can shove off first thing in the morning.'

'We needn't be long. A week, ten days, should do it.'

'I'm due three weeks. Take as long as you like.'

For all his winks and lascivious red lips, Hennie seemed in no hurry to get back to the wife who was too much for any man. Who might welcome him ardently. Or not: who could say? And Cal was paying, after all.

Later, the sun well down, Cal went for a stroll. On the landing pad Hennie's baby stood.

Admiring her was the first thing he'd had to do when they'd met in Marree.

'What d'you think of her, heh?'

Cal had stared up at the helicopter. 'It's big.'

'Damn right. They need to be when you're hauling freight.'

'What is it?'

'Four seater Bell. Picked her up from one of the Bass Strait oil rigs. Gets you into places you'd never be able to go with an aircraft. And manoeuvrable . . . Wait till you see how I can chuck her around the sky.' He had laughed exultantly. 'I'll soon get rid of your lunch for you.'

They had climbed aboard.

Hennie had started the engine, wound up the revs. 'It's got only one problem . . . '

'What's that?'

'One of these mothers hits the deck, next thing you're toast.'

Cal had stared at him. 'How do you avoid it?'

Hennie had laughed. 'By not hitting the deck.'

And had taken off, northward bound.

Now Cal remembered Stella saying, *He's mad* . . . Thanks for telling me, he thought. Thanks very much.

Beyond the wire it was as Hennie had said. The land, flat and featureless, stretched away: desert country. Here the steel ecstasies of technology ruled. From the top of mast-like chimneys, gas flares painted the fading sky.

Cal walked a hundred metres and stopped. He stared north. The wilderness beat its ardent drums inside his head. Feeling the north wind barely touching his lips, Cal went ahead of his body, eagerly seeking the fulfilment of those stony canyons, those plains of fire. There, in the emptiness, he would find meaning and artistic fulfilment. He knew it with a certainty that transcended knowledge. There he would go, and Kathryn, whom he loved, would go with him.

★   ★   ★

Early the next morning the two men climbed into the chopper. Rotor thrashing, they took off into an opalescent dawn. The sun was still below the horizon but, as they climbed, the earth's dark rim fell away and the red orb came swimming up through layers of night to meet them.

Cal watched as Hennie banked, settling the chopper on course, and saw the land, like a mysterious shadow, stretching away on all sides until it merged with the twilight, horizonless. The sun's first rays flowed across it so that every undulation stood out in stark relief. The contrast of contour and shade made the landscape even more mysterious, while overhead the stars bled pinpoints of dying light. The sun flushed the cockpit with primrose that turned first to chrome and then to gold. In the newness of the day, the sunlight advancing below them in gigantic strides across a landscape as old as time, the helicopter flew north.

★   ★   ★

A week after Cal's visit, there was a dinner for the victims of the fire. Claude, prodded by his wife, made up a party. A cousin and his wife, down from Crystal Brook. Marge's brother, Dave Holt, had to be invited but, mercifully, declined. Mr and Mrs Chivers. Kathryn, with Charles, who was on his best behaviour. Made one or two jokes, stiffly, at which, stiffly, they laughed. He apologised for the presence of his mobile.

'In case of emergencies,' he explained.

Kathryn sat, and smiled, and was silent. Marge could have shaken her.

Some writer fellow, on a visit to the district, told a story. Of the fire and a farmer's wife. Marge did not follow it too closely; like her daughter, she knew how to smile and not hear. At the end of the evening, she made sure that Kathryn was left alone with Charles, whose mobile had not rung.

I've done the best I can, she thought, as Claude drove her home. I can't propose for him.

Or tuck them up in bed together. Although would have done both, had it been possible.

Perhaps tonight . . .

It was such an ideal solution. She would not give up hope, despite all.

In the meantime, sitting in his car, looking at the town pond where ducks floated,

Charles, at last, was proposing.

Kathryn had felt the moment coming, had done what she could to head him off. In vain.

Despite his consideration for his patients, Charles was not totally immune to the medical profession's disease of arrogance. 'I'm no good at expressing my feelings,' he said truthfully, 'but I do care for you. Nothing would make me happier than for us to be married.'

His sincerity, stiff as new boots, creaked. She hesitated. She wanted a man, children, a life more than her present life. All of which Charles might be able to provide. It was not as though she were inundated with offers; Cal had tried to make love to her, but that was all. No commitment there.

Charles was decent, loyal, considerate, respected . . . His qualities would fill a book.

Yet . . . *I shall be here.*

Her promise confined her. She was close to tears. She said, 'I'm very fond of you — '

'I see.'

For a moment she hoped he might be angry, but Charles knew how to conceal his feelings. If he possessed anything as unreliable as feelings.

'There's no rush. We're right for each other. I'll ask you again.'

If he had truly wanted me, Kathryn

thought, he would have grabbed me, shaken a commitment out of me, but had not. Would not. She longed for violence, in his feelings, even in his body's response, but Charles was not a violent man. Instead he changed the subject, courteously.

'A good evening,' he thought, 'very successful. Although that writer bloke was a bit of an embarrassment.'

How can he? she thought. But knew why. Reality armoured him. Charles was aware what he had to offer, believed she was too sensible to refuse him forever. He would wait; he would ask again; she would accept.

His certainty and lack of passion terrified her. Worst of all, she was afraid he was right, that the net was cast, that struggling against it would be futile or, worse, embarrassing.

He dropped her off, presented a brotherly kiss, as tasteless as chastity, to demonstrate how he had forgiven her. She couldn't wait to get out of the car. The air, warm, cropscented, was sweet.

In the house a light burned: her mother busy with a tapestry on which she had not worked for months.

'Good evening, dear?'

'Fine, thanks.'

Marge waited, in vain. Kathryn was resigned to the fact that soon, in the miraculous way of mothers, she would know all about the proposal and her rejection of it, but would tell her nothing now. Time for that later.

The next day, to her horror, Charles came to see her again. They walked, they talked of nothing, awkwardly, she wishing more than anything that he would leave her alone. He had heard something, that was plain. Would not speak of it, but encircled her with his presence, hoping to out-wait her into saying something.

Which, resolutely, she refused to do.

At last he stopped, and coughed, and stared for a while at his boots. Eventually he said, 'I want you to promise me one thing . . . '

'What?' Eagerly. She would have agreed to almost anything to remove the tension between them.

'If you're committed elsewhere. If you've made up your mind. If I have no hope . . . '

She thought. And thought. *So falls my life.*

Said, 'We need to talk.'

He, watching distance. 'So talk.'

She went and sat on a fallen tree trunk. Patted it. 'Come and sit with me.'

So he did, but separately. Waited.

'I have met someone,' she said.

'You feel for him.' It was not a question.

'I feel for him,' she agreed, 'but am not sure he is right.'

'Second-best.'

His words were bitter; she did not understand.

'How so?'

'You will wait for him. This man. If things work out, that will be fine. If they don't, you'll come back to me. That's what you mean, isn't it? I'm the back-up in case things go wrong. Second-best, as I said.'

'It's not like that!'

Passionately she sought to reassure him, to salvage the pride she had wounded so badly. Could not; he was right and they both knew it. It was terrible. She did not know how to mend the hurt, which he had in no way deserved.

'It isn't you.' *Not only you.* 'It's the way of life here.' *The way we would live if I married you.* 'There's a world out there. I need to see it before I settle down. I'm not ready.'

'You could travel. I suppose. If you really want that.' Dubiously, unable to see the point in gawping at other places, the way other people lived their lives.

It was not that, either. The physical fact of travel was unimportant. She would have explained, but it was impossible to put into words her feelings, her passionate anxiety to seize life by the throat.

'This place, the way we live here, has always been enough for me.'

He spoke humbly, as though acknowledging his fault in being as he was.

'Don't!'

There was no fault in accepting the cards he had drawn in life. In being content.

Like a pudding.

So, talking to her mother, she had dismissed it, contemptuously. Yet here was a man, solid and abiding. He acknowledged his roots, his ancestors buried behind the church, would in time be content to add his body to theirs. He would influence this land in a way that she, skating superficially across its surface, would not.

Despairingly, Kathryn thought that Charles was the better person, yet knew, despairingly, that being better had no relevance. She was as she was, different. She regretted it, but the fact remained. If she settled down now, with Charles, the loss of what might have been would gnaw and gnaw. And, in the end, destroy not only her life but Charles's, too.

She would do it to him no more than to herself.

She put her hand on his knee, seeking not to console but to communicate. 'Second-best has nothing to do with it. I need to see, first.

I need to feel. I need — ' how passionately she felt it ' — to be.' She tightened her hand on his leg. 'Do you understand?'

He did not. His face reflected his pain in trying to do so but failing. With Kathryn beside him, his life here would be complete. A place in which to set his feet, as his forebears had done; a woman he respected, for whom he cared; the opportunity to be of service. A world complete in itself. All else was words and, in his heart, Charles had never trusted words. Which could conceal so much.

'You need more time . . . '

'Yes! Yes!'

If it had been no more than that . . . For the moment, Kathryn was happy to accept even so limited a measure of comprehension.

'Time to be,' said Charles, as though he really understood. He smiled crookedly. 'Better get on with it, then. Or we'll both be waiting forever.'

No hint of reproach. His generosity made her heart weep, although her eyes were dry. She squeezed his hand, knowing she was closer to him now than ever before. Would have kissed him warmly, even passionately, but did not. There was a limit to what even Charles would accept.

He stood. 'I shall be here.' His hand groped helplessly for what might lie on the other side of pain. 'If you ever need to talk . . . '

They walked back, together yet apart. She watched as he drove away. She waved. She had expected relief; instead there was only weariness and sorrow for Charles and herself, that she had been unable to accept the offer of a good man.

She went into the house. Her mother, who understood very clearly what had not been said, waited. Teeth sharpened by disappointment, she would have found relief in words, but words needed two and Kathryn would not give that satisfaction.

'Skip it, ma.'

Went on down the corridor. Her door closed. Marge went in search of her husband, who was an easier target.

10

For over a fortnight Cal and Hennie crossed and re-crossed the Interior. Outback towns, stiff with heat and dust; stations isolated from their neighbours by a hundred miles of emptiness. They flew low over the gibber plains of the Sturt, the mirror-like stones as red as fire under the unrelenting sun. They crossed the southern boundary of the Simpson, saw the sand dunes stretching away northwards like the rollers of a vast and smouldering sea.

From time to time storms ruptured the sky. Rain poured with a frenzy that cut off all vision, all sensation, for perhaps four hours, before stopping as abruptly as it had begun.

'I warned you,' Hennie said. 'Bad news, the rain this time of year. Like being under Vic Falls and makes the ground like glue. You can't walk a yard.'

Bad news in other ways, too. During the storms the electricity knocked out the radio.

Once, the rain caught them as they were landing and Hennie had to feel his way to the ground without being able to see it. He laughed, delighted by the adrenalin rush of danger, but Cal wiped away sweat.

'I hope like hell you know what you're doing.'

'Don't worry about it. This sort of thing keeps you young.'

'Or makes sure you never grow old.'

And again Hennie laughed.

One night they stayed, by permission of the station owner's wife, in a deserted bunk-house, the men who lived there swallowed by the immensity in which they worked. Their presence remained. On a noticeboard a pin-up flaunted balloon breasts tight with silicone, a vapid smile. A pointed tongue, pink and luscious, offered promises that would never be kept.

They ate steaks, courtesy of the station, slept under a roof for the first time in days. Beyond the dusty window the land waited.

In the middle of nowhere, they shared their fire with a bunch of station hands, white and black, who rode in to check out the strangers. To a man they were tall, lean, sun-dried. They sat around the flames and talked cricket. Down in Adelaide the Poms were getting a bashing. Cricket apart, they didn't give a damn what was going on in the rest of the world. Someone mentioned Canberra, was at once jeered into silence.

'Them bloody nig-nogs . . . '

It was still early when the hands left. Before sleep Cal walked a little way. It was cold, the stars sparkled frostily. In the silence he sensed once again a breathless expectation. It is here, he thought, what I have come to find.

Here, too, he would return, bring Kathryn into the remoteness. With the thought, she smiled at him, her hand touched his, her dark cap of hair glossy in the starlight.

When he got back to the fire Hennie, wrapped in his blanket, was already asleep.

Without the chopper and Hennie's expertise, none of it would have been possible. The casual-seeming skill with which the pilot handled the controls fascinated Cal. If he'd handled his wife half as well, Cal thought, he'd have had no trouble. But Hennie was the worst of romantics, wedded to a concept of air and flight and, perhaps, to the oblivion of silence. The sea coast and the woman who lived there meant little to a man whose true love affair was with the empty plains of the Outback.

The two men developed a strange relationship. In the air they hardly spoke; even on the ground they didn't say much. At night, over the fires they lit to arm themselves against darkness and cold, Hennie took refuge in the same stale banter with which he had greeted Cal two weeks before, about Stella and the sexual games that Cal was supposed to play with her.

Cal, too, was insulated by distance. Stella's ardent body moved sinuously beneath his own; he remembered sweat, strangled cries, the open, seeking mouth. He went along with the cuckold's truthful fantasies as though they were indeed the figments of Hennie's overheated imagination.

Yet was exasperated by them. If he thinks about her so much, he thought, why doesn't he do something about it? Came slowly to realise that Hennie did not want to, that for him talk was more potent than the physical act could ever be. He doesn't want Stella at all, Cal thought, only this idea of a woman lost in the rhythms of desire and release.

From memory he drew the pilot at the controls of the chopper, mastery explicit in every line; another drawing showed him beside the nightly fire, features reddened by flame, imagination reddened by visions. Loneliness, Cal thought. Perhaps, for some, there was fulfilment in that, too. And tried to incorporate it in his drawings, a component of the Outback's brooding isolation.

Whenever they were on the ground during the day, the heat savaged them. Hennie had been right about that, too. Each day the temperature neared fifty and, after the storms, the humidity was close to absolute. It was certainly no place for a picnic.

In that flat country, Cal could see for what seemed a hundred miles. He tasted with open mouth the isolation and the silence.

To paint the silence, he thought. That will be the first step. And paced the dusty ground, not so much thinking as holding himself open to impressions, the flowering of the subconscious. There is something here, he thought. In time it will come.

The trouble was that they'd gone far beyond the week or ten days that he'd anticipated. Two more days and Hennie's leave would be up; he'd have to report back to Moomba. Once again Stella would be left to conduct her solitary, or not so solitary, vigil by the sea.

They left the Simpson with its fire-red rollers and flew south, saw the white blink of salt lakes. In the distance, away to the east, were the folded strata of a range of mountains.

'What's over there?'

'Gammon Ranges,' Hennie said. 'Part of the North Flinders. Harsh country, that.'

After so much flat land, Cal was hungry for the variations in perspective created by the hills.

'Can we have a look?'

Hennie looked at his watch, shook his head. 'Maybe tomorrow.'

'What's the rush?'

'If we're not at Emu Tank on time they'll come looking for us, and I don't need a boot in the arse from Moomba for being off-course.'

'What's there?'

'Nothing much. A shack and a bore. An old-timer called Jock.'

'What's he doing out here?'

'There's an old mine, hasn't been worked for years. I reckon he does a bit of fossicking. I heard him mention sapphire once.'

An hour later they were there. Hennie put them down pin-neat on a scrap of open ground outside a low cluster of buildings the colour of sand. Jock stood waiting, a hand raised to shield his eyes against the gale vomiting from the chopper's rotors.

Hennie switched off and they heard the sibilant voice of the wind. They climbed out into a tyrannical heat and walked over to the old man standing as motionless as the bibs and bobs of abandoned machinery that lay scattered here and there behind him. He was pole thin. A pair of old trousers flopped about naked ankles, a tuft of grey hair showed above a mud-coloured singlet from which emerged bare arms as thin as twigs.

At once Cal knew he wanted to draw him and, later, he did.

'Who the hell would want to look at my ugly mug?' Jock wondered, voice roughened by age and sand; by solitude, too, perhaps.

'I'll make you so beautiful, half the women in Australia will come looking for you.'

'Bloody hell, you got a job on, you want to do that.'

But sat there, grinning toothlessly for the artist, as though he truly expected the sheilas to come running.

Soon it was dark. Cal put his materials away and they all turned in.

During the night it rained. The dawn broke sullen and dark. Even with the cloud cover the heat was already a bastard; worse, the humidity was back, bleeding oxygen from the air, leaving a blanket of moisture that, by the time they were ready to leave, weighed like bricks.

Cal, who had wanted sunlight to bring out the colours of the landscape, was outraged.

'On our last day? I don't need this!' Like a spoilt brat.

Hennie shrugged philosophically. 'Be thankful we don't have to walk.'

It was barely light, but neither of them could wait to get out of there. They said tooroo to Jock.

'Make sure you go straight home now,' he instructed them. 'Like good boys.'

Hennie grinned. 'Might take a look at a waterhole I know, if the weather clears.'

'Don't forget to let me have a copy of me picture,' Jack told Cal.

They climbed aboard. Cal worried, privately, about the chopper. If you couldn't walk perhaps you couldn't take off, but Hennie got them away without any dramas.

As the helicopter climbed, the dreadful heat fell away. The sun shone momentarily although ahead the clouds still hung, rage-black. To the south the Gammon Ranges bared their jagged teeth.

'Still want to have a look?' Hennie said.

Cal looked dubiously at the clouds. 'What about the weather?'

Hennie whistled beneath his breath, discarding the weather. 'Be in and out before it breaks. You want to see them, this is your last chance.'

Which was true, certainly.

'Just in and out, then, okay?'

'You're the boss.'

Hennie tried to radio Moomba to tell them of the change of course, but the storm's electric curtain hung between them and he could not get through.

'What the hell,' he decided. 'It's only for an hour.'

And swung the chopper south-east. To their right was the salt blink of Lake Torrens, behind them Lake Eyre faded into haze.

Lake Eyre, Cal thought. The huge salt pan, thousands of square kilometres of it. That was another memory.

They had flown over it a week earlier, the diamond glitter of salt reaching to the horizon. Cal had thought that it had to be one of the remotest-seeming places in the universe, more alien even than the stars. Perhaps that is how I should paint it, he thought, the glare of salt mirroring the night sky. He remembered the painting he had called Fox By Moonlight, of snow beneath the moon, the loping fox, Gianetta.

With astonishment he realised that he had not thought of her for days. Did so now, not with horror and remorse, but with the warm memory of happiness and shared affection.

Perhaps I am free of the agony at last, he thought.

Again he studied the salt shield below them. 'No chance of putting down, I suppose?'

Hennie laughed. 'On the salt? We can try, if you like. Mind you, pick the wrong spot, we might go straight through. They say it's miles deep, nothing under the salt but slime. What a way to go, heh?'

At once he put the chopper into a dive, rotors thrashing. He flew so low it seemed they might scrape the surface.

Cal was appalled. If it were really possible to go through the crust . . . He stared at Hennie, who laughed.

'One way to sort out the men from the boys.'

And went, if anything, lower.

Courage was one thing; idiocy something else. 'For God's sake, Hennie!'

At this height the heat was a killer, but it was not only the heat that brought the sweat to Cal's body. He twisted in his seat and looked behind him, seeing salt crystals whirling like fine snow in their wake.

The shore was lined with dunes as high as cliffs. As they approached, Hennie touched the controls, the helicopter lifted in a roar, Lake Eyre was gone.

Hennie slapped his knee with a gleeful hand.

'Got to change your underpants, don't feel bad about it, heh? You wouldn't be the first.'

He was cackling, but Cal was so furious he could not speak. A salt lake a million miles from anywhere, a crust that might or might not support them, a cowboy at the controls. Who needed it?

Yet they had survived.

A memory, indeed. Now Cal looked down again. As they neared the mountains, the character of the land was changing. A thin scurf of shaggy vegetation barely disturbed the stark symmetry of the cornelian ridges. The colour that in the distance had seemed a uniform grey resolved into a rainbow of muted tints: black and silver and navy, plum and olive brown, with immense fields of sand flowering in yellow drifts between the rocks. The harsh character of the land consumed all. From this height it was patterned with the sinews of dried-up stream beds beneath a sky of violent blue.

That was another key, Cal thought. The relationship between the earth and sky, the weight of the blue immensity pressing down . . . He could sense the land's personality: ancient, withdrawn, abiding. People could do to it what they liked and it would make no difference. It knew everything there was to know, everything that would ever be known. It had existed since the beginning and, long after humanity and all its works were gone, it would abide.

How the hell shall I ever paint this? Cal wondered, awed by the immensity of the task he had set himself. Wondered if it would be sacrilege even to try, to seek what could never be captured, the immense and brooding spirit of the land.

I have no right.

The moment passed. Provided I work with reverence . . .

Hennie was pointing ahead. 'There they are.'

The ranges were very close now: stark, dangerous-looking, enormous after all the flatness they had seen.

Cal was fascinated by the colours, tried to work out the palette he would need to bring what he was seeing to the canvas. Prussian blue, he thought. No, that's not quite right. You'll have to mix it with something, ultramarine, perhaps. And the bronzes, you must get them in. Red and yellow . . . Burnt sienna, maybe, with a touch of red. And the sky . . . also blue, but different altogether from the violet and mauve of the mountains.

And felt excitement at the idea of getting to work.

To Cal's eye the clouds were closer than ever but, for the moment, the sun had come out again. It highlighted the rock formations that soared and twisted crazily, the strata fractured here and everywhere into a turmoil of stone. And old . . . Even from this height, the mountains spoke of the unimaginable aeons through which they had remained.

Hennie swung the chopper over the middle of the range. Cal stared down. It was like coming through a door into a past that had been old millions of years before the first dinosaur walked the earth.

'Yes,' he said. 'Yes.'

This was what he had come to see, the past from which later pasts, the present and the future, all hung. It was the extra characteristic, what the painters at the beginning of the century had called the fourth dimension. Time, made manifest.

And the colours . . . Matisse himself could hardly have imagined such reds and golds and blues. All alive, all blazing in the harsh, yellow sunlight.

Cal stared down, yearning. Everywhere dark canyons opened like wounds. Some of them looked hundreds of feet deep, yet so narrow that a man would find it hard to make his way along them.

A gust of wind came, buffeting.

'Want to go down?'

More than anything he wanted it.

'You sure it's safe?'

'Safe?' Hennie was laughing, exultant. Danger was a drug, and he was as high as the stars. 'Why shouldn't it be safe?'

'And the weather?'

Hennie barely squinted at the clouds,

repeated what he had said earlier. 'Don't worry, we'll be in and out before you know it.'

'Let's do it, then.'

'That's my boy!'

And down they went.

On both sides the rock was so close that it was like flying down a chimney. The cliffs amplified the engine noise until it seemed to fill the universe. They drew closer and closer, yet Hennie never hesitated. Hands sure on the controls, eyes laughing, youthful with excitement, he took them down.

'Like Auntie threading a needle . . . '

They passed through bands of shadow and into the sun again, the light as fractured as the rocks. Below them the land lay tilted in every direction; Cal could see no level ground at all.

'Where are we going to land?'

'I've been here before. I know a place.'

They were clear of the chimney now. A touch of the controls and they entered a narrow gorge enclosed by high cliffs. There was a narrow creek, the blink of water. Beside the creek, a patch of level sand as white as bone.

The helicopter hovered, sank. The engine roar shattered the stillness, sent sand and leaves and debris flying. They touched. Cal discovered he had been holding his breath.

He relaxed and opened his eyes wide.

'Phew . . . '

'Made it!' Hennie, beaming, triumphant. 'I told you.'

He killed the engine. Silence, bruised and savaged, returned.

'You haven't got long,' Hennie said. 'Once that cloud gets over the sun, you'll lose the colour.'

Cal opened the door, went to climb down.

'Best put your boots on,' Hennie warned him. 'It's rough stuff out there.'

Cal saw that he was right. Obediently he changed runners for mountain boots, laced them up, dropped to the ground. The air was hot and humid. He could hear nothing but the faint noise of flowing water; above and all around, the ranges held their breath.

On either side of the creek, gum trees stretched their branches skywards. Further off there were more, leaves forming a mist of green against a wall of brown and purple rock. In the creek the water was brown and clear but, between the pools, its channel disappeared under boulders and clumps of coarse, spear-bladed grass. Along the valley walls the shadows lay dark, velvet-soft, the trunks of gums as pallid as ghosts. Everywhere lay shattered rock, like the debris of a cosmic explosion.

Notebook in hand, eyes devouring every-thing, Cal clambered over the rocks, feeling the texture of the trees, the grass, the air. His mind buzzed with colour, and everywhere he could sense distance, not of kilometres but of centuries, of tens of thousands of centuries. Time bound the rocks, trees, water, himself, into one universal silence.

Ahead of him the gorge twisted out of sight between towering cliffs of gold and purple and a dark brown flushed with rose. He was hungry to see what lay beyond the turn but, before he could get there, the sunlight went out and the colours vanished. Now everything was a uniform and ominous grey.

Behind him Hennie was shouting. 'Time to go!'

Cal turned. He had come a lot further than he'd intended. Overhead the clouds had arrived, hanging so low that they seemed almost to brush the tops of the hills.

Hennie gestured. 'Come on!' There was urgency in his voice, this man who normally was troubled by nothing.

Cal went back as fast as he could, splashing through the shallow pools, hopping from rock to rock.

By the time he got back, Hennie was aboard, eyes watching the clouds, from which a few warm drops were already beginning to fall.

Cal joined him, panting, and hauled up the door behind him.

Hennie said, 'Let's get out of here . . . '

And fired the engine.

The rain was falling steadily now, still manageable, but definitely much harder than before.

Hennie ran up the revs, the concussion of the rotors beating furiously against their ears even inside the cabin. They settled themselves securely in their seats, tightened their belts and Hennie took them up.

Back along the valley, dark and sombre now in the rain. Around the corner and into the space between the rock walls down which they had come like a lift down a shaft. They hovered momentarily so that Hennie could orientate himself, then up they went, not fast, not recklessly, but gaining height with every second. Cal watched the ground fall away beneath them. Twenty feet, forty, fifty.

The rain came in a concussion of pearl-grey water that wiped out visibility in an instant. It was as though they had flown into a waterfall.

The combined noise of rain and engine was indescribable.

'Watch out your side,' Hennie screamed. 'Tell me if we get too close.'

Cal did so but could see virtually nothing, only water and, intermittently, the dark and streaming wall of the gorge. Now wind came with the rain, flinging them to and fro. The cliff swung close. Cal opened his mouth to shout a warning, shut it again as the next moment took them away again. Away and back, away and, sickeningly, back once more.

'Watch out! You're going to hit it!'

Hennie was screaming brilliant blue oaths as he wrestled with the controls. The wind thrashed them, howling; the rain redoubled its fury. Now Cal could see clearly the interstices of the rock, the rain cascading down every cranny. He shut his eyes as again the chopper lurched closer.

He felt the blow, gentle at first, then violent. The machine swung around, crashed again and then again against the rock face. The engine screamed, climbing the octaves as the rotor blades broke, then cut out as it seized. The helicopter fell, smashing and bouncing against the wall, landing in a final crash of metal and the stench of fuel at the bottom of the cliff.

11

He was alive, just. He tried to seize hold of that idea: *alive, just*, but could not come to grips with it. Between one instant and the next, all movement had ceased, violently; the howling cacophony of sound had ceased, yet still he was alive. Miraculously, they had landed upright; he was still in his seat. He felt pain where the straps had bitten into his shoulders but welcomed it, evidence of the miracle.

He turned to look at Hennie. The pilot was lolling in his harness. His hands were still on the controls but he was out, a livid mark on his forehead showing where, despite the harness, he had struck his head.

The stench of leaking fuel, pungent, potentially lethal, brought him back to reality. He remembered Hennie showing off his new toy, chortling.

They got only one problem. One of these mothers hits the deck, you're toast.

Panic. He wrestled with his harness, managed to unclip it. He tried to open the hatch. It wouldn't budge. Cursing, he raised his feet — thank God he was still wearing boots — and lashed out with all his strength. Once. Twice. The hatch flew back. He turned, unclipped Hennie's harness and tried to drag him clear. He would not come. Cursing, sweat pouring, Cal hunted, found that one of Hennie's feet was jammed under the controls. He managed to push himself down, head first, to reach the pedals, twisting and wrenching frantically until the foot was free. He worked his way out again, dragged Hennie clear by the shoulders and let him drop to the ground.

The death reek of spilled fuel was everywhere.

With the strength of terror, he tossed Hennie's body over his shoulder. Half-running, half-staggering, he put distance between himself and the wreck.

Suddenly, a thought.

He dropped Hennie, sprinted back to the helicopter, grabbed the two water bottles with trembling hands and got out again, running full-pelt. He was halfway back to the pilot when the chopper blew. There was a dull thud. In the same instant, the shock wave hit him squarely in the back. He was flat on his face upon the broken scree of the valley floor, no idea how he'd got there. He rolled over in time to see the fireball, orange and red and black, cascading skywards. Flame bellowed.

He lay, poleaxed by heat, shock, the expiring scream of adrenalin through his veins. So easily they might have been inside. Had he been knocked out, too . . .

But he had not.

He staggered to his feet. Hennie was crumpled on the ground a hundred metres away. He, too, was alive. They had water in the bottles, in the creek. They would have a deal of walking to do, but it wasn't the end of the world.

Not that they had much to feel cheerful about, either. He had seen from the chopper what the ranges looked like. Hennie had called it harsh country. It was certainly that. They had no food, the heat was savage, they were an unknown distance from aid.

Now the real struggle would begin.

★ ★ ★

Suddenly, between dream and dawning, Kathryn was awake.

Her heart was pounding. She lay tense, listening. The morning's immaculate stillness was accentuated rather than broken by the distant crying of the sheep.

Something was wrong.

Her heart told her, the uneasy flooding of her blood. That damned second sight again

. . . She got out of bed, pulled on a robe, walked outside. It was half-past seven, the sun well clear of the horizon. It would be warm later but, for the moment, a cool breeze blew from the east. She turned her head, staring northwards. Out there, there would be no cooling breeze, only immensity and silence, the indifference of fearsome heat.

She sent her thoughts, the delicate tendrils of her instinct, winging into the vastness. What had woken her, she who never woke until she was ready? A scent of roses wafted on the breeze. There was nothing, she told herself. Go back to bed.

But could not. She walked to the end of the verandah, came back; walked slowly around the tennis court, came back.

Foolish how they continued to call it that, she thought. No one had played on it for years. The net posts and netting were rotten now, all that remained of her childhood's energy and sweat, the rosy flesh shining, the cries of triumph and despair. The tennis court, she thought. What relevance does it have? What relevance do I have?

She walked round and round the earth rectangle, while the wind stirred the fig tree's brittle leaves. She could not settle, forced herself eventually to sit in one of the verandah chairs, pitting her will against the nervous fluttering of her stomach. Waited for the sunlight, gathering heat with every minute, to dispel the forebodings of the dawn.

It is so still, she thought, yet in reality we are rushing through space. The scientists say that if the earth stopped, we would all fly into the void. As Cal has flown into the void. Yet is so close I can feel his breath, the warmth of his presence. This instant he is beside me. When I turn my head, he smiles.

Our lives are like a journey. One of many we might have taken, might indeed be taking; other lives beneath the skin of this life. In those other lives, I might already be dead, I might be married to Charles, I might be a man. Or a star.

As it is . . . I am myself. Am Cal, too. I am the dawn that separates and unites us. We have travelled far together and shall go further; upon this verandah, in the morning light, in the Outback's silence. Because for us there can be no isolation, neither now nor in the future, in this life or all the other lives. Our spirits touch. I am with him to the ending, not of this world, but of all worlds.

If forever means what it says, then that is where we shall be. In another of our lives we were one, now are one again. Which is why I know without knowledge, am certain without evidence. My flesh and spirit know it. In the vastness beyond the northern horizon, something is wrong.

Time passed. And passed.

Her heartbeat was quieter now, resigned to whatever had woken her. Whatever it was, this was also part of the whole.

Footsteps inside the house. Her father. Now that reaping was over, Claude Fanning had been catching up on his sleep. Water ran. Floorboards creaked. He went out the back, towards the sheds. She heard the diminishing sound of the ute as he drove away along the track to the upper paddocks.

It was five to eight. She went indoors, as though going to an appointment. She switched on the radio, listened to the news, awaiting the inevitable.

Nothing.

There was no comfort in it. All it meant was that the authorities were still unaware. She alone knew, and would wait, not for unneeded confirmation, but because she could do nothing else.

Now the radio was playing classical music. She turned it off and went back to her bedroom. She closed the door behind her, lay upon the bed. Her eyes watched the ceiling. And beyond.

'The beacon,' Hennie muttered, over and over. 'That'll bring them in.'

He had been out for almost half an hour; now, three hours later, his voice was still slurred, as though his teeth were loose in his mouth. The bruise covered half his forehead, to remind them both what a hell of a smack it had been.

Cal had half-carried, half-dragged him to the patch of sand where the helicopter had landed when they had first come here. He had bathed his head, made him as comfortable as he could, waited. As soon as Hennie came to, he had started talking about the beacon that every aircraft carried, how it would bring the searchers to them amid these tangled hills.

Cal knew there was no beacon, no signal. The helicopter was now a heap of grey metal, radiating heat in vicious little spurts of flame. Neither the beacon nor anything else would have survived the fire. He said nothing. Let Hennie go on kidding himself a little longer; time enough for the truth when he'd regained his strength.

There would be searchers, certainly. When they were logged overdue, Moomba would send an aircraft to look for them, but in this valley they were not only far off course but virtually invisible from the air. There was no realistic hope of anyone finding them. The authorities might decide to send a ground party, but Cal doubted it very much. After the rain, as Hennie was always saying, the ground would be like glue. Besides, the Gammon Ranges covered a vast area; no-one was going to find them here except by luck.

Cal believed in making his own luck. Sitting here on the million-to-one chance that someone might stumble on them made no sense at all. The accepted wisdom was that you never, *never*, left your vehicle after an accident, but this was one occasion when, as far as Cal could see, they had no choice.

Though how they were going to set about things, without food or map or compass and with one man injured, he had no idea. Hennie had lived in the Outback for years; perhaps, when he'd had a chance to recover, he might have some suggestions. For now, he was sleeping. As far as Cal could tell, it was good sleep. When he awoke they would decide what had to be done. At least they had water.

The day dragged past. Hennie still slept. Cal walked to where the gorge made its left-hand turn. The going looked terribly rough.

Towards evening he thought he heard the faint sound of an aircraft, but the hills enclosed them as tight as a fist and he could see nothing. Not that it would have helped; they were too far away. Even if the plane had flown directly overhead, Cal doubted it would have seen them. Eventually the sound, so faint that Cal could not be sure he'd heard it at all, died away.

The darkness came stealing. Soon it would be cold. On clear nights the temperatures in these parts dropped close to zero, even in mid-summer, but there was no help for it. There was material for a fire, but no way to light it. They would have to sit it out as best they could.

★　★　★

All day Kathryn waited, listening to the bulletins as they fell due. In the evening came confirmation of what she had known.

'In the far north of the State, a helicopter is overdue on a flight from Emu Tank, south-east of Lake Eyre, to Moomba. A search plane sent out along the helicopter's scheduled path has found no trace of the missing aircraft or its two passengers. The search will resume in the morning.'

210

12

In the morning the bruise was still livid on Hennie's face but in himself he seemed much better. He remembered little of what had happened, so Cal filled him in on the details.

'Pity about the beacon,' Hennie said, 'but it won't matter. They'll come over later this morning and spot us, then they'll send a chopper. They'll have us out of here in no time.'

He sounded as though he believed what he was saying; Cal did not.

'How they going to spot us in this lot?'

'We'll make sure they do. Listen: they'll fly the route we told them, right? Not much cover there. No ways they could miss us. When they don't find us, they'll know we got to be some place else. Only one place we can be, heh? So they'll come south, have a look here.'

'And see us?' Cal was exasperated by Hennie's optimism. 'How are they going to do that?'

Hennie pointed beyond the end of the gorge to where a sharply-pointed crest stood against the sky. 'We get up there, somewhere like that, they'll be sure to see us.'

Cal didn't believe a word of it. 'There must be a hundred peaks like that. A thousand.'

Hennie was not fazed by Cal's disbelief; on the contrary, seemed to enjoy the chance to show off his superior knowledge.

'We take a couple of bits of aluminium from the wreck, polish them up. When the plane comes we use them like mirrors. What d'you think? You're flying over the ranges, suddenly something's shining in your eyes. You're bound to go see what it is.'

It might work, at that. Cal felt better, looked at Hennie with new respect.

'I'll go and get some.'

He found two pieces that were large enough to make decent mirrors, small enough to carry without too much drama.

'Better get moving,' Hennie said. 'We want to be up there when our mates arrive, otherwise they'll miss us.'

He still sounded confident — aggressively so, as though determined to raise a wall between themselves and despair. Cal had seen the nature of the ground in the gorge. What lay beyond, where the ground started to rise, might be worse. It didn't bear thinking about. But Hennie was right; to do it, and now, was their best chance. Miss the search plane and they would have to walk out. Much better to get themselves rescued, if they could.

They strapped the water bottles around their waists, picked up the aluminium mirrors and began to move up the valley towards the higher ground.

★ ★ ★

An endless-seeming night yet, somehow, it had passed. In the morning Kathryn had to go to work, which was probably a blessing.

All through the day she fled to the radio when she could, hoping — dreading — to hear more, but there was nothing. She thought of phoning Moomba or even the CFS, but did not, frightened of what she might hear.

She was determined to be cheerful. Before I get home tonight, she told herself, there will be a message.

There was not. Knowing her mother's views, fearful of hurt, of giving hurt, of a row that might fracture their relationship, she said nothing, listening to what could not be heard. The distant heartbeat of the man. The awareness of his pulse, the rhythmic stirring of his breath. The knowledge that he was.

In which case, why don't I phone?

But could not, caught between certainty and fear.

★ ★ ★

It was a climb out of nightmare.

Unlike Cal, Hennie was wearing ordinary shoes. Before they had even reached the bend in the gorge, as he slipped and stumbled over the rocks, it became clear that the shoes were going to cause trouble, but there was nothing to be done.

Beyond the bend the climb grew steeper until, after an hour, they were scrambling on all fours over and around splintered rocks the size of houses. The surface of the rocks had been knobbed and gnarled by the millennia into a moonscape as dangerous as it was unwelcoming. The giant rocks — umber, sienna, tawny gold — lay in confusion, as though they had been chucked down on the first day of creation. Patches of sage-coloured brush clung to the occasional crevice but for the most part the slopes were bare, beginning to bake in the sun that shone blindingly into the men's eyes as they strained and fought and cursed their way upwards. It was no place for a man, even in boots; for someone wearing light shoes, every step became a nightmare prospect of twisted and broken ankles. Either, in country like this, would mean death.

For the twentieth time in no more than a kilometre, Cal thrust a boot between two mighty rocks and hauled himself upwards. Eyes stinging, half-blinded by sweat, he tried to see where they were going. The change of direction meant that the sharp-pointed peak was no longer visible, but he could still see the ridge leading to it, stark and clear and razor-edged against a sky of blinding blue. It seemed as far away as ever.

He turned to look back down the slope up which they had come. The trees along the creek were out of sight, but the corner where the gorge had twisted and started to climb seemed no distance at all. It was barely credible that they had expended so much energy in covering so little ground. Again he stared up at the ridge which, by contrast, looked very far away. We're never going to make it, he thought, and at once suppressed the idea, fiercely. They had to; there was no choice.

All the same . . .

Twenty yards behind him, Hennie hauled himself over a boulder big enough to dam rivers, its surface as ragged as raw pumice. He was gasping, already close to exhaustion, the bruise on his forehead a livid stain against a face the colour of blood. His pants were badly ripped. Through the holes Cal could see traces of blood, where a stumble had ripped the skin from Hennie's knees.

His own good boots had preserved him from falling but, in other respects, Cal was not sure that he was in much better shape himself.

We have hardly started, he thought.

He waited until Hennie caught up with him, managed a grin.

'Nice day for a stroll.'

Hennie collapsed beside him. Sweat had stained his bush shirt black. His stomach sagged over the waistband of his pants. By the sound of his breath, he could be looking at a heart attack within minutes. He was unable to speak but half sat, half leaned, against the tilted surface of the boulder that represented only the first of the ten thousand obstacles remaining to be circumvented before they were out of the gorge.

Assuming we can get out of it at all, Cal thought. It was quite possible that around the next bend, or the next, or the one after that, the valley might end in an impassable wall. If that happened, they would have to climb all the way down again and strike off in another direction. God knew there was no shortage of choices; they had passed the mouths of three

216

subsidiary valleys on their way up here, each as boulder-clogged and impenetrable as the one they were in.

Stop it! he instructed himself. Stop thinking like that. For all you know, things will ease off around the next corner.

But knew there was no chance of that. The ridge was still far above their heads, the invisible peak further still, and the only way was up.

Dear God, he thought.

Hennie was mumbling.

'What?'

'Gotta have a drink . . . '

They had lost the creek far below. Ahead there was no sign of water.

'Best be careful,' Cal cautioned, 'until we find some more.'

But Hennie was fumbling frantically at his water bottle. Cal watched as he gulped, throat straining.

The liquid sound of the water reminded Cal how thirsty he himself was. For a moment he almost followed Hennie's example, then thought, No, I can hang on a bit longer, and put temptation away from him. It made him feel good, knowing he still had the will to resist.

He looked again at Hennie and frowned. 'Where's your mirror?'

Hennie gulped again, screwed the top back

on the bottle with obvious reluctance.

'I dumped it back there, somewhere. I couldn't manage it.'

Cal was exasperated by Hennie's lack of endurance at what was little more than the start of their journey. He reminded himself that the pilot was still suffering from concussion, that he was a lot older than Cal, that he wasn't in good shape, that he wasn't wearing boots . . .

All of it was true, but made no difference. The slope was there, it had to be climbed and there was no way that Cal would be able to carry him.

The plane, when it comes, *if* it comes, had better damn well spot us, he thought. Otherwise God knows how we're going to get out of this.

There was no chance of its spotting them where they were. The only way that would happen would be if they were up on the ridge when it came. Again he looked up at its sharp outline, so clear and far away.

'You're going to have to go ahead without me,' Hennie said.

'I can't leave you here.'

'You must. Once the plane sees you, it won't matter. You can come back for me. But you've got to be up there before it comes or we've had it.'

It seemed dangerous to pin all their hopes on a plane that might never arrive, that might not see them if it did. Even if, by a miracle, he managed to get up there, if, by another miracle, the plane came, how realistic was it to hope that it would find them? On one ridge out of ten thousand? The idea of the aluminium mirrors had been a good one; it meant they were in with a chance but, realistically, no more than that. They had to keep some hope in reserve in case they needed it later.

Although how it would be possible to walk unassisted out of country like this, Cal could not imagine. Perhaps Hennie was the realistic one, he thought. The search plane would have to find them, otherwise things would be impossible.

'You push on,' Hennie said. 'Don't wait for me. It's the only way.'

He was right.

'What will you do in the meantime?'

'I'll wait here. Find a patch of shade. I'll be fine.'

'Don't drink all your water.'

A grim smile in the port-wine face. 'I can always climb back down for a refill.'

Alone, Cal made better time and realised that, unconsciously, he had been holding himself back for the older man. Even so, it wasn't easy going. The climb grew if anything steeper, the boulders were no smaller and, with the sun now high overhead, the heat was awesome.

Yet he was making progress. When he looked back, Hennie was out of sight. It made him uneasy. How would he ever find him again in this lot? But there was no help for it. He had to get up to the ridge before the plane came. Nothing else mattered.

Cal climbed and climbed. Twice, when his legs would carry him no further, he rested. The gorge was opening up; now the walls were half a kilometre apart, the ground between them a litter of broken stone. There were no more gigantic boulders. It made the going easier but, without them, there was no shade. The heat was a burden beyond anything he would have thought possible yet, when he looked at his watch, it was still three-quarters of an hour short of midday. Still he had not drunk, and thirst, too, was becoming intolerable.

I'll have a drink when I get there, he thought. When I reach the ridge.

At last it seemed nearer, but he wasn't there yet.

It's only here, he told himself, in the middle of it, that you get an idea of the immensity of the landscape. Pity the poor pilot; a needle in a haystack is nothing on this place.

Even the colours were changing. Now quartz was mixed with the granite. It winked and flashed punishingly in the sunlight and he remembered reading somewhere that it was possible to get sunstroke through the eyes. All I need, he thought. It created another, potentially far more serious problem. With quartz deposits all over the range, how would the pilot, if there were a pilot, be able to distinguish the flash of an aluminium mirror from any other flash?

Three hours after leaving Hennie, Cal rounded yet another corner. The cliffs had closed in again but beyond them, at last, he could see open country. It was still a fair way off, the going as steep as ever, but now it was not a question of whether he could make it, but when he would arrive.

Another hour, he thought, and I'll be there.

There was one more ridge of red stone, covered with the remains of dead brush. Grey branches stuck up in all directions, savage as barbed wire, but somehow he found his way through with little more than a few scratches. Beyond the ridge a gully, ten metres deep, crossed his path. It had been ripped through the ground by water in some bygone age and its edges were razor-sharp. Teetering always on the edge of falling, he inched his way down until he reached the smooth channel at the bottom. A snake slithered; only God knew what food it would find up here. On the far side of the channel he clambered up the opposite bank, at the top stood swaying on rubber legs.

Now he, too, was close to exhaustion. He had a few seconds to wonder how Hennie, far below him now, might be doing, but the thought passed as quickly as it had come. He had no energy to think, to do anything but push on up the slope. All else had become meaningless. Even the idea of the plane had ceased to be relevant. The only purpose in life was to climb, and to climb, and to climb.

Just then, out of a sky that had long lost its morning clarity and now quivered with heat, came the distant sound of a plane.

Oh God, Cal thought. I am so close to the top, but I won't be there for another hour. Please don't come yet. If you were going to come, why didn't you do it three hours ago and save me all my trouble?

He grew angry. Stay away, he ordered the plane that, until a minute before, he had wanted more than anything in life. Stay away for another hour. For half an hour. Ten minutes. Even in ten minutes I may be able to get out into open ground so that I can use my mirror to draw the pilot to me. Ten minutes is not so long. Stay away.

But the sound grew louder and louder, and he knew that he was not going to have ten minutes or five or even one. Frantically he manipulated the square of aluminium, trying to focus the sun in its polished surface and, with a sudden roar, the plane was on him.

Engine bellowing, it passed half a mile up the valley. It looked as though it were heading straight for the ridge towards which Cal had striven for so long. He could have wept. From down here the plane looked like a hawk, but the mouse for which it was hunting was too small, too far away. In seconds the plane had passed beyond the ridge and was gone.

With all the immensity of the range to search, Cal knew there was no chance of its coming back.

He could have screamed, cursed, wept, but did not. He stood under the hammer blows of the sun, his mouth open in despair and disbelief. He knew that he was looking at the very real prospect of death, could not believe that after all the hours of agony, he had been too late. If only he had made better time; if only the search plane had come ten minutes later; if only . . .

Futile.

All he could do now was head back down

the gorge, find Hennie, decide what they were going to do next. Not that they had any choice.

He sat on the harsh ground, head between his knees, trying to come to terms with the situation. They had water; not much but, perhaps, if they were careful, enough. On the other hand they had no food or likelihood of finding any.

They had eaten nothing since Emu Tank, thirty hours earlier. By now he should have been ravenous, but was not. The idea of eating did not interest him at all. Just as well, he thought. All the same, lack of food was bound to weaken them, in time. Another day, after that another day ... How long, realistically, could they hope to survive in country like this, in these temperatures?

As long as it takes, he told himself. Water we must have, but food can wait. If we get really desperate, we can always eat the grass.

He raised his head, staring about him at the gorge full of boulders, the rock walls rising vertically on either side. The rock was a medley of russet and gold, with high up a thin line of red where the strata ran obliquely upwards. Here and there across the floor of the gorge were the contorted shapes of bushes and thin trees, their leathery foliage a mixture of grey and the palest green. No sign of moisture. No sign of grass.

Cancel the order for grass, he thought. We can manage without grass. If we don't eat there'll be that much less weight for us to carry.

One thing he knew. He was not willing to give up.

He stood, feeling the complaint of legs already weary from the unaccustomed climbing they had done that day. The ridge was not far away. Get up there and he'd be able to see what the country was like on the other side. And — the sneaky thought, hope, prayer, lingering treacherously even as he told himself it was nonsense — it was just possible that the plane might come back, after all.

Once again he forced his body into the climb.

It was nearer than he had thought. Fifteen minutes later he reached the ridge. He uncapped his water bottle. He took several deep breaths, deliberately, put the bottle to his mouth and drank. Three careful mouthfuls, no more. He stopped, recapped the bottle and looked out at what lay before him.

Ahead was a cataclysm of arid peaks, red and blue and brown, glowing like multicoloured fire. Immediately below him was a ridge, beyond it another — a succession of ridges in waves like a stone sea, the valleys in between black with shadow. From here the valleys looked hundreds of feet deep. Each ridge was higher than the last, climbing away from him in a deepening fiery haze, until the final ridge of all, saw-toothed, stood up starkly against the empty brilliance of the sky.

Not a path, no sign of humanity at all. The only evidence of life was the grey-green foliage of the scattered trees.

As for the plane . . . Nothing.

The echo of his thoughts came back to him. *Cancel the order for grass. If we don't eat there'll be that much less weight to carry.*

Bravado, he thought now. His heart was grey with the idea of trying to walk out of such a place.

Cal turned and began to work his way back down the slope. It was harder even than it had been coming up; in no time the muscles of his thighs were telling him all about it.

Without boots, he thought, it would have been impossible, and wondered how Hennie was doing. Once again he crossed the watercourse, forced his way through the brush covering the red stone ridge and saw, a hundred metres below, the pilot struggling up to meet him.

He raised his hand, but Hennie showed no sign of having seen him. Cal waited, watching the pilot's slow progress. He came on, but barely. It was a quarter of an hour before he arrived. He was sucking air through his open mouth in great, noisy gasps as, earlier, Cal had watched him suck water.

'I thought you'd have been back down by the creek by now.'

Beyond speech, Hennie did not answer. He half sat, half fell at Cal's feet, a sack of lard spilling across the rocky slope.

Cal waited.

Eventually Hennie said, 'No point . . . '

'Why?'

'I heard the plane. When it didn't come back, I knew it must've missed us, so there was nothing for it but push on up here to join you . . . ' Bloodshot blue eyes stared up at Cal. 'We'll have to walk out. You know that, don't you?'

'I climbed as far as the ridge. It's hellish country on the other side. Like the moon. I'm not sure we'll be able to manage it.'

Hennie's body might be collapsing, but his spirit burned as bright as ever.

'Manage it? Of course we'll blerry manage it. What choice have we got?'

Words were cheap. Cal shook his head dubiously. 'I don't see how . . . '

'I'll tell you how we're going to do it,' Hennie said. He fumbled in the breast pocket of his bush shirt, pulled out treasure.

'Something me old dad taught me. Never go nowhere without a compass. So this is what we do, you see. We know more or less the direction we got to take to get us out, right?'

'You're the pilot,' Cal said.

'Damn right. First thing, we climb up to that ridge. From there we take a bearing on a peak in more or less the direction we want. We follow the bearing until we get there, take another one on the next place, walk to that. Over and over. Keep it up long enough, we'll be out in no time.'

Which was all very well, Cal thought, if you hadn't seen the country. If you didn't know that to walk from point to point you had first to climb down into the depths and up again.

'Some of those slopes are damn near vertical — '

'Listen. It'll be a doddle. You know that? Like a walk in the park. The Gammon Ranges National Park. That's why it's got the name, see?'

'So we can stroll in it?'

'Damn right.'

In one sense Hennie was right; it was the only way they would get out. Whether it would be possible was another story.

'How're your feet?'

'Good for a thousand miles. Heh, it's my

blerry gut's killing me, not my feet. Own fault; I always knew I should go on a diet.'

'You're on a diet now,' Cal said. 'Like it or not.'

'Damn right. Think how fit we'll be, time we gets out of here.'

Cal laughed. 'It's madness. I suppose you realise that?'

'Mad?' Hennie grinned back at him. 'Hell, man, if we wasn't mad we wouldn't be here.'

'Even so — '

'Even so nothing. Listen, I'm telling you. We'll stroll along, look at the scenery. When we're tired we'll take a rest. I'll tell you stories of the old *Suid Afrika*, before you know it we'll be eating steak and chips at Arkaroola.'

'You tell me stories, I'll be asleep before I know it.'

'People walk best when they're asleep. Ask me, I'm an expert. You ever hear of a bloke called van der Merwe?'

'No.'

'Great South African hero. Thickest thing on legs. I tell you stories about him, you'll die laughing.'

'As good a way as any, I suppose.'

So they chatted and joked to heal the hurt of the plane having missed them and their apprehension at what was to come, which they both knew would be no joking matter at all.

At length Hennie struggled to his feet. Even that small effort made him puff, but he was grinning, despite all. He punched Cal lightly on the shoulder. 'Best get on with it, heh? I'd hate to waste away altogether.'

It took them an hour to gain the ridge. Long before they reached it, there was no more breath for jokes. They rested on the summit. Later Hennie took fresh bearings with his compass, and they began to clamber down into the gorge below.

It went better than Cal had dared hope.

As they headed north-east down the slope, the sun was hidden almost at once by the ridge they had just left. Down they went into the shadows. Soon the ridges both in front and behind them were high above their heads. Two hours after they had set out, with darkness beginning to fall, they reached the bottom of the gorge.

There were some tea trees along what was obviously a watercourse, although there was no sign of water now. On the far side of the gorge, the slope was patterned with isolated native pines seemingly growing directly out of rock that now, in the shadows, glowed with a sombre red fire. Above and beyond them, the ochre cliffs were darkening to purple as the daylight seeped away.

'No water,' Cal said.

Water was the one essential commodity. He could tell himself they could manage without anything else, could almost believe it, but water they had to have. He had drunk his fill before setting out, since then had swallowed only the three disciplined mouthfuls when he had reached the ridge for the first time. That was all, yet the bottle felt much lighter than it had at the start. As for Hennie . . . Judging by the rate he'd been drinking, his bottle must be half empty by now.

'Don't be too sure there's no water. These ranges are full of surprises.'

Hennie seemed much stronger after their downhill journey but, in the back of Cal's mind, the reverse slope of the gorge still loomed, formidably.

'I'd noticed,' he said, thinking of the crash.

'Good surprises,' Hennie insisted. 'They say there's no end of water if you know where to find it.'

Which was the point, of course.

'Listen,' Hennie said. 'You wait here. Take the weight off your feet. I'll go and have a look-see, check out if there's any water around here.'

And began to work his way cheerfully along the creek bed.

It was hard to imagine a greater contrast: Hennie as he was now and the half-crippled man who had barely survived the climb. Of course it was early days yet. They would be doing a lot more climbing before they were through. Even if they found water, Cal couldn't help wondering how they would manage without food.

His body cried out for rest, but there was still one more thing that had to be done before it got too dark to see. He left Hennie to his water hunt and crossed the dried-up watercourse, hopping precariously over boulders as shiny as glass. When he reached the far side, he forced his way back up the gorge, looking for a way out. In the morning they had to go on, and to climb the cliff that faced them was impossible. There had to be a way around; he could not bring himself to imagine what it might mean if there were not.

Yet the unforgiving cliff ran without a break; indeed, the higher he climbed, the steeper it grew. It was like looking for a way through Ayers Rock. *Uluru*, he corrected himself, and grinned, feeling his lips chapped and sore. Let us build a monument to political correctness in the middle of the Gammon Ranges, he thought. Never mind what you call it. The whole eastern wall of the gorge was a bloody great rock; there didn't seem any way of getting around it.

He looked back. No sign of Hennie. Let's hope he's having better luck.

He had certainly come to life over the downhill stage. It was a huge relief. By the time they had reached the ridge, Cal had been wondering what he would have to do about him. Hennie had looked close to collapse. To abandon him would be unthinkable, yet to carry him would be impossible.

The stark options — to go, to stay — had cast a dark shadow over his mind. Now, if only for the moment, he need worry about it no longer.

Hell, he thought, if he keeps this up, he'll be carrying me before we're through.

It was nonsense, of course. By morning all the old doubts and problems would have re-emerged but, for now, it was sufficient not to have to think about them at all. I shall find a gully leading uphill in the direction we want to go, he told himself. It will be smooth, with patches of grass here and there so that we can dine on grass, after all, if that is what we want to do. The way will be easy, not too steep, with positively no huge boulders to get around. We shall stroll along until we reach the summit, and then we shall see the planes looking for us.

It was a nice thought. As much nonsense as the rest, of course, but he did not want to know about that.

In the meantime the rock face continued as before, straight and harsh and unclimbable, and Cal knew that if they could not find a way out, their confidence would burst like a ruptured balloon, their courage would whistle away, they would die. Because to go back the way they had come, all the way up and then all the way down again, to start all over from the beginning with nothing in their stomachs but bile, would be impossible. Not physically, perhaps, but psychologically it would be out of the question. Even to think about it turned his courage to soup. There had to be a way; had to be.

He pushed on, turned yet another corner and there it was. Facing him was the gully that he had been seeking.

It was not in the least as he had told himself it would be. It was steep and boulder-choked, and there was not a blade of grass to be seen. It was very steep and, at least at the beginning, headed south-east, a long way from the direction they wanted. None of that mattered. It was a way out, it reopened the door to hope, and he was delighted to see it.

Delighted was not the right word, Cal thought. Delight was not a feature of their lives at the moment. Pleased and relieved, yes. Neither was quite as sensational as delight, but would do. Would do very well, in the circumstances.

He went quickly back down the gorge to the place he had left Hennie. The pilot was there before him, his face one big grin.

'I told you . . . '

And held up a bottle brimming with water.

'A kilometre down the gorge,' he explained. 'A ledge of rock, slap against the face of the cliff. This side of it there's a pool where the ledge has trapped the water.'

'Is it any good?'

'Sweet as a nut. Deep, too. Deep enough to swim.'

It all sounded delightful. That word again, Cal thought, but this time it seemed the right one.

'What are we waiting for, then?'

He followed Hennie as, proudly, the pilot showed him the way. He had something to be proud about, Cal thought. They both had. Hennie had found water, he had found a way out of the gorge. Hope had returned to their lives. Delightful, indeed, if only for the moment.

The water was indeed there. They stripped off and got into the little pool. Around them the rocks were a mixture of purple and russet and umber, with traces here and there of madder and cinnabar. The silky cool water was dark and shining, almost black. The tap roots of plants extended across the face of the rock into the water; here and there upon the cliffs above them a number of plants spread emerald leaves.

It was paradise.

Eventually they got out, used their shirts to dry themselves, struggled back into their clothes. Hennie was cursing softly under his breath.

'What's up?'

'I think I'll leave my shoes until the morning.'

Cal looked at Hennie's feet, saw ruin. The skin was broken in a dozen places, blood oozed between toes as fat as apricots. To Cal it was miraculous that he was able to put his feet on the ground at all. All that way, he thought. Up that damn gorge to the ridge and now down this side and never gave a hint of what he must have been feeling. And I never even thought to ask.

'How you going to manage?' he asked.

Hennie threw him a larrikin grin. 'Tell you tomorrow.' Saw Cal's sober face and laughed.

236

'Don't you fret, my mate. I'll be hokay.'

Between the high rock walls it was almost dark; they decided to stay where they were for the night.

'Pity we can't make a fire,' Hennie said. 'Cheer the place up a bit.'

'How did the blacks manage?' Cal wondered.

'I heard they rubbed sticks together.'

'Tried it?'

'Once.'

'Did it work?'

'No.'

That would be right, Cal thought. We've grown so far from our roots that we can no longer survive without our matches, our take-away stores, our television sets. Yet our ancestors, too, must once have kindled fire in the wilderness. We've learned other things, of course, that on balance are much more knowledgeable — which is not to say wiser — but it's a pity we've forgotten so much as well. Especially now. Hennie's right; a fire would have been good.

They made themselves as comfortable as they could, which was not very comfortable at all. After the exertions of the day, Cal had thought he would go to sleep at once, but found himself wide awake, conscious of a dozen pieces of rock digging holes in him.

After the day's blazing heat, it was cold. He huddled as close into himself as he could; to take his mind off discomfort, he tried to focus on other things.

All his sketches, his notes, had gone up in the fire. It was a nuisance, but no more than that. His brain was filled with ideas as hard and bright as Ayers Rock itself. When they got out, it would not be a problem to get them down on paper again. *When we get out*, he told himself. *I like that. When* sounds so much better than *if*.

Let me think about what I shall do when we get out. Two things mattered, each as important as the other. The work and Kathryn.

The work was easy. His head was clear now, all the cogs and wheels working. He would get down to it straight away, would capture on paper every one of the things he had seen in the last three weeks. Including the crash, he thought. The burning helicopter and the cliff down which it had fallen, the creek with the rocks and tufts of grass here and there, the patch of white sand beside it. How I wish I had some white sand here now, he thought, but knew he had no reason to complain; their circumstances were almost miraculously better than he would have dared imagine.

Apart from Hennie's feet, he thought. There is a huge problem. It won't have gone away by morning, either. It is very bad and will get much worse. It might even end up killing the pair of us, if I allow it.

Once again, firmly, he put away any thought of what he might have to do if Hennie were unable to walk in the morning. Instead, he thought of the pool of secret water that Hennie had found. It might be the means of saving their lives. Not simply the water itself, but the idea of water, the belief that there was water to be found even in these arid hills. That was very important. They had to have faith. Believe in themselves and they might somehow manage to survive, although it would certainly not be easy. Lose confidence and they would die.

He remembered reading of a sailing ship that had sunk in the Atlantic. The weather had been calm, the sea warm, there were no sharks. There were enough life rafts and jackets, yet almost the entire crew had died because they'd had no faith in their ability to stay alive.

Let us learn from that, he thought. Let us take this one step at a time. Never mind the nature of the terrain. Let us believe in ourselves and the Ranges' hidden treasures of water. As long as we continue to hope, we shall make it.

We'll be damn hungry by the end of it, he thought. The plunge in the pool had refreshed him, but had also reminded him how hungry he was. Not surprising. Now it was forty hours without eating. Almost two full days. Lack of food would be bound to weaken them, eventually. His stomach cramped painfully at the thought. He turned, trying to find a more comfortable position, knowing that hunger and its implications were two more things he could not permit himself to think about.

★   ★   ★

Once again the long night's vigil. Kathryn lay in her room, watching, listening, feeling. For minutes at a time thought she could no longer hear him, that he and everything he represented had gone from her into the dark.

It was hot. She lay naked on her back upon the bed, a sheet covering her to the waist. She needed sleep but could not, would not. Instead, she watched her thoughts as they trod their weary path through her brain.

My mother thinks I'm a fool to turn my back on what she calls security, yet some forms of security do not depend on money.

With Cal I shall be with the one man who can offer me fulfilment.

I know he may be so involved in his work that I shall exist only on the edge of his awareness, but I am willing to risk that. I know that, after being his companion during all the good and bad years of our youth, I may have to face old age with memory my only companion. I am willing to risk even that. But I never bargained on this, the not-knowing. Dear God, what a terrible thing it is.

She listened again, desperately, heard only the beating of her own heart.

He is gone.

Would not permit herself to believe it. Because in that case the void was bottomless. She thought, I must go to him, to the places he showed me. His spirit will be strongest there.

Suddenly it was of vital importance that she should get there as quickly as possible. Now. She looked at her watch. Four o'clock. Was at once out of bed, chucking on clothes, grabbing a bag which she stuffed with things she would need. She scribbled a note, left it propped on the kitchen table, went out to her car. She would phone the Uni when she got there, make some excuse. For the moment she, who had always been responsible, cared nothing for that.

It took two hours, a journey that was normally half an hour longer. She had intended going straight to her uncle's house, but instead drove up the rutted track to Cal's studio.

He had shown her where he hid the key; she opened up and went inside. Its emptiness seemed more significant than the simple fact of no-one being there. She walked slowly around the room, breathing the smell of turpentine and paint. One by one, she looked at the paintings he had done, had partly done. Most of all she looked at the paintings he had not done but would, she knew, because now the contact had been restored. Again she felt his presence; again she held his soul in her hand, her watchful eyes willing his safe return.

Later, she went to the house. Inside, curled on the settee, was at once deeply asleep. At peace.

★   ★   ★

So that's the first thing, Cal thought. When I get out of here, I'll work. What else do we have to think about? As though he had any doubt. Let us think about Kathryn. There certainly was a lot to think about with Kathryn.

If Dave hadn't talked me into going to *Rheingold* . . . , he thought. A month ago I did not even know she existed. Neither Kathryn nor her parents nor Charles Chivers. I beg your pardon. Doctor Charles Chivers. The boyfriend I have not seen. The boyfriend she has not mentioned. There are times when I wonder if he exists at all. But he does. Oh yes, I can feel him there, in the background.

I don't think I have to worry about Doctor Charles Chivers. Silently he addressed the cliffs, rising like slabs of darkness on the far side of the pool. I believe I have sorted him out. Her mother hates my guts, though. Doesn't she just? He could have hated her in return, not because he cared what she thought, but for how her enmity might damage him with her daughter.

Be fair to her, he told himself. Look at it from her point of view. Would you want your daughter to get involved with a bloke like you?

The idea of having a grown-up daughter to worry about was so alien that he could not pursue the notion. Nor was it important to him. What mattered was how Kathryn felt, and how he felt, and to hell with everything else.

What shall we do when we get out of here? I'll tell you what we'll do, he told the night. We shall stock up *Jester* and sail along the coast, putting in anywhere we fancy. We shall sail east along the South Australian coast, then along the Victorian coast until we turn the corner and head north towards Queensland. There are lots of inlets along that coast, lots of little harbours. We'll put in wherever we feel like stopping. There will be creeks to explore, and lakes. Behind the lakes, as we go north, we shall see mountains. Not like the Gammon Ranges; those mountains will be green and covered in forest, with trails winding through them. We shall hire a car and drive along the trails through the forest. We'll see kangaroos and wallabies and maybe, if we're lucky, the odd echidna. Odd is right, he thought. Very odd; like little scurrying bushes. We shall drive into the highlands. When we get there we shall find a hotel; I've heard there are plenty up there to choose from. We shall eat good food and drink good wine and go to bed between good white sheets and make love. And in the morning the air will be fresh and cold and clean and there will be sunshine gleaming on cobwebs strung between the trees and the grass will be dew-wet and oh God how I wish we were there now.

Kathryn, he said silently, and turned and held her close on the rock shelf in the darkness. Kathryn, Kathryn, Kathryn.

13

Cal awoke to the crystalline stillness of the dawn.

He turned his head. Hennie was already awake, if he had ever slept, lying on his back with his eyes staring at nothing. His eyes were so wide, he lay so still that, for a terrible moment, Cal thought he was dead. He must have made some movement because Hennie turned his head to look at him, and Cal breathed easier.

'You okay?' Cal asked.

'Sure.'

But there was a deadness in his voice that Cal didn't like, as though something had broken in the night and the mechanism was functioning no more. Hennie's port-wine redness had diminished, but the bruise on his head looked more livid than ever in the morning light.

'How's the head?'

'Still there.'

Hennie gathered himself and stood, awkwardly, painfully. From the way he held his head, like a glass filled to the brim that he was afraid might spill, Cal knew it was

246

troubling him but said nothing. There was nothing either of them could do about it, however badly it hurt. Cal stood up, too. He stretched, reaching as high as he could, before bending stiff-legged to place his hands flat on the ground. His muscles were sore, but that was to be expected. Once on the move they would soon loosen up.

He picked up both water bottles and went to the pool. He splashed water on his face and over his shirt, liberally, feeling his skin cringe at its coldness. He drank and drank until his stomach would take no more, filled both bottles, screwed the caps securely and went back to where Hennie was standing, shoulders slumped, looking disconsolately at the distant ridge to which they would have to climb.

He proffered the water bottle.

'Coffee, my lord.'

Hennie did not turn his head or speak, and again Cal felt a tug of apprehension.

'Or champagne, if his lordship would prefer.'

Somehow it seemed important to continue with the foolish game, to go on pretending the reality of what was not.

'Non-vintage, I'm afraid, but — '

'Why don't you just shut up?'

At once there was silence, as brittle as ice, between them.

After a moment, deliberately, Cal said, 'I have ordered breakfast for two at Arkaroola. Fried eggs, farmhouse sausage, all the trimmings. Just a short stroll over the ranges. The views, they tell me, are remarkable.'

The pilot took a deep breath. Taut as wire, Cal watched him. Then Hennie sighed gustily and his shoulders slumped again. Still he did not smile.

'Farmhouse sausage,' he said. 'In South Africa we used to call it *boerewors*.'

There was a weariness in his voice that Cal didn't like.

'I'm sure they'll be able to organise a special order.'

Still he persisted in the stupid game, but Hennie did not smile or respond in any way. Even the anger seemed to have died in him. That would be the worst thing of all, if true. Without anger and will, how would they ever drag themselves over the mountains to safety?

I shall do it, Cal told himself. With him or without him, I shall do it. I've got too much to lose if I don't.

'Let's get on, then,' he said.

Without waiting for a response, he turned on his heel, water bottle bumping against his hip, and began to pick his way over the dark rocks towards the defile leading to the high ground. After fifty metres he glanced back, wondering what he would see, but Hennie was on the move, too. Limping, head down, moving terribly slowly, but following.

I never remembered to ask about his feet, he thought. I never even noticed him put his shoes on. I don't know how he manages at all, those shoes in this country, but once again there was nothing either of them could do about it. So many things they could do nothing about. Perhaps it's as well I said nothing. All we can do is put our heads down, not think, and just walk and walk. What other options are there?

By midday Cal himself was running out of steam. They had been climbing for four-and-a-half hours, and it felt like a year. First, up to the crest upon which Hennie had taken yesterday's bearing. A fresh bearing upon a peak on the far side of the valley, then down another slope of neck-cringing steepness. Beneath them space dragged at their bodies, making their eyes stand out in their sockets.

Now they were at the bottom, the fearsome ridge behind them. They rested for a while in the shade of an immense boulder but, even here, the heat was too great to tolerate for long. They had no strength to talk but panted, and tried to wipe away sweat, and waited for the night.

If the ground had been less broken, Cal

thought, they might have tried to walk at night, to avoid the worst of the heat, but no-one could have done a night march over terrain like this.

Eventually, without speaking, they struggled to their feet and set out wearily together across the valley. It was several kilometres wide at this point, a wilderness of broken rock and dried-up watercourses, of stunted trees as warped as the landscape. They forced their way over a succession of tormented ridges, disputing every step with ground littered with ankle-breaking rocks that waited in ambush like an enemy. The sun blazed down. Clouds were gathering, the humidity climbing like a cageful of monkeys.

By mid-afternoon they reached the other side. Here the ground began to rise again. The slopes of the foothills resembled a petrified sea; the naked rock swirled in crests and hollows, rising and falling like combers. It absorbed the heat and threw it back at them like a gigantic and malignant oven. The sun disappeared behind the swiftly-gathering clouds, yet still the heat continued. It was awful, unrelenting, sapping strength and will, leaving them barely enough energy to breathe.

The two men stood side by side, staring at the rising ground before them. For the hundredth time they squared their shoulders, dragged the baking air into their lungs and pushed on up the slope.

The ground was fearsome, the worst they had encountered. First came a fringe of scrubby trees, their contorted branches as white as bone. Beyond the trees an overhanging ridge was dark with shadow. To the right of the ridge the way lay open between a series of cliffs, bare and terrible, that rose in a succession of steps towards the summit of the range. On the upper slopes the ground was devoid of vegetation, its surface harsh-knuckled and broken, the nearly-vertical cliffs casting gashes of shadow across ground that was coloured chocolate and ginger and fawn, overlaid with a hint of green where patches of lichen caught the light.

There was a defile that ran between the cliffs. From this distance it looked simple enough, even easy, but Cal knew that in these ranges nothing was easy, that it was likely to be choked with more and yet more boulders, that beyond the summit ridge, assuming they were able to reach it, would be another valley, another rise, that beyond that —

Stop it, he told himself. Don't think. Thinking, in these circumstances, was the enemy. Thinking, potentially, was death.

They had passed the trees and were halfway to the nearer of the two ridges when the rain began. By the time they reached the shelter of a massive overhang, it was falling in torrents, blotting out all sound and sensation.

They huddled as close to the cliff as they could and watched the cataracts of rain, the swiftly-spreading floodwater that nibbled at the edges of the rocks, spilling like a tide across the naked surfaces over which they had just struggled. Below them the branches of the distant trees tossed like a grey sea.

'We are *fokked*,' Hennie said.

He had been from the time they had set out that morning; barely able to walk, complaining as the day wore on of a splitting headache, double vision. Any number of times Cal had thought he would be unable to keep going at all, but somehow he had. Lurching on ruined feet, blaspheming in a voice almost too weak to hear, he had still managed to cover the ground, but Cal could see that now he had reached his limit. We both have, he thought, except that I do not accept the existence of limits. One step at a time, that's the way we do it. One step, and then another step. On and on. As long as we think only of the next step and not the millions that lie beyond, we shall be right.

By enormous effort of will, he summoned Kathryn to his side. This is somewhere I shall not bring you, he told her. Not because I don't think you'll be able to handle it, but because I won't. Get out of here and I shan't be coming back. One trip like this is enough to last a lifetime. It's likely to be a very short lifetime, anyway, the way things look at the moment.

Hennie was hunched on the wet ground, hands clasping the shoes that were now as close to falling apart as the men themselves.

'Take them off,' Cal suggested. 'Give your feet a break.'

Hennie shook his head. 'I'll never get them on again.'

He was probably right.

The rain fell, and fell. Finally, in late afternoon, it stopped.

Cal forced himself to stand. For a moment, as he struggled upright, the mountains swerved vertiginously about him. He shut his eyes and shook his head; when he looked again, the landscape was still once more.

'Let's get on,' he said. 'Before the sun comes out.'

'No ways.' Hennie's throat sounded clogged with phlegm. 'The ground will be like glue.' His favourite battle cry.

'It's rock. There's nothing to turn to glue.'

'Then it'll be slippery as *fokking* glass.'

No doubt it would be; all the same, Cal was determined to move on. Movement was good for its own sake; a kilometre, half, even a hundred metres. All were good, a demonstration of the will that would not be defeated.

'Just to the top of the ridge,' he said, as though it really were no more than the casual stroll they had spoken of that morning. 'Have a look at what we can expect tomorrow.'

Once again he set off without waiting for a response but, this time, when he looked back, Hennie had not moved.

Cal stopped. 'Come on!'

Nothing.

'We've got to keep going.'

Or we'll die.

That was what he was afraid of; that if they stopped, even for an hour, if they released their hold on the situation even to that extent, the will would die. Let that happen and they would follow. Movement, for the moment, was life.

Still Hennie did not move. Cal was suddenly furious, glad to indulge it. In these circumstances anger, like movement, was also life.

'Get your arse into gear,' he shouted. 'Or I'll come back and bloody drag you.'

Would have done it, too.

Saw with relief that Hennie was indeed trying to stand, was struggling, struggling.

First on both knees, then on one; inch by agonised inch, his back straightened until he was upright.

'What a hero,' Cal shouted down to him. 'That's the way. Now: one step. Come on, you can do it.'

Hearing his foolish encouragement echo back at him out of the emptiness and not caring. Hennie had to come on by himself, had somehow to drag from himself the courage to continue. Only he could do it, which was why Cal would not go back for him. Ultimately, they would make it, or not, under their own steam and no-one else's.

He watched. One step was all it would take. Once Hennie had taken that, the rest would follow; the lock that presently imprisoned him would be broken.

'One step!' So he hectored him, watching the swaying, struggling figure. 'Come on, Hennie! Come on!'

Hennie lifted one foot, uncertainly. Cal watched, holding his breath. The leg stretched out, straightened. The foot rested on the ground half a metre in front of the other foot.

'You've done it!' Cal as pleased as though Hennie had run a hundred metres. 'Now it's easy.'

Hennie looked up the slope, but at an angle, seeing not Cal but darkness. He said something that Cal was too far away to hear, took three or four rapid steps, almost running, and collided with the face of the cliff. As though he had been shot, he fell heavily forward on his face.

★ ★ ★

'The *Ring*,' Kathryn said.

Beyond the window of her uncle's study, the distant sea glittered in the afternoon sun.

'What about it?' Dave's face guarded, as his voice was guarded.

'You took Cal to *Rheingold* . . . '

She groped for something her instincts knew was there.

Dave sat, the shadows of the room across his face. He said nothing, gave her no help.

'You knew I'd be there. I'd told you. Yet when we met . . . '

The room was so still. One of Cal's pictures hung above the desk, the harvest scene of sky and dust and violence. Like its owner, the picture watched her endeavours, revealing nothing. She knew the hand that had drawn it yet, studying it, felt she knew nothing of the artist himself. The idea terrified her. Her composure might have cracked, had she let it.

'You acted like it was something extraordinary. Unexpected. Why?' she demanded of the still and shrouded face. 'Why?'

Dave rose, walked two paces to the window, stood staring out, silently.

'I do not understand what you're asking me,' he said at length, his back to the room.

'I think . . . I think maybe you set up the whole thing. Deliberately.'

Her words were harsh, emphatic. Yet still a question.

'I felt Cal needed something to lift him out of himself. Something to shake off all the terrors he had lived with so long.'

Outrage painted her cheeks. 'And I was handy. Is that it? You used me,' she accused.

Now he turned. 'Not you. *Rheingold.*'

'But you knew I would be there. You hoped — '

'A little,' he conceded. 'I thought you would be good for him. And he for you, perhaps.'

'You never thought of me!' Scornfully.

'Not much; you've always been capable of looking after yourself. Whereas Cal — '

'I've never known anyone more self-sufficient than Cal.'

'Now, perhaps. Because you've made him so. You restored him to what he was before.'

'Before Paris.'

'Before Paris,' he agreed. 'But when you met him . . . No.'

'You used me,' she accused again, bitterly.

He would admit nothing. 'How did I use you? I introduced you, that was all. The rest was up to the pair of you. But I would have done it, if I could.'

'Why?'

'Because I have a responsibility. I told him so myself, once.' He smiled, reminiscently. 'He was not pleased, I remember.'

'You are responsible to *Cal*?'

'To art. I believe Cal Jessop has the potential to be a very great artist. One of the greatest, perhaps. Anything I can do to help him achieve it, I shall.' His eyebrows challenged her, bushily. 'You would sacrifice yourself.'

'I have that right. Whereas you . . . '

Yet she spoke uncertainly, unsure even of her own outrage.

'It was the right thing for you, too. I was thinking more of him. Of course. I admit it. But I was hoping you'd get together and you did. Good. I'm glad. It's what he needs.' Again his eyes assessed her. 'You, too, I think.'

She said nothing, unwilling to admit, unable to deny.

'That doctor fellow,' Dave said, 'is no good for you.'

'You've never even met him.'

'I've been meeting men like him all my life. You don't love him. You can't. You love Cal.'

It was an intrusion she would not tolerate.

'Cal is missing. He may be dead. Don't you think that talking about him like this may be wrong?'

May tempt providence was what she meant.

Her uncle watched her, eyes hawk-bright in the soft face. Nodded, satisfied. 'You do love him.'

'And what use is that,' Kathryn cried, 'if he is dead?'

And ran. With tears.

Later Dave found her in the garden.

'I did not mean to hurt you.'

She blinked at him, managing a smile.

'It wasn't you . . . '

He watched the petunias. 'I know myself very well,' he said. 'I cannot tolerate too much civilisation.' He saw she did not understand. 'Art is its highest manifestation and that has been my life. But when it comes to consideration for others . . . ' He shook his head. 'Civilisation shows me up, you see. It spells out all my inadequacies.'

As an apology it wasn't much, yet Kathryn could not resent for long the man who had brought her Cal.

'I want you to do something for me,' she said. 'I want you to take me through Cal's studio, explain to me what I'm seeing.'

'Why?' He watched her, promising nothing.

'Because Cal is in his paintings. I need to know them if I'm going to know him.'

Dave was dubious. 'He's planning to dump most of them, anyway.'

'He won't.' Kathryn was positive. 'You'll see; they'll be very well thought of, one of these days.'

'You believe that, you don't need me to explain them to you.'

She smiled at him, caught his hand. 'Humour me.'

★   ★   ★

'Anonymity in the use of pigment,' Dave said. He gestured at a painting that leant against the studio wall. 'It was the hardest thing of all for Cal to learn. His personality is so wrapped up in his work. He had to learn to be objective; it didn't come naturally to him. He was heading in that direction when the Paris business cropped up.'

'It must have been a terrible time for him,' she said sadly.

'It nearly killed him. Literally. I was afraid that one day I'd come here and find he'd done away with himself. Artists feel things more intensely than the rest of us. Even men like Picasso, who behave like monsters in order to protect themselves.'

He walked around the room, touching paintings here and there with his fingertips.

'They're all saying, Look at me, look at me. They're clever, of course. Too clever. He was inclined to be that, at the beginning. He was getting out of it; then, after Paris, he went straight back. All these' — his flung arm discarded them — 'are too indulgent. Too full of self-pity.'

She could not bear it. She had asked Dave to come here, yet now found that this dissection of Cal's work was like picking over the bones of a man whom they did not even know was dead.

'Self-pity? Or pity of humanity generally? The human condition?'

He turned to stare at her, looked back at the stacked paintings.

'Perhaps some,' he admitted, grudgingly. 'He was beginning to get over it again, even before he met you. You see,' he gestured. 'Here. And here. He is very disciplined, you know. You hear about his wildness, all the garbage the media loves. It's crap. He works harder than any artist I know.'

He moved on, picked up another canvas.

'The tonal construction is so important. The freshness of colour. He told me he saw a lot of Matisse when he was in Europe. You can see it, yet what he is doing here is absolutely original. He captures the emotion, you see. The painting *is* the emotion. He uses unconventional means to provide texture. He is a very tactile artist. It's why he went to Paris, to study engraving. He experiments with materials, too. Here.' He showed her another painting. 'Sand, embedded in emulsion. He's always pushing into new areas.'

'Into utter darkness,' said Kathryn, remembering.

'What?'

'He told me about it. The darkness where no-one has been before.'

'Exactly,' Dave said. 'He's never believed in being safe.'

All this was technique. It meant nothing to Kathryn, who wanted to discover not the artist, but the man. If it were possible to differentiate between the two.

Perhaps, after all, there were other ways.

She went to the island, to the long, flat stone that Cal had called his sacrificial altar. Sat. The sea's silence howled.

Oppressively, amid the grey shapes of rocks, the foaming heads of seas, the desert stretched away. The dunes of red sand beat like drums under a remorseless sky in which were reflected all hope, all dreams, all desire. The mountains reared implacably.

He is not dead.

The sluggish sea broke.

You love Cal . . .

Her uncle's voice amid a cacophony of gulls.

He will live. He will come back. To me.

Sea and gulls wove their rhythmic dance above the blood-red land. And faded, faded, leaving the distorted image of the man striding beneath a sun the size of the sky. A fragile skein of footprints stretched behind him, across shattered rock, the tufts of wire-like grass, the cliffs and defiles that rose steeply into the pitiless air. The pigments — red and blue and brown — were on fire behind him. An infinity of stone, the devouring maw of wilderness.

The lichen on the spray-dark rocks would have mocked, had she permitted.

★ ★ ★

Once again Cal was filled with the awful fear that Hennie was dead. He ran to him, turned him over. The pilot's eyes were open, his face purple. He was breathing, a steady, snoring sound that enhanced horror.

'Hennie . . . Hennie . . . ?'

Nothing.

Cal sat on his heels and studied him. This was more than fatigue. He remembered the terrible crack on the head Hennie had taken when they crashed and wondered whether there might have been some form of brain damage that was only now coming to light.

He did not know what to do, whether in fact there was anything that could be done, and was filled with the most terrible sense of powerlessness. He tried to move the pilot, to make him more comfortable, knew even as he did so that it would mean nothing at all to a man so deeply unconscious.

He stared up at the ridge. He had been so determined to get there before dark, to find out what lay on the other side. He looked again at the pilot. No change. He thought he might as well make the climb to the ridge, see what lay beyond and then come back. It was most unlikely that Hennie would come round while he was away; if he did, he would just have to wait.

He opened the breast pocket of Hennie's shirt and took out the precious compass. He put it in his own pocket, buttoned the flap carefully. He turned and started to climb.

Again he found that he made better time by himself. It was as though, while they were together, Hennie's clumsy presence held him back. The ground was still very rough, but he was able to find his way with far less difficulty than when he had first climbed alone. He skirted the first cliff, leaving it behind him as he forced his way up the boulder-littered defile that led steeply to the high ground.

At last he came out on the ridge and looked at what faced them: another steep descent, another valley, and beyond it yet another line of hills.

They were as lost, as far from civilisation, as ever.

'Good night's rest, I'll eat you up,' he told the valley, the blue ranges. Of Hennie he would not think; do so and he would be forced to accept that Hennie, even if he came round, would never be able to make it to this point, never mind continue beyond it on what was beginning to seem like an endless, futile march into oblivion. He put the thought away from him; did not wish to be confronted by it, not now that he was tired, not tonight.

There seemed to be more and more things he could not permit himself to think about. The forbidden subjects hemmed him in, crowding closer and closer until it seemed sometimes that it was impossible to think about anything at all.

He took out the compass and drew a

bearing on the furthest ridge. The setting sun was warm on his neck. He squinted across the top of the compass, bringing the needle into line with the highest point of the ridge and reading the degrees off the scale. Fifty degrees. Still on course, he thought. Still heading more or less north-east.

Then he spun on his heel as a sudden thought struck him.

Behind him, on the far side of the valley, the sun was going down in a haze of golden light. He looked at the sun, then back at the ridge upon which he had just taken the bearing.

The sun had to be setting in the west. Which meant that the ridge towards which he had intended to march in the morning should have been at a pronounced angle to the north. He lifted the compass, again read the bearing. Fifty degrees. As before. Yet it was not. Standing with his back to the setting sun the ridge was immediately facing him. Due east.

The compass was out. They were more lost even than he had feared.

★   ★   ★

Now the third day was almost over.

On every newscast, the television had gone

266

on and on about the planes searching the Outback, how still no trace had been found of the missing men. The sombre-voiced reporter spoke of temperatures in the high forties and more, of the impossibility of sustaining human life in such conditions beyond a few days.

They had trotted out a doctor, complete with white coat and stethoscope, looking like an advertisement for pain killers. Four days, the doctor had said, gloomy as a pall bearer. Five for tops.

They had interviewed her uncle. Dave Holt had described Cal as the brightest in the constellation of Australia's artists. He had called him a dear, close friend whose loss, if he were indeed lost, would be a tragedy to art.

It had been terrible, terrible.

'I don't care about bloody art!' Kathryn had screamed at the smug images. She could have massacred them all. *What about me?*

But that she did not say.

The media did not interview her. They did not know she existed. She watched the news. Had they found his body, there would have been a report, but there was not. Instead she saw Monica Lewinsky prancing, thought, thank God.

Cal had told her about his parents, his

Dad's tricks. Had pointed out their house, one of a row two streets back from the harbour. It had looked too small for Cal himself, never mind for the three of them. They must have lived in each other's pockets, she thought.

Earlier that afternoon, trembling, in trepidation, she had gone to see them.

Em stood in the doorway; doughy face, suspicious eyes. 'Yes?'

'I'm a friend of Cal's.'

Em's expression did not change, but she stood back from the door. 'His dad's here. You'd best come in.'

It was clear they didn't know what to make of her, wavered between resentment and indifference. Cal, their manner said, had known lots of girls. What made her special?

It was a question to which she did not know the answer.

She had imagined they might be able to comfort each other, each with a son or lover missing in the far-north, but the parents made it clear that Cal no longer meant much to them. If he ever had.

Mick, over sixty and thinking about giving fishing away, hanging on only because he was scared of shutting the door on life, now carried a grudge that he was only too willing to parade for her benefit. 'Raise a boy to take over when the time comes,' he said, 'then he buggers off and leaves you to get on with it. Not good enough. Not by a long bloody chalk.'

He licked thirsty lips and eyed the clock surreptitiously, hoping to sneak away to the pub, to bellyache to mates who had given up listening long ago.

Cal had moved on; that was what Mick resented. Em was resigned, had watched her son, like life itself, leave her stranded. She had expected nothing else, did not think of life as something over which she had control.

'Gunna get a paper,' said Mick, and left them to get on with it.

'Got mates down the pub,' Em explained. 'He dunno what to do with himself now he's given up the fishing. Always sayin' he'll go back to it. That's why he's hung on to the licence. Could get a good price for it nowadays, but. Goes his own way,' she declared, fatalistic yet clearly proud of her difficult man. 'Always has, always will.'

She made them a cup of tea, moving painfully on feet that, like life, had let her down. Now she was willing to chat, but defensively, guarding herself against the intrusive woman she did not know.

'Cal had a good life here. Dunno why he turned his back on us. His Dad didn't like it, not one bit. When he found he was going into this painting lark, he kicked him out, told him not to come back.' She cackled at the antics of the violent man who had dominated her life. 'Can't blame him. What's a son for if he's not going to take over the business from his old man? Mind you, I don't complain. Slips me a quid now and then — not that I ask, but it helps. Don't let on to his Dad, mind. Lose his rag if he found out.'

Kathryn didn't understand. 'Why should he mind Cal helping you?'

'Not his place, is it? His dad ain't a cot case, not by a long shot. Up to the husband to look after his wife, i'n' it?'

'I hope and pray Cal is safe,' Kathryn said.

'He'll be right. Take a deal of killing, my Cal.' Topped up the teacups. 'Nothing we can do about it, either way.'

'I would sacrifice myself willingly,' Kathryn told her, 'if it meant he was safe.'

'Yeah?' Em's eyes acknowledged the gulf that separated them. 'You think like that when you're young. Get a bit older, you'll find there ain't nothing you can do about things. They just happen.'

Kathryn left, more tired than when she'd arrived.

Now she watched a reporter once again talking about the missing men in the far-north. Suddenly, a change as he began to interview the pilot's wife.

Kathryn remembered walking with Cal along the path past the little island, the house with its face turned to the sea. She heard Cal's voice. *Stella. The wife. She makes out all right.*

So she did, apparently. Kathryn watched her composure as she answered the interviewer's questions: Yes, you could say they lived apart. He worked out of the gas plant, whereas she preferred to stay here, by the sea. Someone had to look after the house, after all.

The reporter, who worked for a channel that prided itself on its liberal views, was nevertheless uncomfortable with the idea of a wife who chose not to follow her husband.

'Doesn't it get lonely, down here by yourself?'

There were daggers in Stella's laugh. Her dark eyes gashed him. 'You making me an offer?'

Kathryn, watching, believed the wife was going through the motions, was not as tough as she made out. But strong, certainly. Perhaps I could gain strength from her, she thought. God knows I need it.

★   ★   ★

271

Stella Loots was the daughter of a shearer who was home so seldom that her conception might have been an act of God or at least of Neptune. She never saw the sea until she was ten. Her mother, sick of keeping house for a man who was never there, took off one spring day with Stella and a battered suitcase, leaving the briefest of notes — *I'm off. See ya.* — and a pile of ironed shirts. Found a willing truckie, swopped a free ride to the coast for half an hour in the back of the cab, walked with her daughter along a beach quaking with the drum roll of the surf.

Stella, enchanted by this new world of spray and space, walked at one with the sea of whose existence she had barely been aware.

The sea wooed and overthrew her, the rhythms of the surf entered her being.

How they lived she did not know. When she grew older and learned about things, about the dole, a bit of grape-picking, the occasional bloke, she didn't care. Knew only that she had been wedded to the sea from the womb, that even there, swirling, had answered its insistence. She entered into its lightness, married a man, beer-bellied, much older than herself, who had charmed her by his total commitment to air and flight, the shared mystery of freedom from the mundane land.

Her mother took off with her latest bloke, Hennie proved so wedded to flight that he left her for months at a time in the house on the island beset by water. I am repeating my mother's experience, she thought. She took Cal for a lover because his need matched her own; the spirit of the sea moved in him as in her. When they made love it was as though the sea itself entered her; she experienced the ecstasy of salt in the thrusting body of the man.

She lost him, turned again to the sea, her true lover, regained Cal, briefly. Yet knew that in truth he was gone from her, however much he might deny it. The sea entered and possessed her, shaking her once more in its powerful embrace.

A knock on the door brought Stella hurrying.

A young woman she did not know. She thought, Not another one.

People were always doing it. They saw the house overlooking the sea and came, cool as you please, to inspect. As though house and occupants were exhibits. One couple had even walked through the unguarded door to check out the view, they said, from the living room.

Stella in no mood for nonsense like that.

'Can I help you?'

Her razor smile offered nothing of the sort.

'I'm sorry to trouble you. Especially now . . .'

Stella endured the limping apologies, wondered what was going on.

'I wanted to meet you.'

On guard, eyes narrowed. 'Why?'

'Your husband is also missing . . .' Sensing Stella's exasperation, she said simply, 'I am a friend of Cal's.'

Stella thought, so that is what this is about. With gathering anger, she remembered the evening, four weeks before, when first she had suspected something.

Something's happened . . .

He had denied it. Now this.

The bastard.

She looked at her visitor with new eyes. *My God, she's beautiful. She's like I was ten years ago. The skin, the hair, the eyes. The innocence. Unbearable.*

She smiled unpleasantly. 'Cal's done it this time, hasn't he?'

'Maybe they'll be right.'

She noted *they*. As though anyone gave a damn about Hennie. 'You know better than that.' She was prepared to hate this woman whose image painted, more graphically than Cal could have done, the sour ravages of time. 'Why have you come here, anyway?'

'Because I heard you were his friend. Because your own husband is also involved.'

Friend, Stella thought. That's one word for it. And studied her from behind her smile. She knows nothing. *Nothing*. But perhaps is beginning to suspect.

As for Cal . . . Trust him to pick a ripe one.

'Come in,' she said. 'Tell me about you and Cal.'

Got her to sit down. Tried to ease confidences from her, but discovered soon enough that this one would say only what she wished.

'Have you known him long?'

Had Kathryn learned to guard her eyes as she had her tongue, Stella would have discovered nothing.

'Not long, no.'

'But you care for him?'

'He is a friend,' Kathryn allowed. She opened her guard a chink. 'I am worried,' she said.

'Aren't we all?' But still did not understand why the girl was here.

'They wouldn't just forget them, would they? They've been sending out search parties. If they'd found out anything, they'd be sure to let you know. Your husband's involved, after all. I have no status, you see.' A wan smile. 'They probably don't even know I exist.'

So it was news she was after. Liking would be impossible, looking as she did, but at least it made it easier to tolerate her.

'They haven't told me much. They've been sending out aircraft, but so far they haven't found anything. Hennie's chopper's got a homing beacon, but it doesn't seem to be working. There's no sign of them on the route they were supposed to be flying. And of course there've been lots of storms, which won't have helped. I'm sure they're doing all they can.'

'It's this business of not knowing,' said Kathryn. 'Although I have no doubts.'

The two men were almost certainly dead, and this child said she had no doubts.

'How do you work that out?'

'I know he's still out there. I can feel him. I talk to him.'

Stella watched. You could never tell. They come on as sane as can be, while all the time . . . 'You talk to him?'

'I can't explain it. I feel in touch, somehow. If anything happened, I'd know.'

'You must care for him a lot.' Which Kathryn neither denied nor confirmed.

Stella was angry, spiteful. That this unknown woman should come here, parading her youth, her concern . . . There had been times when Stella had believed she could have loved Cal, had she allowed herself.

She resolved to punish. If Cal were truly dead, as after three days he surely must be, her own life would be diminished. What was worse, she would never be able to talk about it, to ease her feelings by parading them, as this young woman seemed willing to do. No, she would have to endure in silence. Well, for the moment there was perhaps another option.

She stood. 'Come with me.'

And led the way swiftly through the house to a door opening onto the tumble of rocks that formed the island, separating the house from the sea. Brushing aside Kathryn's protests, she followed a track that scratched the cliff edge before zigzagging up a scrambling slope to the top, a pinnacle of weathered stone that hung suspended between wind and water at the seaward end of the island.

Behind her Kathryn was slipping and clutching above the gaping maw of the rock-fanged drop, but Stella ran as light as air. She ducked under the capstone where there was a space large enough for two to stand sheltered from the elements.

Kathryn joined her, breathless. From beyond the rock came the hollow boom of the surf. Beneath the canopy was a stone tray, damp and mossy, with ferns. Shells arranged before it, like a votive offering.

'A shrine,' Stella said.

Kathryn looked at it, and her, uncertainly. 'For your husband?'

Brassy Stella laughed. 'For Cal.'

Kathryn's heart gave one thud. Stopped, as her breath stopped.

Stella said, cruelly, 'Every day I pray for his return.'

'I see.' Lips white.

Stella seized her by the arm, shaking her. 'For a year he nearly died of grief. I helped him, then.' Released her. Said scornfully, 'Did you think you were the only one who had a claim?'

'But you are — ' Was going to say *married*, but it sounded too foolish. She stopped, helplessly.

Stella understood. 'I am married, yes. If you can call it a marriage, when I hardly see my husband from one year to the next. Cal was desperate,' she insisted harshly, 'close to dying. I helped him when no-one else could. Neither you nor anyone.'

'I did not know him then.'

'Whatever . . . '

Suddenly Stella's anger died. She was weary, weary. Whatever she did or said, however she felt, her time with Cal was over. This child, how clearly she could read it, had stolen the future. If there had ever been a future. Now she felt only resignation, knew she had been expecting this moment for a long time.

The bastard, she thought again. Waits until he's dead before he tells me we're through.

'Come back to the house,' she said heavily. 'Let's have a cup of coffee or something.'

She thought that Kathryn would refuse; indeed, she said as much, but now Stella did not want to be alone. She persisted and eventually Kathryn stayed. They had coffee together, and sat, and said little, but the fact of being together was a comfort.

Eventually, after they had washed up, Kathryn left. Stella watched her as she crossed the bridge and disappeared down the path towards the town.

Later, she knew, she would weep.

★   ★   ★

The pilot was conscious; more, he was aware. Panic stained the haggard corners of his mouth.

'I thought you'd done a runner . . . '

Cal laughed unconvincingly. 'I was having a look at what's on the other side of the ridge.'

'What's it like?' Anxiety flecked Hennie's lips with spit.

'Much easier,' he lied. 'Get across this lot, it'll be a doddle. Like you always said.'

'Great . . . ' But dully; he did not believe, Cal saw, was willing to pretend only to make Cal happier.

'A good night's rest,' Cal persisted, 'we'll be right.'

A rusty creak as Hennie laughed. 'Going to paint it, are you? All this?'

'Of course. That's why we're here.'

'We're here because I *fokked* up.'

'It wasn't you. The storm — '

'I should have allowed for the storm.'

Now it was almost dark. Cal sensed an ebbing in the prostrate body, a settling into the rock on which it lay.

Out of silence Hennie said, 'Know something? I'm not hungry at all.'

'Neither am I.'

In Cal's case it was not true but, in a conspiracy of lies, it was as good a thing to say as any.

'How many days is it now?'

It took a surprising effort to work it out.

'Tomorrow will be the fourth.'

'The one that kills you. That's what they say, isn't it? You can last until then, as long as you've got water, but the fourth day finishes you off.' Again Hennie's fractured laugh whispered in the darkness. 'If I live so long.'

Cal felt he had to act out the ritual of encouragement. 'No need to talk like that. There's no magic about the fourth day or the fifth or the sixth. Remember what we said? We said we'd take it one step at a time. Play it like that, we'll get out okay. You'll see.'

But Hennie said nothing. The night drew close. It was cold. Cal lay on his back staring up at the stars. A speck of light moved steadily across the darkness; one of the many satellites that cluttered the stratosphere. From up there it would look no more than a few metres, he thought. Half a dozen steps to get us out of this place and back to safety. Pity it doesn't work like that in practice.

Once again he thought what he would do when they were out of the Ranges. A drink, he thought. I wouldn't mind that. Half a dozen drinks. Maybe I'll look up that bastard Tolliver and finish the business we started six months ago. Everyone said I was drunk, but I wasn't. I was sober and he was drunk, which was why I beat him. All over a girl I barely knew.

★　★　★

There was a man at the other end of the bar. Big, with heavy shoulders and a gut thrusting the counter. Cal watched him absent-mindedly. Face round and flushed beneath a greasy combing of black hair, head like a cannon ball. He'd seen him somewhere before. Been here quite a while, by the look of him. Cal turned back to his beer. Whoever he was, it was none of his business.

He sensed the stir and looked up to see the man shouldering his way aggressively through the crowd towards him, his face black with anger. He stopped a couple of yards away, head lowered between his shoulders.

Carefully, Cal put his beer down, muscles gathering beneath his plaid shirt, making himself ready without being too obvious about it. Maybe the man had mistaken him for someone else.

The first words put paid to that idea. 'You Cal Jessop?' A voice like a rusty hinge.

Cal said nothing, watching him carefully. He had three inches on Cal and twice his weight. By the look of him, he'd been in a scrap or two in his time, but so had Cal and he was still sober, whereas the stranger, swaying on his feet, was clearly not.

'Cat got your tongue?' the man demanded. 'I spoke to you, mate.'

'I don't know you.'

The answer infuriated the man. 'You're a bloody liar.'

On the instant, Donald the barman was there. 'Take it easy, now. We don't want no fighting in this pub.'

The man took no notice, eyes fixed on Cal's face, a tiny, half-crazed smile at one corner of his mouth.

He's not going to back off, Cal thought. Whoever he is. And felt anger at the sheer stupidity of it. He didn't need this.

'Kylie Tolliver,' the man said. 'Maybe you remember *her*?'

Of course he remembered her. A warm day in May, summer lingering into the end of autumn. A girl from the other side of Kidman's Inlet. They'd gone for a walk on top of the Bushranger. He'd bought her a couple of drinks, run her home in his car. She was young, quite pretty. He'd pulled into a lay-by on the way to her place, kissed her, no more than that, and she'd come on like she'd wanted to rape him. He'd been tempted, of course he had, but she was only a kid, no more than seventeen, and he wasn't in the cradle-snatching business. He'd run her home and her brother, fifteen years older by the look of him, had been waiting, heavy round head thrust into the open window of the car as he ordered her out. She got out

283

fast, like she was scared of him, and scurried indoors without a word. The brother had given Cal a slow, measured glance and followed her, also without a word.

This man.

Cal had not set eyes on him before or since. And now this, a belly full of beer, a stack of who knew what resentments piled up inside him.

'Kylie Tolliver,' the man repeated. 'I suppose you never heard of her, either?'

'I gave her a lift home, couple of months back.'

'What I hear, it wasn't all you give her.'

'I never laid a finger on her.'

'Not what she told me.' The man drained his pot, set it down on the counter with a bang. 'Had your hand up her skirt, she said.'

'She wasn't wearing a skirt, what I remember.'

'Likely not, time you'd finished.'

The other people in the bar had drawn back from them now, not wanting to get involved in the trouble they could all see was coming. The sheer stupidity rekindled Cal's anger.

'There's not a word of truth in any of it,' he said.

Tolliver straightened slowly. 'You calling my sister a liar?'

'We'll have no brawling in this pub.' Donald again, voice agitated, but he was too old, too ineffectual, and Tolliver took no notice. Cal made a last attempt to pacify him.

'I'm not calling your sister anything.'

Tolliver almost caught him. He grabbed the empty glass off the bar, splintered the top against the counter and leapt straight at Cal, broken glass outstretched.

There wasn't more than six feet between them. Cal never knew how he avoided getting the jagged glass full in his face. He wrenched his head sideways, the heavy body cannoned into him and they went backwards across the room, grappling with each other, the hand holding the glass somewhere behind Cal's left shoulder.

He had to settle things before this idiot had the chance to change his grip on the glass and do some real damage. He was big, all right, but by the feel of him not in good condition. Cal feinted to one side and felt Tolliver's weight follow him, straightened and kicked his legs from under him. Tolliver fell on his back with a crash that shook the room. The glass flew from his hand and shattered in a corner. Cal stood over him, fists clenched, but Tolliver was winded and didn't stir.

Donald was shouting from the other side of the bar. 'Stop it, the pair of you!'

'It's stopped.'

Cal picked up a jug of water from the counter and slopped its contents in Tolliver's face. He opened his eyes and groaned.

Cal leant over him, putting his face down into his. 'Get up!'

Tolliver licked heavy lips. He didn't stir.

'Have it your way . . . '

Cal bent, got a grip on the man's great carcass and hauled him to his feet. He spoke contemptuously into the stupid, stunned face. 'Next time you fancy waving broken glass around, choose someone a bit older. Someone around eighty. That's more your mark.'

Tolliver's expression did not change. 'I'll get you, you bastard. I'll get you. Never you fear. I got friends in these parts. I'll get you.'

On and on in an imbecilic monotone until Cal's temper snapped and he clouted him across the face with a blow that nearly took his hand off.

'Shut your mouth!'

And the same, open-handed, on the other cheek. 'Come after me with a broken glass again and I'll kill you.'

Tolliver swayed and would have fallen had Cal not held him up. He yanked open the bar door, half-pushed, half-threw him out into the street and turned back to the silent room in time to see Donald putting down the phone.

One of Tolliver's mates was prepared to swear that Cal had started it. As for the girl ... No-one knew the truth of that. *This bloody artist, thinks he's so damn smart, got a name for trouble where women are concerned. Look at the papers, you don't believe me.*

The cops decided to make something of it and it had ended in court. Some doubt about the evidence saved him. Even so, the magistrate told him he was lucky to have missed a spell in jail.

'We shall not tolerate violence, do you understand me? The fact that you are a well-known personality only makes things worse. You have a responsibility.'

Yes, sir. No, sir. Of course, sir. Cal froze his feelings, his expression, while Tolliver grinned and grinned.

⋆　⋆　⋆

Now Cal watched the stars, remembering. It would be nice to sort him out, certainly. Not that he'd make a very good job of it at the moment. Have to get his strength back first. Knew that in any case he would not waste time and energy in fighting. Those days were over, thank God.

Kathryn, he told the stars. I shall spend my time with Kathryn.

14

The next morning Hennie was alive still, but would not be climbing the iron range at their back, nor any other range.

'How's the feet?'

'I wouldn't know.'

Cal knelt and looked at them. The shoes were wrecked, both soles flapping, the uppers ripped. Above the leather the ankles were puffed and dark. Cal didn't like the look of them at all.

'They're my best shoes,' Hennie said. 'Real leather.'

If they'd been canvas runners, they'd have been a better bet.

'We'd best get them off.'

The previous evening Hennie had refused, indignantly. Now he made little resistance.

'I'll never get them on again.'

He spoke half-heartedly, knowing he was going nowhere.

Cal loosened the laces, tried to ease the shoes off. They would not come. He tugged at them.

Hennie screamed. '*God*, Cal!'

'I'll have to cut them.'

'They're my best shoes . . . '

As though they would be fit for more than the bin, in any case. Yet even now Cal hesitated. To travel on bare feet was clearly impossible; cutting off Hennie's shoes would be like handing him a death sentence. No wonder he wanted to hang on to them.

Once again Cal looked at the ominously swollen ankles, the dark shininess that had travelled an inch or two up the flesh of both Hennie's calves. Made up his mind.

'No help for it, mate. They got to come off.'

He opened his knife. As delicately as possible, he sliced through the ragged leather, pulled the shoes away.

The stench made him sit back. He could barely believe what he was seeing. Hennie's feet were twin explosions of agony. Blood, dark as toffee, had solidified over them like a second, burnished skin. Where the dried blood had cracked, the torn flesh showed yellow, with an overall hue of purple and black. It might have been simply the worst bruising he had ever seen but, with sinking heart, Cal knew it was something far more ominous than that. He turned the left foot with feather-light fingers, while Hennie gasped and writhed with contorted face. From toes like charred meat, veins ran in dark and ominous lines to just above the ankle. He looked at the other foot: the same. The stench brought bile to his throat.

How Hennie had walked on feet like these was beyond comprehension; he would certainly be walking on them no longer. The question was whether they would be able to save them even if they did manage to get out. Which now, with this catastrophic development, seemed less likely than ever.

'I'm *fokked*,' Hennie said again, teeth embedded like nails in the dark rictus of his mouth.

'Not by me you're not.'

So Cal joked, thrusting his defiance at the prostrate man, the rotten feet that threatened both of them, the menacing landscape of crags and ravines they still had to cross. He remembered another occasion when he had made such a challenge and survived:

Amid cascading spray, the sea's violence; Stella's bright face, denying the storm. The yacht rearing and plunging, a whirligig of will. His own voice, raised in challenge.

'I'm taking this yacht in!'

In the extremity of near-death, he understood now that, before this new journey was finished, he might be compelled to know this broken man almost as intimately as he had the woman.

'How much do you weigh?'

'God knows. Too much, anyway. You won't be able to carry me.'

'Who said anything about carrying?'

He had hung onto his piece of aluminium in the hopes that another plane might come. All the previous day they had heard intermittently the distant sound of searching aircraft, but none had come near them and he had given up any thought of rescue. If one came, good; in the meantime, they would struggle on as best they could, alone.

Now the flattened sheet of aluminium might have another use. He picked it up. It was about two and a half feet square with rivet holes around the edge where he had managed to wrench it from the wreck.

'You reckon you'll be able to sit up?'

Hennie frowned. 'What's the game?'

'We're going skiing.'

Or at least tobogganing. Previously it had been Hennie who had known the answers; now it was Cal's turn. He took off his shirt; there was danger in that, in this place of manic sun, but his skin was used to the sun. He ripped the shirt into strips that he plaited into reins. He threaded the reins through two of the holes in the aluminium, made them fast.

'My lord,' he said, reverting to the childish

banter of the previous day to flourish defiance in the face of the dangers that faced them, 'your carriage awaits. I'm afraid the snow conditions are not as we would wish.'

Hennie stared. 'You planning to *tow* me? You got to be mad, my mate. Totally off your rocker.'

'Like you said, if we weren't mad, we wouldn't be here.'

Although God knew how it would be possible to drag him across the miles of broken ground and rocks that lay between them and safety.

'Look at it this way,' Cal said. 'It's pure selfishness. If you can't walk and I can't carry you, how else am I going to get myself out of this mess?'

'By leaving me here and going on by yourself.'

'No.'

'When you get out, you can send someone back for me — '

'No!'

Harshly, this time; for Hennie to wave temptation in his face was too much. If Hennie had to die, at least he would not be alone.

'Then we've both had it.'

'In which case you're going to be stuck with me for the rest of your life.'

Somehow he managed to manoeuvre Hennie's great carcass on to the improvised sledge. Hennie sat hunched forward, hands clasped about his ankles.

'Nice and cosy?' Cal asked.

'It's impossible. You know that?'

'Like they say, miracles we do at once. The impossible takes a little longer.'

He took up the reins and bent them as firmly as he could over his bare shoulders. They weren't long enough but would have to do. He looked at his watch.

'Just after seven. We'll go till half-past. Then we'll stop, give us both a break. In the meantime all you have to do is sit tight and think beautiful thoughts.'

He hunched his head into his shoulders and took up the strain. Step by agonising step, he began to drag them both up the slope that led to the summit.

The only way it might work, he decided, was by detaching himself completely from what was happening. Let his mind dwell on the ludicrous impracticability of what he was doing, and they would be finished. Instead he had to focus on the beautiful thoughts he had prescribed for Hennie, allow his mind somehow to waft above the tormented struggle that took them first a metre, then ten metres, a hundred, while the rocks swam in the sun, the sweat flowed down his back and chest and, somewhere in his semi-consciousness, he could hear Hennie crying beneath his breath like a wounded child.

Every few metres the sledge jammed against a rock and he had to stop to work it loose. Steep rocks over which, it seemed to him now, he had marched with minimal effort during his reconnaissance of the previous evening, were now impassable. Again and again he had to stop, to work a way around obstacles, while the distant ridge seemed to remain as far out of reach as ever, suspended against the harsh blue sky upon which the climbing sun scored its remorseless, fiery trail.

In no time Cal realised that the plaited reins were beginning to rub the skin from his shoulders. He stopped, cut two strips of cloth from the bottom of his trousers and folded them into pads that he put on his shoulders beneath the reins. For a while after that things were better, but very soon the pads became saturated with sweat and would not stay in position. Twice more he replaced them; twice more they slipped. Eventually he shut his mind to the pain and went on. Soon the soreness of the raw skin was submerged beneath a tide of other pains that grew and merged and, long before the half-hour was up, threatened to overwhelm him.

I shall not stop. I shall not.

Nor did he. The hands of his watch moved with desperate slowness, the aluminium sledge scraped and thudded behind him. Inch by inch he worked his way sideways and upwards until, after what seemed an eternity, the watch indicated the half-hour.

Cal stopped, let the reins fall, stood swaying. For several seconds his cramped muscles refused even to let him collapse; then all at once they let go and he was on his knees without knowing how he had got there. He drew deep breaths of blazing air into his lungs, fighting not to recognise what he had known even before they had set out, that Hennie's feet were gangrenous, that the pilot was doomed whatever happened, that if he persisted in this imbecilic attempt to rescue a man who was beyond rescue, he would be writing his own death warrant.

The truth of all this stood over him, as deadly and unavoidable as the heat that, hours before midday, was already almost too much to bear. It was another dimension of the remorseless struggle to survive. Now he had to fight against hatred of the man whose mistake folly bravado had landed them in this mess, who was incapable of walking out and whose stubborn refusal to die now meant Cal's own ruin.

He's doomed, anyway. You could kill him. Or walk away from him. That way at least you'd have a chance.

He should have been shocked at thinking such things, but was not, too tired to worry about abstractions. He knew he was not going to do either of them.

Three choices, he thought. Kill him, abandon him or die with him. Nothing else is going to work. All the rest — this stupid, futile, fight to drag a dying man across an endless, sun-blasted landscape — is nonsense.

He eyed Hennie again. Temptation breathed, insidiously.

No, he told himself. I shall not.

But the idea had taken root and would not go away.

He rubbed his stinging shoulders and saw that his hands were red with fresh blood from the wounds that the reins had inflicted.

One more thing, to be disregarded like the rest.

He wiped his hands on his pants. 'How you going?'

To which Hennie made no reply.

'Nearly there,' Cal persisted cheerily. 'Once we're on top, it'll be plain sailing.' While the ridge, remote-seeming as ever, the memory of what lay ahead of them, mocked.

Hennie muttered something.

Cal came closer. 'What?'

'It hurts. It hurts. It hurts . . . '

On and on, a dirge of pain.

'It hurts . . . '

Hennie's eyes were fixed on madness. There was nothing, nothing that Cal could do. The endless litany was unbearable. He wanted to scream out at the hunched figure of what had been a man.

Stop it! Stop it!

Somehow, biting his lip almost through, he remained kind.

'Let's have a look at those feet . . . '

Even in half an hour, the infection had spread, visibly.

You are torturing him, a voice said. To no purpose. You have your work cut out to save yourself; to save both of you is impossible. If Hennie were in hospital at this minute, it would already be too late.

'Go,' Hennie said.

It took a moment for Cal to realise what he had heard.

'We are going.'

'We are going nowhere. You go on. Leave me one of the water bottles. I'll come on after, at my own pace.'

Cal wished passionately that Hennie would shut up. Even the constant *It hurts, it hurts* would be easier to bear than this business of telling him to do what commonsense had already told him he must do.

'Your own pace,' he said, forcing himself to make a joke of it. 'I bet you'd really go, at that. You'd go like a racehorse. Next thing they'll be calling you Champion of the Gammon Stakes.'

For an instant Hennie smiled. 'This charging about the country is hard on the bones of my arse,' he said apologetically.

His face had relaxed a little, but now drew tight as the pain bit once more. Watching, Cal saw him age twenty years within seconds.

'*God . . . Liefde God!*' After so many years, Hennie had reverted to the language of his birth.

'Stretch out a bit,' Cal suggested desperately. 'Get some rest.'

Hennie remained frozen, a hunched knot of appalling pain, while the devils ripped at him. Cal put his hands on his shoulders, felt the skin on fire beneath the shirt.

'Lie back. I'll help you.'

And Hennie screamed again. There was agony and despair in the sound, the terror of abandonment. He seized Cal's hand in his own.

'Don't leave me!'

No talk of going anywhere, now. Cal tried to free his hand, but Hennie hung on, desperately. Cal turned his back on hope.

'I'm going nowhere,' he said. 'What we have to do is get you into some shade.'

The only shade to be had was under the trees they had passed at the bottom of the slope. The thought of giving up all the ground they had gained that morning was appalling but, if they stayed where they were, with the sun climbing ever higher in the sky, Hennie would fry to death before the gangrene killed him.

With something like death in his own heart, Cal said, 'Let's get on with it, then.'

And once again took up the reins.

It was almost as hard to go back down the slope as it had been to climb it. The rocks were as difficult as ever, the heat greater; with gravity working on it, the sledge was harder to control. Despite everything, Cal persevered, the pain of his wounded shoulders so intense that it was all he could do not to cry out himself.

Much more of this, he thought, I'll be getting gangrene, too. Steadily, perversely, he kept going, dragging Hennie and himself inch by inch over ground that had tormented them so badly on the way up. Now it was the trees that seemed frozen, constantly visible, but drawing no nearer for all his efforts, blurred in a terrible miasma of sweat and pain. All the time he heard behind him Hennie's voice.

'*Dit maak seer . . .* It hurts . . . '

Cal was on his face. He had done nothing to break his fall, but lay with his mouth in the dirt. He was half-stunned, his forehead stinging where the skin had torn. For a minute he lay still, trying to catch hold of what had caused him to fall. At last he struggled to his feet and found that one of the reins had frayed and torn away from the rivet hole to which it had been secured. Hennie had been spilled off the sledge and now lay, fat, ungainly and unmoving, upon the ground beside him.

On top of everything else they had endured, it was too much. Cal watched the tears roll silently down Hennie's fat face; could have wept, himself, but did not. Rage against Hennie, fate, everything and everyone in the world fuelled him now, driving him to his feet, hauling the body of the pilot over his bleeding shoulder, staggering on down the hill towards the dancing blur of sage-green leaves. Twice he fell; twice struggled again to his feet, hauled Hennie once more onto his shoulder, staggered on. The impulse lasted until he reached the patchy shadow of the trees, then evaporated as quickly as it had come. Without stopping even to lower Hennie to the ground, he fell forward and was still.

★   ★   ★

That morning Marge Fanning phoned her delinquent daughter.

'How are you, Kathryn?'

'Good.'

'I am very glad to hear it. We have been so worried.'

The mother was clearly willing to make an issue; Kathryn's hackles awoke.

'I don't see why. You knew where I was. I left a note — '

'Going off like that, in the middle of the night . . . ' Marge ventured a little laugh, making light of what her tone said was a most serious offence.

'I needed to be here.'

Kathryn's response would have closed the door on further discussion had Marge been prepared to be dissuaded.

'I cannot imagine what Charles will have made of it all.'

Kathryn bit back fury. It was not her mother's business what Charles might or might not make of her daughter's actions, nor did she feel disposed to volunteer. To speak at all was painful, yet she ordered herself to do so, to be patient.

If I am merciful, she thought, perhaps Cal will be saved.

She said, 'Charles and I have talked things over — '

'I know. You told me. But — '

'We have agreed that what we do or do not do in our lives is not the other person's business.'

Or yours; but left that unsaid, although Marge Fanning heard the words clearly enough. A few seconds' silence; then Marge spoke brightly, determined to make the best of a sorry situation.

'I really don't think you can say that, dear.' She laughed, deliberately pressing her attack home. 'You might as well say it is none of *our* business, either.' And waited.

The opportunity to strike a mortal blow hovered, but it was a confrontation that Kathryn would not accept. She said nothing.

Mollified, Marge asked, 'When are you coming home?'

'I don't know.'

'Has there been any news? About . . . ?' Even now she found Cal's name difficult.

'No.'

'Do they still hold out any hope?'

The television had said that the fourth day

would offer the last realistic chance of finding the missing men alive. Which meant tomorrow. Of course, as the commentator had said, funereally, if they had no water . . . Kathryn shut her mind to that. *Take a deal of killing, my Cal.* Em's words kindled courage.

'No-one's been in touch with me.'

'I suppose not. You could just as well wait at home,' she suggested. With rare percipience, she added, 'You'd be nearer to him, here.'

Physically, that was true. But Kathryn had not forgotten the loss of awareness that she had experienced at the farm, the sense that Cal had gone from her.

'I think I'll hang on here a bit. For a day or two, anyway.'

After which there would be no hope. Both women acknowledged the unspoken words.

Marge surrendered. 'Whatever you think is best.'

It was so hard to know. In the end Kathryn could only allow her instincts to dictate.

She made a pilgrimage to the beach where Cal had so nearly drowned, where in losing him she might have lost what was worthwhile in her life. A cold front had arrived from the West; it spread its fingers over her, but could not erase the terrible heat, the thirst that dried her heart and brought her almost to the point of despair. Almost, but never quite. Never. Never.

She stood at the far end of the beach, beyond the terrible place of almost-dying. About her were the rocks where she and Cal had lain in the sun. Beneath the water the anchored rocks seemed to flow with the movement of the surf. She raised her open hand, slid it beneath her shirt. Laid it against her own breast. In her touch Cal gentled her.

No, she had said when he pressed her. 'No.'

How she wished . . .

Too late.

She turned abruptly, glaring at the running ocean as at an enemy, the invisible rips plotting treason.

'It is not!' Her raised voice challenged the screeching of the gulls. 'It is not too late! It is not!'

★   ★   ★

For the rest of the day Cal waited. Mostly Hennie was unconscious or at least asleep, came to, briefly, from time to time. When he did, the crying started again.

'*Dit maak seer . . .* '

How Cal welcomed the silence, when unconsciousness returned.

305

It was only a matter of time now, but how long it took was still critical. With every hour his own chances of survival grew less. The temptation to walk away was ever with him, but he fought it, knowing that if he did so he would never escape at all, that the image of the pilot dying, alone and abandoned in the wilderness, would reproach him forever.

So he sat in what had become a trap that, in the freedom of endless space, held him securely. He tried to think of neither the present nor the uncertain and menacing future. Instead, he thought of the past, of how he had come to find himself in this situation.

It was too simple to pin it all on Hennie, even on the storm that had struck so inopportunely. The roots of the present were buried much further back.

He had always felt the need to paint, to draw, had earned a measure of notoriety at high school by his ability to draw vulgar cartoons of teachers. Inevitably it had got him into trouble, but there was nothing new in that. As long as Cal could remember, he and trouble had shared a bed.

It came in many forms. The most extreme example would have landed him in deep grief had he been caught. He had come across a big boy, a notorious bully, attacking a little kid with a stick. Cal, fourteen now and strong for his years, had had a bad day. Told the bully to stop and got a mouthful for his trouble. There was a sack washed up on the beach. He stuffed the boy in it, tied a knot, left him for a couple of hours to think about things. When he let him out, he told him he'd kill him if he breathed a word or tried his nonsense ever again. Said much the same to the victim.

It was only later that it occurred to him that he might easily have killed the boy, anyway. The word got out, as it always does, but vaguely, a rumour that was never brought home to Cal. The bully's father, a bully himself, threatened mayhem but, scared of Mick Jessop, did nothing.

A week later a master got hold of Cal. In his hand one of Cal's caricatures, a lady teacher looking like a spaniel, with pouting breasts.

'I never seen it in my life,' said Cal.

The master smiled. 'Every time I get hold of one, I put it in a file. I've quite a collection by now. I expect them to make me a packet, one of these days.'

It had never occurred to Cal that his drawings might be worth anything.

'You have talent,' the master said. 'It won't do you any good unless you work at it. But I'm hoping you may find it more rewarding than tying kids up in sacks.'

Cal gave him his blank look.

'Try it. There are books in the school library. Have a look, why don't you?'

And left him to think about it.

Cocky Cal did nothing for a while. Then, one day when there was no-one about, slid into the library and had a look at what was on offer.

So it went. The more he read, the more he practised, the stronger grew the urge. Until everyone, even himself, accepted that he really was an artist.

Years later, the Art Club exhibition, the meetings with Dave Holt and Angela Scales.

'Trouble with you,' Angela said, 'you're illiterate.'

It was true that he had never bothered much at school and a fishing boat was no place for catching up. Not that he was about to admit it to this pushy lady.

'I'm a fisherman,' he told her defiantly. 'I know all I need to get by.'

'You're an artist.' Her tone slapped him down. 'Or could be, if you took the trouble.'

How he longed to believe her. But reality said *bullshit*.

'You telling me I need to go back to school?'

'At least do a TAFE course. Learn

something about design.'

He dismissed it; thought about it; did it.

That was the next stage, he thought now. Doing it had triggered a response, not only to the visual arts, but to education generally. He found that the chore of study, that he had detested so much at school, was a chore no longer.

He had learnt and, as he learnt, he thought. It made a difference. Angela got him into the Adelaide School of Art. He absorbed what it had to teach him, moved on. Then came the success of 'Coastal Sequence'.

He could truthfully say that it had never gone to his head. He knew what he had put into it, how much further he had to go; he had no plans to be a prima donna.

He had an up and a downer with Mick, told him to stuff the fishing. He got hold of a tutor to give him the rudiments of French, found he had an aptitude, knew enough to get by when he went off to Paris.

Paris, he thought, let me think about Paris. Because Paris had been much more than Gianetta's death. It had been his first real city but, more important even than that, had shown him the possibilities of life.

To begin with, he had been conscious only of how much it differed from anywhere he had known before.

The smell of French cigarettes was one of the first things he had noticed. Early morning cafes pungent with the fumes of Gitanes and Gauloises. A plunger of coffee, strong and black, on a zinc counter, while about him jostled the sturdy shoulders of morose, blue-shirted men.

From the first he had preferred working men's cafes to the places where students hung out. The men were not friendly, more than ready to turn their backs on someone so evidently a foreigner, but there was a sense of reality about them that the others lacked. He had come a long way from the day Angela had called him illiterate, but was still more comfortable with people who talked racing and football than with those whose idea of a breakfast conversation was Rimbaud and Verlaine. Even though they did not know it, these were his type of people. Back home they'd have been fishermen, too.

For weeks he crisscrossed the city on foot. Not only the obvious places like Montmartre and the Eiffel Tower. He poked his nose everywhere, from Boulevard Haussmann to cité Falguière, where Edith Piaf had been born.

Even then he felt more at home on the streets than in the museums although, conscientiously, he paid his dues there as well. Jeu de Paume, Museé de l'Orangerie, Niarkos Collection, the Louvre . . .

The river at night, the lights of bridges reflecting in the dark water. Bookshops and fruit markets, with the spire of Notre Dame soaring overhead.

With friends, idling away Saturday mornings at pavement cafes, drinking red wine when they could afford it, *Perrier Citron* when they could not.

And everywhere the clatter of French, pervasive as the traffic, the suicidal, maniacal drivers of the Place de la Concorde.

A whore, once; a couple of fellow students; Gianetta at a party. Both of them giving each other the eye until he went across and took her out of there.

Gianetta, he thought, and now Kathryn. I loved Gianetta truly, but she is the past now. Whereas Kathryn . . . What a future we shall have! All I have to do is get out of here alive.

For the rest of the day he stayed put. Twice he thought Hennie was dead; twice his breathing, momentarily interrupted, resumed its hoarse, spastic snore. When the sun went down, he swallowed a miserly mouthful of water. The bottle was less than half full now, and they had seen no sign of water since the waterhole two days ago.

He was weak himself, the landscape

blurred by more than the gathering darkness. He had heard no planes today; probably they'd been written off, another two adventurers swallowed by the immensity. I hope Kathryn has not written me off, he thought. Not yet.

I am coming . . . He wanted to shout the words loud enough for her to hear them, believed that somehow she would hear them, anyway.

Going barmy, he told himself, but did not believe it. Kathryn, the link he had with Kathryn, the faith and hope and trust he had in Kathryn, his love for Kathryn, would bring him home.

It grew dark and cold. Still Hennie snored intermittently; still Cal waited.

If he never comes to, I'll have wasted a whole day. It might make the difference between survival and death.

Yet waited, still. A superstition hovered in the darkness. If I abandon him I, too, shall die.

★   ★   ★

Dave Holt prevailed upon Kathryn to go with him to a get-together: one or two artists, one or two dozen hangers-on. Dave was flying to Europe the next day, so this would be his last opportunity for a while, and he did not want to miss it. Dave was a great one for parties; they provided the oxygen that fuelled his precious eccentricities.

'Go ahead,' Kathryn said. 'Don't mind me.'

'I wouldn't think of it.'

Kathryn had thought she would refuse but, when it came to the point, could not bear the thought of another night of anxiety and dread, chewing her fingernails in darkness. So she let him talk her into it; later wished she had not.

She knew no-one and no-one knew her or, blatantly, wished to do so. Braying laughter slapped the air, the cacophonous clatter of asinine voices. The large-roomed house was an enclosure in which the party-goers guzzled and munched. Beyond the walls lay worlds unknown to them and, therefore, not worth knowing; a calculated indifference to strangers who, by definition, could not be relevant.

On the walls hung reproductions of Australian art produced by artists — some a hundred and fifty years before, some many centuries before that — who had stretched their world by celebrating visions that their mind and eye had seen, visions that these people, tonight, sought to banish through contempt. Because disregard of the new, the unknown, the incorrect, screeched contempt.

313

Kathryn's only consolation was knowing that such attitudes were destined to failure. The inevitability of change was undeniable, even as it was denied.

She stood in a corner of the room, an untasted drink in her hand, and watched the zoo. Beyond the imprisoning walls lay the desert, the sea exploding in smoking pillars stitched with rainbow glints.

She remembered what Dave had said to her the previous day, when they had been in Cal's studio together and she had stared in perplexity at the profusion of canvasses.

'Has he done all these paintings since he got back from Paris?'

'Plus the ones he sent to New York.'

'He must never stop.'

'All successful artists have the same problem,' Dave said. 'They keep on and on, either out of habit or because they need the money. The biggest names have to work the hardest to keep up their reputation, even though they'll tell you they don't care about that. The irony is they know the importance of spiritual solitude, yet never have time for it. Society forces them to become entertainers. There is no space left for dreams. The bravest ones make their own space. That's why Cal has gone. He tells himself it's to discover the Outback and, in one sense, he's right. But his real reason is to find himself.'

'And when he has found himself, will he be changed?' Kathryn asked. How much she wished that this would not be so.

'Probably. All true artists have to change, constantly. They have no choice.'

She picked out one of the paintings, a rectangle of black set against a white ground. 'I like this . . . '

Dave looked at it with her. 'It reminds me a little of a painting by Mondrian, a silhouette merging into darkness. But I suspect this could be beyond Mondrian. Sometimes I think Cal has the potential to go beyond all the artists who have preceded him. He has to, of course, if he is to discover the new worlds he's looking for.'

What about me? Kathryn wanted to ask, like a child. *Where do I fit into all this?* But could not.

Instead said, 'I love him.'

Dave studied her gravely. 'I hope I haven't injured you by bringing the two of you together.'

'Never.' She was resolute in her denial. 'Even if nothing comes of it, if he never comes back, or worse, if he comes back and doesn't want me, I shall never regret what has happened. Even,' smiling ruefully, 'what has not happened. Because he's given me a vision

of how my life should be. Enlightenment . . . '
Again the smile. 'Isn't that what the
Buddhists are supposed to look for? Well, I've
found it. You are the reason it happened, and
I shall never be able to thank you enough.'

Brave talk; yet now, watching the milling
herd, she asked herself what she would do if
Cal had indeed changed and no longer
wanted her. What would she do then?

After returning from the party, Kathryn lay
on the bed in her room at her uncle's house.
She thought:

He is alive, still. He cannot survive much
longer, but I know that, if he dies, I shall be
with him, as I am with him now. In this life,
or another life. This time, or another time.
Past, future, present. All one. I am with him
and shall be, forever. He is my love and I, in
the infinite complexities of the universe, am
his. He comes at night into my room. From
the mouths of ewes, the slink eyes of foxes,
the artist who, even in the face of death, has
contrived a universe. He has gone to a distant
place, has taken me with him. Now, if he has
to go on, I shall go with him, also. It is
inevitable, because I am his. I am his. Even
into the flame and ecstasy of stone.

15

Some time before dawn Hennie awoke.

'Cal.'

'I'm here.'

The pilot relaxed, panting.

'How you feeling?'

'Okay. The pain's gone.'

'Soon have you up and running.'

'Right.'

'The Gammon Stakes. Don't forget; my money's on you.'

Silence drifted; Hennie's hand, cold and damp, clasped in his own.

Out of nowhere, Hennie said, 'Say hi to Stella for me.'

Even now Cal would not admit what they both knew. 'Say it yourself.'

'I know,' Hennie said presently.

A flicker in the mind, the gut. 'Know?'

'About you and Stella. I've known for months.'

Silence, then.

At last Cal said, 'How'd you find out?'

'There's always a friend. Can't wait to tell you, some of these *okies*.' Silence as, painfully, he breathed. 'Couldn't expect much else, I suppose, the way things were. If it hadn't been you, it'd have been someone else.'

A breath of air came coldly out of the north. To the east, beyond the ridge that still remained to be climbed, was the first faint lightening of the sky. The idea of the ridge, still waiting, reminded Cal what had happened when he had been up there a day and a half ago.

'There's something wrong with the compass,' he said. 'We're heading too much to the east.'

'The compass is okay.' The effort of speaking echoed painfully in a voice so faint Cal could barely hear it. 'There's magnetite in the rocks. It throws the needle out. I should have warned you.'

'How do you allow for it?'

'Easy. First thing in the morning, get a fix on the sun. That's east, near enough. Ninety degrees. All you got to do is take the bearing and adjust for the difference. Don't forget to allow for the variation.'

'You'll be able to show me how to do it.'

'When I first heard about you and Stella, I was mad as a snake,' Hennie said. A croaking gasp as he tried to laugh. 'Don't seem to matter much, now.'

Again silence.

'Say hi to her for me,' he said again.

'Sure.'

The light grew stronger, diluting the darkness. Hennie sighed once. Was dead.

'Hennie?'

Too late.

It was impossible to bury him on the rock shelf.

Cal took Hennie's shirt and put it on. Also took his water bottle and emptied the contents carefully into his own. There wasn't much, but even a drop was worth saving. He tidied the body as best he could, wondered whether to say anything. Decided against it, in the end. What was there to say, after all?

He turned again to the ridge, still half-hidden in the darkness, and began to climb.

★   ★   ★

The fifth day. Dave had left; Kathryn had run him to the airport. When she got back she went for a walk, going nowhere. She had been to all the places, had felt Cal in her bones and blood. There was nothing else she could do. Or perhaps one thing, a gesture to challenge fate.

The wind was strong. Along the cliff top the grasses streamed like hair. Her own hair was tugged by its cool fingers while the surf grenades exploded upon the rocks. She found her way down to the water's edge, walked in the iodine aroma of seaweed and damp sand. She clambered onto the black and glass-slick rocks. She picked her way, precariously, to the outer limit of the shelf upon which the seas were breaking. She stood upon the edge, enduring the pounding fist of the seas as again and again they broke over her. It was dangerous, foolhardy, but she did not move. If she permitted herself to endure the frenzy of the waves, if she suffered, Cal would be safe. Alone upon the slippery black rock, she faced the ice-cold spray, the breath-thieving buffeting of water and wind.

Later, drenched through, she went back to the house. Where visitors awaited her.

'We came to see how you were going . . . '

Marge all smiles, eager to commiserate over what Kathryn was determined had not yet happened. Behind her, Charles stood uncomfortably.

'I'm good.'

But her mother was already exclaiming over the state of her clothes.

'Kathryn, you're soaked!'

'It's nothing. Spray.'

'But you're drenched. You have been in the sea,' she accused this daughter, of whom all things were possible.

'I am fine.'

The words neatly spaced, with gaps between them. She could have screamed them in Marge's face, but took a succession of measured breaths and did not. Even managed to smile at Charles.

'How you going?'

Charles was clearly unhappy at being brought here, like a load of washing. Or a husband-in-waiting. Their last meeting breathed.

'There is no news?'

She managed a smile. 'I would be the last to hear. No-one even knows I exist.'

Apparently this was true no longer.

Her mother said, 'There was a mention in the paper . . . ' Which obviously had not pleased her. 'It said there were two women by the coast waiting for news. The other is apparently the pilot's wife.'

'Stella. They must have got it from her.'

'They called you a friend. It made you sound like — '

'A lover?' Kathryn, who had been both lover and non-lover, did not know whether to cry or laugh. But this Marge was not prepared to say.

'I have come to bring you home,' she proclaimed. 'You need your family around you.'

'I shall go and change,' Kathryn said. 'You will stay for lunch?'

She did so, deliberately choosing the brightest of the few things she had brought with her: a plain white skirt, a blouse of red and blue and golden flowers.

She saw that her mother had expected something more sombre, to suit the occasion. Kathryn smiled, said, 'When Cal gets back, we plan to go sailing. I'd better be here when he arrives, or he may decide to go without me.' And laughed, quite merrily, at such a ludicrous idea.

Charles did not know where to put feet or hands.

Kathryn gave them a stew of scallops and prawns, leftovers from the meal she had cooked the previous day as Dave's farewell treat. At the time she had forced herself to do it, to focus her mind at least for an hour or two on something other than Cal, and now was glad. Although her mother expressed surprise that Kathryn should make herself so free with the kitchen of someone else's house.

'Where is my brother, anyway?'

'In Paris.'

Fatal Paris.

Raised eyebrows. 'Leaving you here by yourself?'

'I'm perfectly safe.' Which was not what

Marge had meant. 'I think he trusts me not to steal the spoons,' Kathryn said.

After lunch — 'Very nice, dear' — Marge said she wanted to put her feet up. Kathryn went outside, hungry for air. Charles followed.

'I'm sorry . . . '

She was not at all forgiving. 'You shouldn't have come.'

'I came because I thought you might need me.'

Because he hoped I might need him. The idea made her furious. 'Why should you think that?'

Charles took her hands. 'You realise he is lost?'

Fire, then, to match the Outback's heat. 'If you mean he's dead, you're wrong.'

'How can you be sure?'

'I know. That's all. I know.'

'If you say so . . . '

Charles's patient expression infuriated her. 'You don't believe me!'

'It's five days, now. They've found no trace — '

'They will.' Shutting her mind to all else. 'They will!'

'There is a limit,' he told her. 'For anyone. To go on hoping — '

'It's not a question of hope,' she cried at

him, her own sharp-toothed doubts. 'I know!' She pounded her heart, extravagantly. 'In here!'

They walked slowly, side by side.

'The media will be after you now,' Charles said.

'I shall tell them the same thing.'

'It's the sort of story they love. Human interest — '

She saw that it was the thought of publicity that troubled him. He was afraid of embarrassment in the mid-north, a community without secrets.

'I don't care about the media. I don't care about anything. Only that Cal should be safe.' She stared at him, willing to hurt the man who by coming here had hurt her. 'Only that Cal should be safe,' she repeated brutally, 'and come back to me.'

He sighed, heavily. 'You're right. I shouldn't have come.'

'No,' she agreed, 'you should not.'

'I did so for you,' he defended himself.

But she was willing to be brutal. 'Nothing of the sort. You did it for yourself.'

Her mother, to Kathryn's horror, was staying.

'There is no spare room . . . '

'You say Dave's in Paris. I shall use his room, then. I'm sure he won't object. His own sister . . . We shared a bed plenty of times in the past.' A little laugh. 'Such a ladylike brother . . . I knew I'd be safe.'

Marge enjoyed innuendo, but Kathryn would have none of it. 'You saying he's gay?'

Deftly Marge evaded the question. 'They say your friend's his protégé, don't they?' Smiling, she made much of the word. 'He's a very good-looking man, after all.'

Kathryn went cold. 'That's a disgusting thing to say . . . '

'Disgusting?' Again the tinkling laugh. 'My dear, I'm so sorry. I thought it was quite acceptable, these days.'

'So it is. And not before time. Except that neither of them is like it. And you said it only because to you it *is* disgusting.' She confronted her mother, who would have looked away if she could. 'Would you like me to tell you *why* I know Cal isn't gay?'

Now Mrs Fanning showed the deepest distress. 'Kathryn, darling . . . I came to comfort you. To try and help.'

'The only way you can help is by keeping quiet. I mean it. Otherwise I shall move out.'

'My dear . . . ' So gently she said it. 'You're upset. I understand. But running away solves nothing.'

★   ★   ★

From the top of the ridge, Cal took a bearing on the far side of the valley. To allow for the compass deviation, he had to head midway between north and north-east to maintain the correct course. Assuming the magnetite was evenly distributed throughout the ranges.

If it's concentrated more in some places than others, he thought, I have problems. Resolutely he discarded the thought. All I can do is head in the direction that seems best and hope like hell I'm right.

He trudged forward, endlessly, an ant moving in the vast and empty plain. To take his mind off the heat, the distance separating him from rescue, the near-certainty of his own extinction, he forced himself to focus upon memories.

Strolling at Kathryn's side along a beach cooled by the white tongues of waves. Sitting with dangling feet above the peaceful immensity of the sea. It seemed to him now that the times of his greatest happiness had come in periods without rush, when he had been able to take the time to move slowly and without frenzy along the corridors of his life.

Three years before, he had gone to Malaysia, had seen upon the roads a multitude of wooden carts drawn by water buffalo. They had moved timelessly, in a dream, whereas he, in a hired car, had passed them in a blink of light, a gust of tropical air. Once, driving fast along the rifle-barrel-straight road north of Taiping, he had overtaken one of these carts, a blur of which he retained only an impression of a hunched figure wearing a conical hat that extended almost to the shoulders, two children staring. A minute later he had passed another car heading south. Their combined speeds would have been close to three hundred kilometres an hour and when, seconds later, he looked in the mirror, the other car had already passed the cart that was now the best part of three kilometres behind him. He could see nothing of the cart's occupants, had never at any time seen the slow revolutions of the wooden wheels, heard the steady creak, creak of the wooden frame, yet still it continued at its own pace. Somehow it had seemed to him that the slowly-moving cart, the driver hunched beneath his shoulder-wide hat, the brown faces of the children, possessed a reality greater than his own, screaming towards Penang in a hired car.

Now, pacing himself step by slow step across yet another valley of stone and scrub and heat, he thought that he too had come to reality. God will decide whether I come alive out of this place, he thought. Or whether He or She or It saved me from the water only to destroy me now. If you believed in an interventionist God, one who made the rules only to break them.

Out here it was easy to believe. John the Baptist in the desert, he thought, making straight all the crooked ways. He'd have a job in the Gammon Ranges. He lived on locusts and wild honey, I recall. Not much of either around here. Maybe we can bring some in.

And screamed full-voiced, howling against the emptiness, the distances reverberating with silence, in which his scream died.

For the first time, he realised that he was beginning to lose it. It frightened him, this scream erupting from nowhere; it meant that his mind was wearing out faster than his body. Even as he thought it, he stumbled upon a loose piece of rock and fell heavily. He lay for a while with dirt in his mouth. He was not thinking, not doing anything, but lay motionless, feeling the sun's weight through the borrowed shirt, the stiffness of his shoulders where the welts raised by the plaited reins still throbbed.

After a minute he got slowly to his feet and began to plod on. Once again he remembered the buffalo carts, the sense he had always had that they were not heading towards any specific destination but trundling with infinite slowness towards nowhere at all.

As he, now, was trundling with infinite slowness towards nowhere at all.

The foothills of the next line of ranges rose before him. They were yellow and hard, flecked with patches of green bush, with a shadow over the higher slopes where the sun had gone behind cloud. Cal looked at the height and steepness of the slopes and knew he did not have the strength to climb them. To his left the valley narrowed into a gorge running between red cliffs. As far as he could tell it headed north and, after a moment's consideration, he decided to follow it. If it came to a dead end, too bad; he would just have to come back.

He entered a narrow tunnel where the red cliffs leaned so close on either side that the sky was almost hidden. The bed of the tunnel consisted of yellow, rippled sand. It was obvious that after rain there would be a creek here, but there had been no rain for two days now and, for the moment, the sand was dry.

Further on, the gorge opened up a little. In place of the towering cliffs, there was now a line of contorted trees, leaning inwards, but their white branches and leathery, sage-green leaves the shape of spears gave little shade. It was very hot, the air heavy, and he fell again, twice, as he tried to force his way through the soft and clinging sand.

He knew without conscious thought that he was running out of time. Again he experienced the fatalism that he had felt in the sea, when he had nearly drowned. He was alone. There was no-one else in the world, nor could be ever again. The idea of solitude no longer worried him, because neither it nor the heat nor the impossibility of his quest mattered any longer. Even Kathryn was slipping away from him.

During the day they had spent exploring the coastline around Kidman's Inlet, Kathryn had asked him whether he was ever afraid, whether trying always to do something new in art was not bound at times to fail.

'Of course,' he had told her. 'I've always known that somewhere is a blank wall I won't be able to cross. There is for all of us, the limit of what is possible. I've always been afraid of reaching the wall, but so far I haven't.'

Now that he was getting very close to that wall, he discovered there had never been any reason for fear, after all. It seemed that even the wall did not matter. What would be . . .

Again the sides of the gorge drew in. Ahead of him a cliff, perhaps two hundred feet high, rough with protruding knuckles of stone, reached vertically skywards. Beyond, the peak of yet another mountain beckoned, but he knew he would never be able to climb up to it. On either side the cliffs' strata ran horizontally, but with gnarled and rocky overhangs that gave no promise of handholds.

He had come into a blind valley. There was no way out. He had reached the wall, at last.

He turned to look back the way he had come. The mouth of the gorge stood open, like the mouth of a cave seen from within. It framed the distant ranges, the valley he had crossed to get here. He was surprised, mildly, to see that once again the sun was setting beyond the saw-toothed range that now stood black against the sky. It meant that what had seemed to him like no more than two or three hours had, in fact, been twelve hours, a whole day in which he had wandered and, it seemed, got nowhere.

He turned to look ahead of him at what had become his prison. Beyond the drift of sand on which he stood was an upright stone, almost two metres high and as red as fire, with the walls of the implacable gorge forming a circle beyond it.

Moses's fossilised bush, he thought. From which — who knows? — the voice of God may speak.

He reached the rock, collapsed beside it like a rotten house. No-one, neither God nor Moses, spoke; even the silence said nothing.

Only his harsh panting reverberated.

It was unbearable. He screamed again, trying desperately to people the silence with noise. Abruptly stopped. His chest heaved.

Stop it. *Stop it!*

Panting, panting.

The day sank, melting, along the western horizon. He turned to watch. Beyond the gorge's dark mouth the sun hung amid the flare and spume of incandescence, then slid suddenly below the surface of the day. Its silent going filled the universe. Above Cal's tortured eyes, the first pinpoint star.

In the darkness, swift-plunging, came reason. Now he could drink. And did so in measured gulps. One, two, three. Enough. He shook the bottle, hearing its content slosh feebly. Nearly empty, now.

He breathed the night, seeking rest.

Tomorrow would be the last day. At midday there would be no shade in these burning hills. The idea of walking by night, lying up by day — what use was that when the shattered terrain made it impossible, when there was nowhere to hide from the thunder of the sun?

He knew he had barely made it tonight, had been on the brink of defeat, despite all his brave thoughts. Beyond the limit of endurance lay the unknown. Uncharted country.

That was what life was. Standing always on the brink of the unknown. Because to know tomorrow before tomorrow came was death. Whereas the trackless deserts of the mind . . .

We wander, seeking, he told himself. There cannot be a road, because that would mean that someone had been there before, which would make the journey futile.

He thought, Let us go further into these ranges, then. Let us find a way up and over the wall that is facing us, let us seek out the final landscape of knowledge. Perhaps there we shall discover the answers. Or perhaps shall see only the plain unfolding its arid wings to infinity. Who knows? Because who, ultimately, can find that landscape, find the pass through the mountains that leads to truth?

★   ★   ★

That night a minister of whatever denomination, satin vest, satin voice, spoke on the box of the True Path, of those who had strayed from it and who, in their loss and isolation, were driven by dementia to summon visions of what could not be.

'God will save those lost in the desert, as he

will those lost in sin. Only God. All else is
vanity. If they die, if they are already dead,
that is God's will. Before which we all must
bow.'

Kathryn shoved past her mother, reaching
frantically for the switch. 'Turn that sancti-
monious bastard off!'

★　★　★

Alone in the fifth night, Kathryn waited. The
black demons came upon her. Amid the
screaming night she cried to the cliffs, the
clean-running seas. She knew that she was
losing him, that he was fading from her,
despite all her efforts.

She was angry at what was happening,
would stand and curse fate before she bowed
in submission. Why is it that the good and
holy should be scythed down? she demanded.
While the rubbish flourishes? The world does
not need the knavery of Tom or Kerry, Eric or
Grant or Nigel or Alan or Ingmar, of Norma
and Iseult, Clarice and Lettie, Naomi, Tamsin
and Oona. We shun their shabby corruption
of the spirit. Yet they live and smile and do
not care. We see their faces everywhere.

When Cal left, he went not into the desert
only, but into fulfilment, a universe of time
and space and imagination. To seek the other

selves, the other places, through his journey. To reject the riffraff, those who steal our integrity by their lies, their corruption and collusion and canker. To seek truth.

At least it is true that he will live after all these others. He has already won his place in eternity. Once, the knowledge would have comforted her, but now was not enough. Oh keep him, she prayed. Let him come back to me.

All night, frightened of what she had come to believe was ending, she kept vigil. The demons howled and howled. Until, at length, the long night gave place to day. The sixth day. Beyond which all hope would be gone.

16

Alone before the cliff that frowned implacably through the darkness, Cal breathed the night, seeking rest. He lay on a rock ledge six metres above the creek bed. The sand would have been more comfortable, but after dark it had rained violently for a time and he was afraid the creek might come down during the night. It might not be a bad idea if it does, he thought. At least I'll have water. But had read too much of flash floods to risk being swept away.

At length, muscles bruised and sore from the harsh rock, he saw the return of light. First came a softening of the darkness, then, far overhead, the outline of the cliff top growing steadily sharper against a sky that was grey, then silver, then flushed with rose. The light trembled, still cool, yet with the promise of implacable heat.

I wonder where it'll happen, Cal thought. When willpower is finally overcome by the failure of muscle and blood. The ultimate experience.

He shook his bottle, hearing the feeble slosh of such water as remained. Before starting he would drink half of what was left. He knew he might as well drink all of it, but would not, unwilling even now to accept the inevitability of his own death.

The light formed a trembling meniscus upon the lip of the cliff, spilled over to run downwards until it lay all about him. Only the crevices remained in shadow.

To the right of the rock wall a small fissure disappeared around the corner of the face. He stood, making himself ready.

Now every action was fraught with significance. The last night; the last girding of the will to face the light; the last departure.

He drank half his remaining water, as planned, and pushed his way into the fissure. It continued to curve continuously to the left so that he could not see the end of it. It was no more than two feet wide, shrinking at times to half that, forcing him to fight to squeeze through at all. Underfoot were round stones, smooth as glass, over which he stumbled. It would have been water that had smoothed them, he thought, although whether ten thousand or ten million years ago there was no telling. On either side the cliffs were smooth, devoid of handholds. If a flash flood caught him here, he would drown. The idea did not trouble him. One way or another, he thought. What difference did it make?

He worked his way around another bend, found that immediately in front of him the fissure narrowed to no more than a few inches. There was no way he could get through. He stopped, panting slightly with expended effort and disappointment. Looked again.

A tree's roots were clamped against the rock, a latticework up which it might be possible to climb.

He craned his head to stare upwards. Far above him he could see the outline of leaves against a cerulean sky. Looked again at what was before his nose. He doubted he had the strength to navigate the tangled roots but would try, refusing absolutely to consider the idea of turning back.

He wedged one foot into a gap between the roots and hauled himself up. A start, then.

Slowly he progressed. The fissure closed about him; he jammed his boots against the opposite wall and somehow kicked his way through. It opened out again and he clung to the glassy roots, hunting desperately but unsuccessfully for somewhere to rest.

He had to keep moving. Stop once, and he would never have the strength to start again. The roots thinned, his hold upon them became ever more precarious. Sweat blinded him.

He slipped, dangled from one hand, managed somehow to swing back, to seize hold upon a section of cliff that had been splintered over the years by the probing root systems of the tree. Hung in desperation, feeling strength and resolution leaking through his cramped fingers, while below him a hundred feet of air sucked ravenously.

Somehow his boots found a place upon which to stand, if only temporarily. A minute's rest before once again, teeth clamped, eyes squeezed almost shut, he forced his way upwards.

And upwards.

Time had no meaning; his own draining strength had no meaning. A hand reached out, took hold, the legs and body convulsed, the muscles raised him an inch or two higher. Again. And again. Eyes tight, blood crying shrilly in his head.

He felt the first blow of sunlight. Opened his eyes. Ten feet above him, a ledge beyond which nothing was visible.

He clung, breathing deeply, feeling the shirt wet with sweat against his chest. He reached out again, heaved upwards, again upwards. The lip of the cliff grew nearer. Could at last reach it. The stone was warm beneath his hands. With a final convulsive effort, he hauled himself clear. Lay, more unconscious than not, in a blood-red swirl of utter exhaustion.

★ ★ ★

Dawkins, the pilot of the rescue chopper, repeated his question.

'You sure they gave no clue which way they were heading?'

Jock was not much for talking at the best of times. In particular, hated being questioned and showed it.

'Moomba,' he managed. 'That's where.'

Dawkins stifled a sigh. Others had questioned the old man and got nowhere. Why should he have thought he might have better luck? Yet perverseness made him keep on.

'They never mentioned anywhere else? Anywhere they might have stopped off on the way?'

'They was talkin' 'bout the Gammons. Hennie said he'd been there before.'

'Whereabouts?'

'Dunno nuthin 'bout that.'

The pilot was not so sure. There was something about Jock's look, the way his eyes flickered. Yet why should he lie? No one was blaming him for what had happened. Perhaps he thought they might. In which case . . .

He pressed him. 'You sure?'

Was already turning away when Jock lashed out vehemently, spraying spit. 'I say sumthin, next thing you'll have me in that machine of yours.'

Shit. Dawkins turned back.

He said, 'Where?'

'You ain't takin' me up in that thing . . . '

'No one's taking you anywhere.'

Silence. Jock sucked gums, nervously.

'It might save their lives.'

A cackle. 'After six days?'

'Just tell me, okay?'

Jock dithered. Patience imploded. Dawkins grabbed the old-timer by the shirt, shaking.

'*Where?*'

★　★　★

Eventually Cal mustered enough strength to stand. Beyond the tree, the ground opened up. A scattering of tea trees, a litter of dead trunks flung down by ancient floods upon a bed of gravel and boulders. Beyond the trees, the stern ranges, mottled russet and green, stretched away.

He fished out the compass, took the reading, allowed for deviation.

'Straight ahead,' he told the air.

Into the unknown.

He looked at the landscape ahead. The peaks closed in about him, he could no longer see far enough to have any clear idea where he was going. It made no difference. All he could do was continue.

Again he forced his body to obey. Step by lurching step. At some stage found himself discussing life and love with Kathryn, who was his life and love.

After I'd finished 'Coastal Sequence', I knew I had to move on. 'Sequence' had been good, I shall always be proud of it, but it was *safe*. It broke new ground when I did it, but now it wasn't new any longer. I couldn't go on doing the same thing. I always have to try and do what no-one else has ever done. To paint the wind, the heat, the heart. Not like Picasso or Braque, taking things to pieces like clocks to see how they worked. I want to paint what lies beneath. The spirit, if you believe in spirits. The force that drives and unites all things.

Walking beside him in the desert of stone, Kathryn asked, How can you paint what you can't see?

The question made sense, yet Cal remained confident.

With vision, it might be possible.

The contours of the valley bore away to the left across the foothills of the imprisoning peaks. He had to make an effort to work out what that meant. North, he decided, it's taking me north. Not that it mattered. Direction mattered no more than distance, now. He was weaving like a drunk, following the valley mindlessly, no longer thinking about anything but the inner dialogue that had taken up residence in his mind.

I can't allow myself to stand still. I'm not the only artist out there. Gerard, van Myssen, Alexander Smith. They aren't going to wait for me. I have to move on.

The business with Gianetta had been bad, no doubt about it, but maybe the way I reacted served a purpose, too. Perhaps all this time I've been waiting for something to jolt me into a new way of thinking, of seeing.

Kathryn, he said, your uncle believes it was Wagner who turned the key.

A laugh hacked the dry air, derisively.

Let me tell you something. I've heard the Ring a dozen times. I love it, but it's not *new*. It wasn't Wagner got me going again; it was you. I don't know why. You're not an artist. I'm not sure you even understand what art is about. Yet the fact remains. It was you.

He knew he was straying, meandering.

Could do nothing about it. He fell, repeatedly.

Do you believe in God? he asked her, the iron hills. The God that destroys and creates? The God that lives in the dust storm and the drought, that is more dangerous than either? Do you believe in that? If you do, you must strip yourself naked. Humanity must be naked, mustn't it? Naked before God?

Look at me, the stripped and naked man in the stripped and naked hills. Moses, too, went into a high place to meet his God, the god of fire speaking to him out of a bush of flame. It is in the deserts, the citadels of stone, that we come closest to him. That's when we've got to watch out. That's when things get dangerous.

In the sea, drowning, feeling eternity . . . Which is surely God?

Yet it is also true that God is in my hand when I paint. The image has to come from somewhere. The line emerges on the page. No use asking where it comes from, or why. It is so, that's all. No one knows the answer. The unknown is also God.

★　★　★

Dawkins raised Moomba on the radio.

'I'm going to take a look further south. The old man claims that Hennie said something about a waterhole. Somewhere east of Mount Serle, he said. Although God knows that covers a lot of country.'

There were a hundred places; it wasn't easy, having so many to choose from.

Dawkins set his jaw. 'The bastards got to be somewhere.'

Searched; failed. Searched; failed.

★   ★   ★

Cal stumbled on, past and present inextricably entwined. The truth was that his past life no longer had any significance. The fact of the crash, ineluctable and conclusive, meant that everything that had happened before, everything in the world, had ceased to be of account. Nothing — neither lover nor dinosaur nor painting — had existed before the crash. Now all was new and attainable. Or possibly not, in which case nothing in his life would have been achieved at all. It was true that his paintings would remain, but what of all those he would have painted, had he been permitted?

He told Kathryn, I have seen photographs of the rock art of Africa, the stick-like figures of bushmen running in almost-movement upon the walls of cave and shelter. Their paintings were the membrane that connected their physical and spiritual worlds. In those mountain valleys the colours of the long-dead artist still enable the eland and rhinoceros to pass from that world into this.

I have also seen a reproduction of a rock painting discovered in a shelter on the banks of the East Alligator River, in our own far-north. A prehistoric marsupial tapir, extinct for tens of thousands of years, brought by art glowingly into the present.

If it is possible for art to open the gateway between the present and the past, perhaps it can also link us with the future. Can we use art, which is to say magic, to fly from the cage of what is into the intoxication of might be, could be, into the extra dimension? Where we can walk, and be one?

Cloaked in longing for Kathryn, Cal staggered, and fell, and crawled.

More images came. The uplifted arms, the long hair, Stella's figure crucified upon a rainbow arch of spray. He had betrayed her, seeking her out only to abandon her. Had betrayed her husband, had been unable even to keep the relationship secret from the man who had been his friend. Had betrayed Kathryn, his love. In so doing, had betrayed himself.

Forgive me.

Knowing forgiveness impossible, while he

himself did not forgive.

And so the spastic, weary dance continued, while around him the rocks neither reproved nor judged, but observed in silence. Anything less than eternity was nothing. As the man and his sense of guilt, the man himself, was nothing.

★   ★   ★

In mid-morning her mother came soft-footed to the room where she sat behind drawn curtains staring at the wall. Upon which her visions, too, were now almost too faint to see: the far pinpoint of the eagle spiralling above red cliffs, the prostrate figure of the man.

'There is someone . . . '

Kathryn came silently.

'I wanted to see how you were . . . '

Stella.

'I am fine.'

'You don't mind me being here?'

'I came to you, first.'

'That was before — '

'It doesn't matter.' Nor did it.

They sat, and sat.

Stella said, 'I told him Hennie was a cowboy.'

Kathryn almost nodded. She had nothing to say, and said it.

'Do you hate me?' Stella asked.

To Kathryn it was a question without meaning. 'Why should I?'

'I came close to hating you. I'd thought maybe, with Cal, I might have a life. He made me feel, you know, special. But Hennie . . . ' She thought about it. 'He's not a bad bloke, but I should never have married him. It was the idea of me he wanted, not me. He was never around. Then Cal turned up.' She shrugged. 'I was lonely. He was worse than lonely. Halfway to cutting his throat, I reckon. We . . . comforted each other.' She turned in appeal to the younger woman. 'Is that so bad?'

Kathryn did not answer. She wanted neither to hear nor think about it, would say nothing to encourage this stream of intrusive confidences.

Stella said, 'Then, one day, I knew I'd lost him. That was you, though I didn't know it at the time. Men are bastards,' she burst out. 'They get you to care, then they move on. But you can't just switch off, can you? When Moomba phoned to say they'd gone down, it was like he'd kicked me in the stomach. Because I warned him, see, and still he went. Bastards!' she repeated, savagely.

Again there was silence. Into which Marge

Fanning stuck her beak, bringing a tray of tea.

'I thought you might want something . . . '

Would have stayed, but Kathryn gave her an eye. Went off again with a miffed look, martyred mother banished by her ungrateful daughter.

Who, the door safely shut, wondered, 'That shrine you showed me . . . '

'It wasn't really to bring him back. I knew there was no hope of that. But to ask that someone, somewhere, should look after me.' Now tears sprinkled the words. 'I need that more than anything. Someone strong, someone I can rely on. I never found anyone like that. Only the sea.' She smiled, wryly. 'Some things even the sea can't do for you.'

'You told me you'd made it for Cal.'

'I did say that. Not because I wanted to hurt you . . . ' She paused, then sighed. 'I'm lying. Of course I wanted to hurt you.'

'Because of Cal?'

'Because you're young.'

'Then why come here today?'

'I need to be with someone who knows what I'm going through. I thought you might feel the same.'

Kathryn did indeed need the comfort of someone to share the waiting, now her mother had failed the test. She did not believe this woman had given up hope of winning Cal back, but would handle that when the time came. In the meantime, she felt kindness towards Stella for her courage in coming, her willingness to share grief.

She had no words but stretched out and took Stella's hand.

'The sixth day,' Stella said.

Kathryn tightened her clasp on Stella's thin fingers, shaking them with the intensity of her ardour.

'They will be safe.' Vehemently she proclaimed her faith. 'Safe!'

Stella at last had gone. The sixth day was half over, yet still they had heard nothing. Kathryn returned to the cliffs. Stared across the wild and crying sea.

'We don't measure life's achievement by success,' Cal had told her, speaking of the wall that might block the way to achievement. 'Success is nothing. Failure is what matters. To achieve anything, there must be failure. You have to seek always to go beyond what is known. Often that will mean failure, and suffering, and an endless striving for renewal.'

Alone yet not, she walked with measured steps along the cliff top, bearing in every stride the imprint of the arid hills, the stones casting their painful javelins of reflected light. The harsh gasping of the man's breath tormented her, the spastic weaving of his feet tore her heart. The ranges stood high above her. We must climb them together, she prayed, through rock and bush, the endless agonies of heat, of thirst, the long rituals of death. We must reach the ridge, touch the texture of the sky, look out upon the other side where salvation, perhaps, may be found.

While in the desert of the Gammon Ranges, the bubble-brightness of foam rushed onwards, bearing the forms of dolphins. The fiery rocks reverberated with the thunder of the waves; the spray of their glad progress, endlessly repeated, lashed the sky.

★ ★ ★

'Problem is,' Dawkins said, 'the bastards could be anywhere.'

In any case the endless searching had become pointless. No-one could have survived so long. Stubbornness alone prevented his giving up.

Arch, his observer, thumbed the intercom switch. His voice hissed in Dawkins's headphones.

'The Willina Gorge is down there. I've been there. No waterhole that I know of, but there's a creek.'

351

Dawkins stared out of the window at the blue sprawl of mountains beneath them.

'Might as well take a look.'

The chopper swerved out of the sky, descended between high cliffs.

'What's that?'

Tangled metal, like the nest of a gigantic steel bird. The cliff wall stained with smoke.

'Shit!'

They landed.

Dawkins said, 'No-one will have walked away from that.'

Yet when they searched the cold wreckage, they found no sign of occupants. Cast about the area, discovered a patch of sand sheltered from the rain. In the sand: footprints.

'How many?'

Arch stared, scratching his head.

'Who knows? We need a tracker for this job.'

Dawkins turned slowly on his heel, surveying the gorge.

'Only one way they could have gone.'

And pointed to where the gorge turned sharply out of sight, climbing between parallel cliffs.

'How do we track them in that lot?'

They climbed back into the helicopter. Arch spoke to Moomba.

'We've found the chopper. No people.

We're looking further.'

They followed the gorge up to the ridge and saw nothing. They hovered. Beyond the ridge the valley, gold and green and red in the westering sun, extended into a purple distance.

'Where the hell . . . ?'

Dawkins shrugged. 'You tell me.' Thought, Surely they would show themselves if they were still alive? It was hopeless. He looked at his watch. Once the sun went down, darkness would come swiftly.

'We'll come back in the morning,' he decided.

He raised the collective control stick, twisting the throttle to increase the revs. The chopper lifted and flew away.

★ ★ ★

I don't trust those herons.

The impact of water, endlessly wonderful. Upon the bank, the cool and lovely figure of the girl, the sun-bronzed face laughing beneath its cap of short dark hair.

Come and join me.

'Come and join me,' Cal cried to the silent hills.

A ridge danced before him.

Yes, he thought. Yes.

Upwards, towards the endless landscapes of the sky.

★　★　★

Kathryn went back to the house. To her mother, waiting. Who shook her head heavily.
'Nothing.'

★　★　★

The cameras came, the vulture faces, seeking to tear from her the flesh of her most secret desires.
'What is your relationship?'
'Have you modelled for him?'
'Do you still have hope?'
'Of course.'
'How can you?'
'Because he is alive. I feel it. I know it.'
At once the circling vultures closed in upon her. 'How can you know? Are you saying you are in some kind of psychic contact with him? Do you believe that?' Incredulity in their voices, the polite and silent laughter.
'I believe it, yes.' Kathryn knew herself ravished by their smiling disbelief, the silent, materialistic scoffing of those who knew better. Yet still she fought. 'I daresay you find it strange. But reality is more than what we

can see and touch. I am in touch with him, yes. I feel his pulse.'

'You are that sure he is still alive? After six days in temperatures of over — '

'I am sure.'

★　★　★

Fingernails torn by the unimaginable, final effort to haul himself upwards, to hang onto life, he dragged himself up. Up. About him the air was a scream of pain. Still he would not surrender. One body's length and then another. A broken lizard, crawling upwards. The rocks cut and bruised him, he was aware of a cauldron within himself in which pain bubbled, rising remorselessly. Like the mound spring they had seen on the southern fringes of the Simpson Desert, it would reach the surface, it would overflow, it would inundate him in its scalding heat. But what was pain? Only the price that had to be paid for the celestial vision that awaited him, that beckoned from the summit of the rocky slope on which he lay, the bronze and red and ochre components of a palette that would never be assembled, the great painting that he would never now compose.

Up. Up. Until at last, the very air swinging crazily, he dragged himself onto the ridge.

With sight failing, dust and death in his mouth, he stared at . . .

Infinity.

So, he thought. Beyond the last blue ridge everything continues as before. A landscape containing nothing but vastness, isolation and heat, a silent grey shimmer extending to a horizon as still and smooth as the rim of a bowl. The only movement a distant boiling of dust, wind-blown.

It was for this I came, he thought. It was this I wanted to paint, eternity in the last slow dying of the light. He looked again, trying to force his eyes to take in for the last time the flare of red and green and gold that he knew lay there, concealed beneath the grey veil of heat.

Let me see them one more time, he prayed to what might be. Let me taste once more the ecstasy of colour. And waited, in humility and faith. The day drained nightwards. The sun, sinking behind him, caught fire. The colours came, softly, to illuminate the land. The violets and prussian blues. The ultramarine, umber, sienna; all the glory.

Thank you. He did not know whether it was mind or tongue that spoke. Thank you.

He repeated it again and again; the words, like the rebirth of colour, an exultation and singing.

In his mind he painted feverishly, applying each pigment to the canvas in turn, each separated from the rest to give it room to breathe, to expand. The painting became, not a representation of light, but light itself.

The plume of dust hung motionless.

He thought, *There is no wind.*

He fought to focus haze-dazzled eyes. Failed. A dust-devil, he thought, eating up the motionless plain.

Then doubted. As he watched, it moved again, swinging nearer. *Swing low, sweet chariot, comin' for to carry me home. Come in, then, if you're coming. Come in, number one.* And wondered if he had become mad or was merely dead.

The dust, swirling. The bubbling froth of surf. Colour and form whipped in tumult, coalescing into . . .

The features of the girl, between him and the horizon, him and emptiness. But fading, fading. On his knees, he reached out desperately to her.

Come to me, my only love. Come to me.

Too late. Fading. Too late. Fading.

Gone.

Cal, bereft, staring at emptiness.

For a moment the haze cleared. At the centre of the dust plume, a white shape moved steadily across the valley from right to left. Legs and arms formed exclamation points as he struggled frantically to feet that danced, feebly, upon the rock. He flung out his arms, was at once blown sideways by the wind of his movement. He tried to cry out, could not. Tried to wave. Could not. His arms fell hopelessly. He slumped; first to his knees, then forward on his face. He lay still.

Upon the valley floor the vehicle, tethered to its plume of dust, drove on.

17

Stella sat alone in the salty dark, surrounded by the reverberation of the trampling seas. The hours she had spent with Kathryn Fanning had soothed, but now was the time to think, to feel, for anguish to come rushing into the emptiness that echoed in time with the waves.

Strange how that child had been so sure that Cal was still alive. All the odds were against it, yet it was true that people sometimes knew these things. As for Hennie ... Stella had no feeling, one way or the other.

I have made no attempt to keep in touch, she told herself. I have lost the knack of communication.

For reasons she could not explain, she felt bereft that it was so, as though an opportunity had offered but now was lost beyond recall.

Again she thought of Kathryn. *That child*, she had called her. It seemed to her now that in all the ways that mattered Kathryn was older than she was. She wondered why it should be so, feared it might be because Kathryn loved another person whereas she, Stella, had always loved only herself.

She thought rebelliously, If I don't look after myself . . .

And paused.

That was it. Of course.

I shall pray no more to find someone I can lean upon. Neither Cal nor Hennie nor any man will be my custodian. I, alone, will make my destiny.

Easily said.

At least try, she told herself.

She went slowly out of the house, crossed the spray-wet galaxies of rocks, followed the spider's-web path between sea and dreams, ducked her head beneath the capstone, came with trembling breath to the solemn stillness of the shrine.

And looked.

The ferns were withered, the ranks of shells lustreless. She took them all, scraping every particle into her cupped hands, went out awkwardly, cast the remnants into the air. The wind sucked them away. The sea's pageant rolled on.

'I am free,' she cried, weeping.

Free to make a new life, to be lonely.

She turned and went back into the house. I shall be resolute, she told herself, and wiped away tears. Somehow, somehow, I shall live my life.

★   ★   ★

Marge Fanning came on silent feet. Stood in the doorway. Kathryn lying on her back on the bed in her room. Empty room, empty heart, empty eyes.

'Telephone, Kathryn.'

She did not move but watched beyond the shadowed ceiling the diminishing figure of the man. Whom now, she had to accept, was lost.

'Phone, Kathryn . . . '

She came back. Her eyes focused on her mother's face.

'Who is it?'

'Channel Nine.'

The two women stared at each other.

'Perhaps it is good news.'

A forlorn offering. From the first Marge Fanning had been opposed to the masculine threat of Cal Jessop, but now was frightened of what might be the consequences for her child if the news was not good.

'I'd better go and find out.'

Kathryn forced herself upright, swaying. She walked in dread and ashes to the door. Passed through, while her mother, frightened

361

mouth and eyes, gave her space. Reached the
phone. Took it up. Held it to her ear.

'Hullo?'

Her eyes stared blindly at the cool,
white-painted wall. Against which memory
and hope and grief lay, silent as dust.

'Yes. This is Kathryn Fanning speaking.'

And stood while a man's voice quacked
softly. Marge watched, trying to out-guess the
silence.

'I've heard nothing at all,' Kathryn said.
'Not from the police or anyone. Nothing.'

Again the faint, sibilant quacking.
Kathryn as still and pale as a statue
fashioned in chalk.

'I see. Thank you. Thank you.'

Replaced the phone. Turned, staring at her
mother through a drenching of silent tears.

'Some scientists from the Observatory at
Arkaroola found him in the Gammon
Ranges.' In the air about her Kathryn saw
images: all her hopes, all the glory. Her
dust-grey lips barely moved. 'They were
going to take observations from one of the
peaks in the district and found him there, on
the summit.'

Marge held her breath.

Kathryn turned blindly, almost collided
with the wall. Was still marooned in that place
to which she had retreated during the last

days. And again swayed, breathing.

Beyond the window the dark air carried the tang of salt. Kathryn opened her mouth to taste the awareness of a life restored, of light returning after days of darkness.

'They brought him out,' she said. 'He's alive.'

THE END

We do hope that you have enjoyed reading this large print book.

Did you know that all of our titles are available for purchase?

We publish a wide range of high quality large print books including:
Romances, Mysteries, Classics
General Fiction
Non Fiction and Westerns

Special interest titles available in large print are:
The Little Oxford Dictionary
Music Book
Song Book
Hymn Book
Service Book

Also available from us courtesy of Oxford University Press:
Young Readers' Dictionary
(large print edition)
Young Readers' Thesaurus
(large print edition)

For further information or a free brochure, please contact us at:
Ulverscroft Large Print Books Ltd.,
The Green, Bradgate Road, Anstey,
Leicester, LE7 7FU, England.
Tel: (00 44) **0116 236 4325**
Fax: (00 44) **0116 234 0205**

1194 AD: Appointed by Richard the Lionheart as the first coroner for the county of Devon, Sir John de Wolfe, an ex-crusader, rides out to the moorland village of Widecombe to hold an inquest on an unidentified body. But on his return to Exeter, the Coroner is incensed to find that his own brother-in-law, Sheriff Richard de Revelle, is intent on thwarting the murder investigation. But Crowner John is ready to fight for the truth. Even faced with the combined mights of the all-powerful Church and nobility . . .

SLAUGHTER HORSE

Michael Maguire

The Turf Security Division is surprised and suspicious when playboy Wesley Falloway's second-rate horses develop overnight into winners. Simon Drake investigates, but suddenly there is a new twist — someone is out to steal General O'Hara, the star of British bloodstock, owned by Wesley Falloway's mother. With a few million pounds at stake, lives are cheap; Drake finds himself both hunter and quarry in a murderous chase where even his closest associates may be playing a double game.

Eventide

BEVAN COURT

Selbourne Court

APL		CCS	
Cen		Ear	
Mob		Cou	
ALL		Jub	
WIL		CRE	
Ald		Bel	
Fin		Fol	
Can		STO	
TIL		HCL	